Praise for Brian Conaghan

WINNER OF THE COSTA CHILDREN'S BOOK AWARD

WINNER OF THE AN POST IRISH BOOK AWARDS TEEN/YOUNG ADULT BOOK OF THE YEAR

WINNER OF THE UKLA BOOK AWARD
(WITH SARAH CROSSAN)

SHORTLISTED FOR THE CILIP CARNEGIE MEDAL

'So much heart [his writing] bounces off the page'
Irish Independent

'Conaghan is a sublime storyteller who can make the reader hang on his every last word (and all of the others)'
The Times

'Laughter is inevitable'
Irish Times

'[Writing] packed with energy and a brilliant distinctive voice'
Bookseller

SWIMMING on the MOON

Books by Brian Conaghan

Cardboard Cowboys
Swimming on the Moon

For older readers
When Mr Dog Bites
The Bombs That Brought Us Together
The Weight of a Thousand Feathers
The M Word

And with Sarah Crossan
We Come Apart

SWIMMING
on the
MOON

BRIAN CONAGHAN

BLOOMSBURY
CHILDREN'S BOOKS
LONDON OXFORD NEW YORK NEW DELHI SYDNEY

BLOOMSBURY CHILDREN'S BOOKS
Bloomsbury Publishing Plc
50 Bedford Square, London WC1B 3DP, UK
29 Earlsfort Terrace, Dublin 2, Ireland

BLOOMSBURY, BLOOMSBURY CHILDREN'S BOOKS and the Diana
logo are trademarks of Bloomsbury Publishing Plc

First published in Great Britain in 2023 by Bloomsbury Publishing Plc

A catalogue record for this book is available from the British Library

ISBN: PB: 978-1-5266-5392-5; eBook: 978-1-5266-5390-1;
ePDF: 978-1-5266-5391-8

2 4 6 8 10 9 7 5 3 1

Typeset by RefineCatch Limited, Bungay, Suffolk
Printed and bound in Great Britain by CPI Group (UK) Ltd, Croydon CR0 4YY

To find out more about our authors and books visit www.bloomsbury.com
and sign up for our newsletters

For Rosie and Larry

One

Here I am once again. Sitting on the edge of the bed. Just sitting. I gnaw on a loose pinky nail. Staring. Thinking. Dreaming. Hoping. There's space on my bedroom wall for another poster. Or maybe a family photo. A happy-snappy one with tons of teeth on show. Maybe from that camper-van holiday we went on two years ago.

'This thing's a tent on wheels,' I remember Dad saying.

He used to be dead funny. These days not so much. I can't remember what Mum said in return, but the laughing caused the camper-van seats to bob up and down. She's dead funny too. Or *was*. I used to be a *proper wee comedian* myself, but now I just stare. Think. Dream. Hope. It's really hard knowing there won't be any more family holidays. Like so hard it makes you cry. It's worse wishing for them though. It's so bad that I'd even settle for an actual *tent on wheels* one again.

My mind takes me back there loads. I remember how the colours in the sky were different to the sky outside my bedroom window at home and how the smell of sun cream didn't leave my hands the entire time we were there. I want the salty taste of the seaside to touch my tongue again. I want the moon to be so huge and close that I can reach up and touch it. Dance on it. Swim on it. I'm always imagining what it'd be like to go back ... I stare hard at the empty section of my bedroom wall until I see it. Like actually see it. Our family picture slowly appears. We're all in it, bursting with joy.

Right, so, we're all in this big clapped-out camper van. Mum and Dad are up front while me and Anto are bouncing around in the back. It's scorching outside, but we're definitely somewhere in Scotland. One of those summer days where everything looks hazy yellow, and all the adults talk about wanting to live in it forever. The windows are open and Mum's singing like a champion to the music, her tonsils going like the clappers. She does have some voice. In another world she'd have been the lead singer in a wedding band instead of working in Asda.

'But she's high up in Asda,' Dad always said to anyone who'd listen.

By *high up* he meant that she works directly above

2

the food section, in clothes. It's not exactly a laugh-out-loud joke, but it never failed to crack him up.

Dad's elbow is half in, half out. He's blowing cigarette smoke towards the sun. Green menthols, which don't damage you as much. At least, that's what he's told us. *It's like smoking Polo mints.* When finished, he flicks the butt over the roof and starts drumming the camper-van door. He should have been the wedding band's drummer instead of being a baker in Greggs.

'Someone's got to put all those sausage rolls into the oven,' Mum used to say to the neighbours.

Me and Anto like our neighbours.

Mum's singing gets louder. Dad's drumming fiercer. They look at each other. Lots of back-and-forth smiling. Their eyes are filled with sun. I imagine that if me and Anto weren't here Dad would've probably pulled over for a big sloppy kiss. I notice Mum's hand resting on Dad's knee, she taps her finger off it. A new song comes on now, a much slower number, one of those rap ballad things. Halfway through the second verse she moves her hand to the back of his neck. I taste menthol everywhere, it's clinging to my new blouse. George at Asda, obviously. I smack my tongue off my lips. Polo mints my eye! Mum tickles the little hairs on my dad's neck. Anto, who's next to me, sticks his tongue out as if he's about

3

to cover my face with the contents of his stomach. The fish and chips we had on the beach. Erm, no thanks. I glare at him and point to his face as if to say: *Don't even think about it.* Anto might be the same age, but if it came down to it, I'd more than fancy my chances. I've seen enough *Bullies Getting Owned* YouTube videos to know how to handle annoying boys. We might've been born on the same day, in the same hospital, from the same mother, but technically I'm his big sister since I popped out a full six minutes before he did. So that's sister, with a capital BIG. But, whatever happened in those six minutes is beyond me, beyond Mum, beyond Dad and beyond the doctors. Anto is another story. He's just, well, Anto.

I squeeze my eyes shut and the picture disappears. Magic!

I let myself fall backwards so that I'm lying on the bed. My head's squished too close to the headboard but my imagination covers me like a soft, warm duvet; especially when I return to our holiday, remembering when Mum and Dad seemed to be bouncing around in a happy bubble …

Dad takes his hand off the steering wheel and drops it on to Mum's bare knee. She's wearing a fluttery dress. The George summer range. Staff discount. The dress matches her headband.

When I grow up I want to look exactly like my mum. Beautiful, cool. But I won't. Everyone says I'm the spit of Dad. It's Anto who got Mum's dark hair and velvet skin. Both of them could pass for a Spanish Italian any day of the week. Dad just looks Scottish. Pink in summer. Sad in winter.

She thinks I don't hear when she leans into him and whispers, *Love you, honey*. And he replies, *Love you too, chicken*, before taking his hand off her knee cos we're coming up to a roundabout. My stomach goes all woozy. Anto's as well. I know the look on his face when his tummy tumbles. Maybe it's a twin thing.

Suddenly our shabby camper van has transformed into this mega-cracking jalopy; one you only see in American films and stuff. Like, you could dance in it if you wanted to, that's how big we're talking. And we're driving all the way towards the sun.

One big, mega-cracking family.

'Anna!'

Driving in the hazy yellow.

'Anna!'

Everyone touching necks and knees and loving each other.

'ANNA!'

I break from my trance. My breathing is heavy. The thud of the stairs is loud. Anto thudding down. Mum thudding up. And that's me back in normal land, with a bash. When the door crashes open I jump. Dreamtime over.

'Anna, I've been down there shouting on you for ages.' Mum's standing at my door squeezing the life out of a dish towel. 'Your dad's back and dinner's on the table.'

'Right.'

'Did you not hear me shouting?'

'I must have dozed.'

'Dozed,' Mum scoffs. 'Twelve-year-olds don't doze, Anna.' She looks up at the stars on my ceiling. 'Dozed, would you listen to it.'

'OK, I fell asleep then,' I say.

'Right, well, your dinner's getting cold.' Mum shakes her head and goes to leave.

'Mum,' I shout, mainly cos I don't want her to leave. She stops. 'What are we having?'

'Sausage roll and chips.'

I should have known, it is Saturday after all. Although sometimes Dad brings us a couple on a Friday too. Anto doesn't like much, but sausage rolls, well, he could eat them like sweets.

'I'll be down in a jiffy,' I say.

'Tonight, no reading to one in the morning, got it?'

'I've finished my book anyway,' I tell her.

Mum looks at the stars once more, twirls the dish towel and leaves.

What's the point looking at the ceiling? All the stars have lost their power to glow. I'm far too old for new ones.

I tiptoe down the stairs.

Another night, another sausage roll. These ones are a bit flaky. Probably been drying out in the shop window all day long. Another night, another dinner where no one speaks. Only Anto chomping on food like a starving wildebeest breaks the silence. The three of us who *can* speak don't utter a thing.

Wish I was still on that holiday.

Two

It was three weeks ago when we first found out something wasn't right. The 7th of June to be exact – the day after our twelfth birthday. I got new trainers. Anto'd got more Lego.

Actually it was past midnight so it was really the 8th. Saturday night or Sunday morning, whichever you prefer. Nancy Drew was about to find out who had written the mysterious letter when I heard their voices sneak into my room. I stopped reading on the line *You gotta be kiddin' me* when I heard Mum say, *Think this is all one big joke, do you?* I sat my book on top of my belly. Listened for more. When Dad said, *I'm not laughing at you, I wouldn't do that,* I got out of bed and slid into my birthday present. Vans. Checkerboard, size four. Classics.

Doing my best slinking-mouse impression, I crept out of my room. Anto was already perched on the top stair when I got there; rocking and banging his coat hanger off the side of his head. I put my finger to my lips to shoosh him, but the coat hanger sped up. I mimed the word NO with a swipe and he stopped. He hates when I swipe. I sat down next to him and he placed the coat hanger across our legs, just as Gran and Papa do with their tartan shawl at the park. And, like an electricity flow, we were connected. From the top stair, with Anto's coat-hanger shawl protecting us, we listened as Mum and Dad whisper-shouted to each other.

'You know what, Tony?' Mum went.

'No, but I suppose you're gonna tell me,' Dad said.

'You're full of excuses. It's always someone else's fault.'

'That's not true.'

'Take responsibility for your actions.'

'You think I haven't done that, Liz? I'm trying to be as responsible as I can.'

'Not hard enough.'

'It's not just me I'm thinking about here.'

We heard Mum snort, even though there wasn't anything funny being said.

'God, would you listen to this,' she went.

'Do you even know the meaning of the word *listen*?'

Mum did another two laughy snorts. She was definitely trying to get on Dad's wick.

'Oh, so that was it, was it? You wanted someone to *listen* to you? Aww.'

I pictured Mum with her hands across her chest, like she does.

'You wouldn't understand.'

Mum took a drink of something. Dad too. He swooshed open a can. We could hear their gulps from where we were sitting. They weren't happy gulps.

'No crime has been committed here, Liz.'

'That's how you justify it to yourself, is it?' Mum had her teeth clenched. I'd heard that voice loads, she sounded well up for a battle.

'I'm just saying, it's a misjudgement. It's a … just something that happened. I haven't killed anyone.'

There was a dead long pause which made me hold my breath and worry that Anto might have given our game away.

'Just this family,' Mum said.

Dad drank more of his can. He puffed his cigarette too cos we could smell the menthol wafting up to us.

'I don't think this is good for either of us, Liz.'

'Well, if I were you I'd get on to Rightmove and sort yourself out.'

'YOU GET ON TO RIGHTMOVE,' Dad screamed.

'Tony! The kids.'

'Anna's not stupid, Liz. She knows what going on.'

'And what about Anthony?'

I held the coat hanger tight against my thigh in case Anto needed to start rattling it off his head again. Mum's right, I'm not stupid, but I actually didn't know what was going on. Not at all. I was confused. And scared.

'Go to bed, Liz.'

Neither of them went to bed after that. We heard Mum potter around the kitchen, taking her anger out on the dishwasher. Dad took his out on Netflix. I know the *da-dum* sound it makes when it starts up. The silence lasted for about five minutes and then they went for it again, only louder this time. I cupped my ears, but I released my hands one time and it seemed as if they were playing swear tennis. Worst. Sport. Ever.

More silence followed, but we did wait for it all to kick off again. It didn't. I knew Anto was desperate to make a sound, any noise that would let everyone know he was steaming with rage, but he zipped up his mouth really well; squeezing every face muscle so hard. I was dead proud of him.

'K ... K ... K ... K,' Anto sounded, which means one of two things: cuddle or cosy-in. I nodded. He rested his head on my shoulder. A cosy-in is what he was after. Me too. I didn't put my arm around him cos that makes his body all

11

tense. He tapped the coat hanger off my thigh to take away his stress and tension. Gentle taps.

Anto didn't want to go back to bed, and neither did I. Our heads were far too fizzy for sleep. I switched on his lamp, fixed his sheets and I left him on his bedroom floor surrounded by a million coloured pieces of his birthday present. He was bang in the middle of building a Lego Land Rover. Before leaving him there I put my arms out and said 'K … K … K … K?' Anto looked up at me and shook his head.

'You OK, Anto?' He double-blinked a yes. 'Don't worry, all mums and dads argue. It's just the bad part of being married.' He did a long, angry blink. 'What we heard was love talking, that's what it sounds like sometimes.' He started clicking bricks together. I definitely knew that in the morning a new Land Rover would be parked up on his floor. And then he'd destroy it and build it back up again.

I couldn't be doing with Nancy Drew. Couldn't care less who wrote that mysterious letter. The last thing I remember of that night was looking at the clock. Three forty-eight. By far the latest I've ever been awake. I hadn't even taken off the checkerboard Vans. I had my dance group in the morning. How was I going to move, never mind dance?

I lay in my bed thinking and thinking and thinking. I felt it under my ribs. The fear. I couldn't allow it to happen, I couldn't allow Mum and Dad to throw everything away on a game of swear tennis. Me and Anto had to work some Lego magic on them.

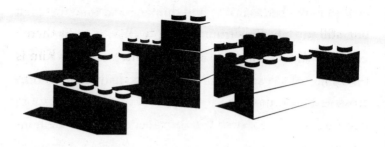

Three

Since the arguments started I've begun trying to change everything: I've been doing tons of chats at the dinner table. Told them how school has been this past year, and no one my age talks to their parents about school. Not ever. Told them in really major detail about my experience at Adventureland, the place we went to on our last day of school before breaking up for the summer holidays. I couldn't stop laughing when telling them how Karen McAfee screamed her head off when she was dangling on the zipline and how I had to cuddle her shaking body back to calmness when she came down. Miss Dunne said that I was *a really compassionate friend* and that my *parents would be so proud*.

I've not asked *for the twentieth time, Anna*, if we're gonna go anywhere at the end of the summer; or a last-minute deal in July or something. Obviously I know the answer, but, still, there's no harm in asking twenty times, is there?

I've told them about all the new dance routines Kim is teaching us at MadCrew, and how many fingers I'm crossing that I make the squad who'll be going to Italy in late August. Yesterday I even mortified myself by demonstrating a really cool routine we're working on in front of everyone. They gave me a small applause, said, *That's fantastic, sweetheart*, and then went straight back to their phones. Anto watched my living-room takeover through slitted fingers, but I knew by his scrunched-up face afterwards that he loved it.

There's loads of things I've done: I've filled the dishwasher without needing to be asked. I've brushed my teeth for the full two minutes. I've had more than one bath a week. I've not sulked when people give Anto things and forget about me. I haven't said anything to Gran or Papa. What would I say?

But nothing changes, we still sit at the top of the stairs in the dark and listen to them. The fear still rests, snuggled up, under my ribs. I can't remember the last time they looked each other in the eye and had a normal conversation. I mean, Dad used to wrap his arms around Mum's waist when she was chopping onions and stuff for dinner; and she used to put her feet on his legs when watching

15

24 Hours in A&E, then he'd rub her ankles and they'd make comments about all the accidents until the programme ended. See, all that touching, it used to make me feel yucky with embarrassment inside. But if it happened now I'd be doing tumbles all over the house.

There's no chance of acrobatics these days though. It's all about silent sausage-roll dinners that lead to silent cleaning up and a few clicks at the TV remote before popping off silently to bed. A life in silence. Until, that is, me and Anto are safely tucked up in bed, out of harm's way, and the arguing breaks it. I know their tricks.

It's clear that I need to up my game.

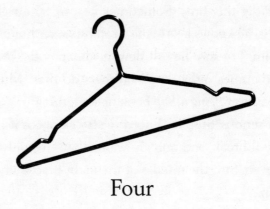

Four

It's the morning after another round of swear tennis and I'm dozing. I've been in and out of sleep most of the night. Anto pushes my door open. I quickly shut my eyes tight and pretend to baby snore. He doesn't care for things like people's sleep patterns; he starts jabbing his knuckle into my shoulder. He won't stop, even when I open my eyes. His jabs are deep and sore. My brother doesn't know his own strength; he's twelve with a fifteen-year-old's biceps. I swipe him to pack it in. 'No!' I say.

He shakes his head to remove the hair from his eyes. It's getting long; looks like a bunch of wild snakes. Wild snakes on top of a Minecraft onesie. Good luck with trying to get him into a barber's chair though. He's so funny, but I dare not laugh. I swipe once more. He jabs me again.

'Anto, stop it,' I say. But he does it again, more like a

17

proper dig this time. Sometimes he can be a right pain. Thing is, he knows he's being a total spanner but it doesn't stop him. I'm sure he just does it to annoy the life out of me sometimes. Why do all brothers do that? Must be in their *Rules to Being a Sap* book or something.

'I'm serious. Stop it.' I need to stay calm cos if I snap at him he'll break, and nobody wants that. 'It's only twenty past seven. Still the middle of the night practically. I need to sleep.'

He moans and stamps his foot. I've seen this look on his face a million times, he's about to explode. I point to the bottom of my bed.

'Go there.'

He grunts a no. If his body was a volcano, the lava level would be around his chest area at this moment. He stomps twice more.

'Anto, go lie there.' He clenches his fists and groans through gritted teeth. 'You better shoosh or Mum and Dad'll hear you.'

I heave myself up to give him some space at the bottom of the bed.

'Go,' I tell him.

Anto scowls before curling himself into a ball at the bottom of my bed; he turns his back on me and stares at the wall. Nothing new there.

18

I know exactly why he's here at this time in the morning. Things aren't good when he's tired and bothered. His breathing is loud. Reminds me of a bull waiting to charge the red rag. I crawl up to him. Plonk myself near, not touching. His eyes are wide. One blink would make a tear fall.

'They didn't mean it, Anto,' I say. He twists his body closer to the wall. 'We always hear them saying things that aren't facts.' He moans. 'Don't believe any of that stuff they said last night; it's not true. They'd never ever do that. No way.' He starts bouncing his head off the mattress. Quicker and quicker. More violent.

Oh, no, I should've noticed; I scoot off the bed and go find it. In his room I'm careful not to step on anything Lego-related. There would be war if I trod on the garage he's just built.

I find it sitting on his pillow.

'Here.'

I place his coat hanger in the V space between his knees and stomach. Anto takes it and pulls it to his chest, as if he's kind of spooning it. It works. His eyes close. Not one tear falls. I lie down beside him and run my hand through the snakes on his head. He's OK with that. It works too. He no longer sounds like the bull. Now all I need is for him to be a lamb. His hair is so thick, it's pretty amazing really. If he went to my school I bet all the girls in my year would think the same. Probably some in the year above too.

'Let's be lambs, Anto,' I whisper. I bleat my little-lost-lamb sound into his ear. 'Think of little lambs. Those lambs in the farm we went to with Gran and Papa.' I make more soft bleating sounds. 'The lambs we saw from Dad's car.' Another little bleat near his ear. 'The Lego lambs that you have, think of them. Remember that farmyard you built?' Anto snuggles into the coat hanger and lets out the gentlest of lamb sounds. I hand-comb his hair until he starts falling asleep.

The Minecraft figures on his onesie rise and fall as his sleep gets deeper. I often wonder what his dreams look like. If they always happen in magical fantasy lands or just in someone's kitchen. Is he a total blabbermouth in them? You know, like a Scottish chatterbox. In mine he's simply our Anto; full of facial expressions and wild gestures only. Still, his gestures and expressions make so much noise, it's like a different form of talking anyway. Funny thing is, I'll never get to meet the version of Anto who appears in his own dreams, which is fine cos I meet my own version whenever he pops up in mine. The sad thing though is that in my dreams Anto is full of joy, but when I'm done dreaming, and open my eyes, I always manage to kill that joy. If only I could save a smidgeon of it for his real life.

It's hard not to hate Mum and Dad for what they said last night. I wish we hadn't been on those stairs this time. OK, so we might share all the weird twin things about us, especially when one feels pain and the other feels it the exact same way, in the exact same place. But now, in this moment, I feel Anto's pain cos I heard it with my own two ears. And I can't stop playing it over in my head.

'Oh, you don't need to tell me,' Mum fired at Dad last night. 'I know you'd much rather be at work. Anything to get away from here.'

'Away from you, you mean?' Dad shot back.

'Yeah, well, the feeling's mutual, Tony.'

'All I've done is work hard for this family.'

'What, and I haven't?'

'Am I saying that?'

'You don't have to.'

'Look, Liz, it's hard for everyone here—'

'Don't you dare blame Anthony for this.'

That made Dad's voice boom. 'Did I say anything about Anthony? Did I?'

Anto's shoulders jerked. Mine too.

'You don't have to, Tony. It's written all over your face.' Mum added her own boom to the show.

'Written all over my … What are you talking about?'

'He's a problem for you.'

21

'Put a sock in it, Liz, will you.'

'An embarrassment.'

'Stop! I mean it.' Dad was now on his feet, I could tell. 'Just stop.'

'He always has been.'

It seemed as if they didn't care if we heard them or not. I guess they were tired of whisper-arguing all the time. Dad laughed loudly. It wasn't his usual stomach laugh. No, this was all throat.

'You're such a hypocrite, Liz. You know that?' I think he was close to Mum's face. 'Let's not forget that I've seen how you are when you're out and about with him. I've seen it for years. I know he makes you feel like a failure. So don't stand there and tell me that he's only my problem.'

I thought the coat hanger was going to leave bruises on Anto's head. I tapped my knee so he knew that he could rest it there and connect us, if he wanted to. He didn't. Don't blame him.

Now it was Mum's turn to laugh from the throat. Honestly, these were the ugliest laughs ever. Laughs that would be good for a Halloween party and nothing else.

'You won't even take him to the football in case he embarrasses you in front of your so-called mates,' she said.

'Rubbish.'

22

'OK, so tell me the last game you took him to then?' I knew Mum was standing with one hand on her hip; she does that when she's right about something. I think she was right about this. 'Go on, I'm waiting.' The wait is long. Nothing happens in the silence. 'You've never even taken him to join a football team.'

'That's because he doesn't play,' Dad snapped.

'No, Tony, it's not, it's because his father has zoned out of his son's life.'

'Zoned out? Who got him into Lego?'

'You also left him to figure it out alone.'

'I do Lego with him occasionally. Truth is, he prefers to do it on his own.'

'And he's told you this, has he?' Mum tutted a big one.

I know they were only saying these things to make the other feel in the depths of despair. Each desperate to hit the bullseye and score the highest points. They don't mean it; it's part of their rubbish game, which you can see through like a blown-up balloon.

A bit of time passed without shouting. I held my breath.

'None of that is right,' Mum finally said. Her voice soft and shaky. 'You know I'd die for the pair of them.'

Dad coughed as if he was trying to free a melon from his throat.

'I know you would,' he said. His voice had a similar

23

softness and shakiness to Mum's. 'You're his biggest supporter, Liz. I know that.'

'We both are.'

'You're the one who's always backing and protecting him.'

'You are as well, Tony,' Mum said. 'The two of them, not just Anthony.'

They were silent for twenty-three seconds. I counted in my head. That's a really long time with nothing being said. I gestured for Anto to shoosh cos I knew he could've killed this peace at any time.

But it was Mum who broke it, her voice still dead soft.

'He'll be more secure being here with me,' she said, which put an end to the truce. Didn't last long, did it?

'You think so?'

'I know so.'

'Yeah, don't worry, he'll be with me half of the week.'

'Excuse me?'

I heard Dad spark a match – one of the long ones Mum uses for her candles – and light his cigarette. Anto twitched his nose, then sucked his nostrils together. He can do that. He can do most things. I tapped a finger off my lips again to let him know how serious this moment was, and not to make a sound.

'Tony, don't think you're going to take Anthony away from—'

'You think I'm just going to let you keep them both and I get nothing?' He sucked on his cigarette really hard. 'That isn't going to happen.'

Mum mumbled something under her breath, which was tough to make out. I think it was something to do with Dad only wanting to have one of us … *and it isn't Anthony*. I'm sure Anto heard it as well. My brother's hearing is unreal. He could tell if a kitten was miaowing in a wind tunnel. Mum's mumbling made Dad slap his hand down on the sofa.

'I have rights, Liz, and I know them, so don't push me.'

'This is exhausting,' Mum said.

'You can't handle him on your own.'

'And you can? You spend more time at work than with him.'

'It'll be a doddle for me to arrange my work shifts around all this.'

'Oh, I've seen how much of a doddle that's been for you over the years. Or maybe that was just another one of your lies.'

Dad blew out the cigarette smoke as if he was blowing out the candles on our tenth birthday cake, which took some puff cos there were twenty of them on there.

'You're right, this is exhausting,' Dad said. 'I'm going to my bed.'

Anto shot off to his room before Dad made it to the bottom of the stairs. I followed, but when I got to his room he was already under the covers. In his very own bed tent. I didn't put the light off or say goodnight.

'Don't worry, Anto,' I mutter to him now. The Minecraft figures are still rising and falling, my hands still combing. 'I'll never let them take you away from me. Not in a million years. Or a billion days. I don't have a new plan yet, but don't worry, I'll get one. One for all four of us.'

Five

'Wake up, Anna.' Dad's standing at my bed holding a glass of water, flicking some of it on to my face. Has he gone completely tonto? 'Come on, you're going to be late.'

I can't find Anto's messy hair so I reach out to feel for him and hit only cold duvet; his stinky breath isn't wafting up my nose. He's gone. He must've bolted after I fell back to sleep.

'Hey, stop that,' I say, pulling the covers over my head but still trying to catch some air.

'You're going to be late,' Dad says.

I glance at the time. Ten to ten. 'For what?'

'MadCrew.'

'That's not until three.'

'Not for those going to Italy, it's not.'

I slide the covers down from my head and stare up at him.

'Seems a nice wee Italian trip is on the cards for you, Anna,' he says.

As soon as I hear the words *Italian trip* it's like I've just been struck by a flash of lightning. I feel the surge shoot from my toes right up to my head.

'Say that again, Dad.'

'Kim phoned ten minutes ago.'

'Really?'

'Really. So I'd get up if I were you.' He heads for the door.

'Wait,' I shout. He's grinning like one of those cream-licking cats. 'What did she say?'

'Who?'

'DAD!'

'You made it, Anna.'

'Honestly? No joke?'

'Would I joke?'

Not these days, no. But anyway.

'You better not be,' I warn him.

'You've made the squad.'

'Dad, if you're kidding me on, I'll kill you.'

'That's a bit much.'

'And I'd know how to do it too.' I sit up and mime strangling him. He mimes being strangled, wonky eyes and everything.

'Kim wants to see all those who made it at half ten.' He leaves, then quickly pops his head around the door again. 'So you'd better get up.' For a sec I thought he was about to tell me how proud he is of me. No, he just smiles and winks, which is the same thing really.

I catapult myself from the bed and start bouncing. Screaming too. Anto comes back in, covering his ears. I jump off and try to do a-ring-a-ring-o'-roses with him. Bad move. Anyway … I'm going to Italy.

I mean … Italy!

I bump into Tanya Breen outside the hall and we practically fall into each other's arms. She's not my BFF or anything, but she'd definitely be a member of my gang if I had one.

'Can you believe it?' she says.

'No, can you?'

'I knew you'd make it, Anna.'

'Really?'

'Well, not exactly, but I'm glad you'll be going too.'

'Shut up, you're not.'

'Shut up, I am.' Tanya punches me on the shoulder. 'I mean, it'll be amazing, Anna. Italy! We're actually going to Italy.' She widens her eyes and mouth as far as they can go and lets out a silent squeal.

'I know! Mental, isn't it?'

'It-al-y.' She writes in the air.

Tanya was born to be in MadCrew. When she's older she wants to become an actor, a singer, a choreographer and a primary school teacher. In that order. But last week she told me she wanted to work on an ice-cream van, so who knows what to believe.

'And we're going on an airplane,' I say.

'Have you ever been out of Scotland, Anna?'

'We went to Center Parcs in France a couple of years ago,' I tell her, peacock proud.

'Yeah, but I mean to a proper country?'

It's not fair, Tanya's been everywhere. Last Christmas she went to Dubai, apparently they've the *best air conditioners in the world*, and in October she's going to Marbella for a *cheeky week* with *the girls*. Well, her and her mum.

'God, I wish we were going tomorrow,' she says.

'I wonder if we'll be staying in a swanky hotel.'

'I hope we're sharing if we are.'

'Think they'll have a pool?'

'They better have, or some heads will be getting cracked.'

'I can't wait,' I say.

'Talk about heads.' Tanya nods behind mine. I turn to see who she's locked her eyes on to. Although there's no need to look. I know who she's talking about.

It gives me a severe earache to say it, but Evan Flynn is by far MadCrew's best and most creative dancer. It's just the constant performing and the 'SEE ME!' attitude that annoys the life out of me. I heard a teacher once say that *someone should turn down the volume on that laddie*. But still, I'd go as far as saying he's super-brilliant. Along with Kim, he practically designed the piece that won us our place in Italy: this amazing hip-hop routine where we danced to beats we created ourselves by bashing old buckets and empty cans off the floor. It sounds horrendous but it was really special. Mum said she'd *never seen anything like it in my life*. Dad said he thought we were all *trying to murder a gang of rats*. Both said that MadCrew should be on *Britain's Got Talent*. Anto didn't see it, he was with Gran and Papa.

Since winning, Tanya's been all over Evan like salt on a chip. She told him that he should *totally become a proper dance teacher when he's older*; that he could be Scotland's version of Bruno Tonioli. Yes, she actually said that. That was before her weak knees gave way and she collapsed on the ground right in front of him. Of course, that bit didn't happen, but you get the drift.

'Can't believe you pair of muppets made it,' Evan says, coming towards us. All jazz hands and smiles.

'It's some news!' I say.

'Hi, Evan,' Tanya says, all lashes and smiles. Seriously, if there was a bin close by I think I'd puke in it. Or dunk Tanya's head deep inside. 'It's amazing, isn't it?'

'Amazing?' He then brushes past us, eager to meet the others and no doubt suck up to Kim. Nothing worse than a teacher's pet. He turns back just before he enters the hall. 'It's the second best thing that's happened this year.'

Tanya twists her mouth, all confused.

'What's the first?' she shouts after him.

'When we win the whole thing.' He puts his hands up to his open mouth and does a comedy face.

Tanya's still smiling when he's out of sight.

'The cheek of him,' I spit. 'He's so confident—'

'And a brilliant mover,' Tanya interrupts. She turns into Little Miss Weirdo whenever he's around.

'Mover?' I squint an eye at her. 'I think *dancer* is the word you're looking for, Tanya.'

'He's going places, Anna.'

'Yeah, in to see Kim.'

'We've been getting some cheeky practising in,' Tanya says.

'Who? You and Evan?'

Tanya wiggles her eyebrows and trots after Evan as if she's impersonating a pony. I walk. Where is that bin again?

Kim hands us all our new hoodies. Black. MadCrew's written on the front above a silhouette of someone break-dancing like it's a rainbow. Then the best bit: the name ANNA is printed on the back in big yellow writing.

I keep the hoodie on my lap, but all I want to do is bring it up to my face and hug the life out of it. I can't believe I'm going to be dancing in another country. Me, Anna Quinn, competing in the European Street Dance Championships. Me, Anna Quinn, from the poor council schemes. No Mum or Dad. No Anto. No noise. No eggshells. No trying to glue everything back together again. Not worrying if losing a rogue Lego brick will start a World War Whatever. Just me and my hoodie.

I look up at the long strip light on the ceiling and try to imagine what being inside Italy will look like. And all the other squads as well. I mean, what do dance squads from Hungary and Germany talk about? I then wonder if some girl from Sweden is thinking about what we're like in Scotland. Life is daft. The strip light changes: now it's a giant cloud, shaped like an upside-down teddy bear. I see Mum and Dad's face appear from the mist, ear-to-ear grins on them; dead proud of their wee daughter.

They fade back into the cloud and it reminds me that nothing is normal these days, and might not be again for a very long time. It also reminds me that I still haven't got a plan together, but something's starting to bubble away in my thoughts.

'OK, squad.' Kim raises her voice in order to punch through the excitement in the hall, as well as all the questions being fired at her. She claps her hands three times. 'Silence, squad, SILENCE!' Everything comes to a hush. 'Just some basic housekeeping before we get started. It might answer some of your questions.'

'When do we leave, Kim?' Lucy Goldsmith asks.

'The morning of the tenth of August,' Kim says. 'We'll arrive in Rome around midday. That's only six weeks, guys.'

'What time specifically?' Lucy continues.

'Your parents have been emailed the specifics. And information about what paperwork you'll need, as well as an itinerary.'

'What's *itinerary* mean?' Tanya whispers.

'The stuff we'll be doing,' I whisper back.

'Kim? Kim? Kim?'

Honest to God, you'd think Lucy Goldsmith has never been out in public before.

'Yes, Lucy.'

'Do we have to make our own way to the airport or are we getting a minibus?' I've a feeling that Kim's already regretting that she put this question monster in the squad. But I could have told Kim that. She's the exact same at school.

Tanya puts up her hand.

'I'm allergic to kiwi fruit, Kim,' she says. People chuckle. I want to laugh too. Tanya looks at everyone's reaction. 'What? I am. Not my fault.'

'We've asked all parents to provide us with facts like that, Tanya. All special requirements. It'll all be covered. Don't worry.'

'Who's worrying?' Tanya whispers to me, and tuts. 'She's a spacer.'

'Oh, and congratulations, everyone,' Kim adds.

She takes us through some of the major do's and don'ts of the Italy trip. It's basically like this:

- DON'T do anything that will get you or someone else brutally killed.
- DO be kind to everyone you meet … apart from someone you suspect might want to brutally kill you.
- DON'T pick a fight with anyone from another country. Or your own.
- DO be respectful of other cultures … If you hear anyone shout *mamma mia!* in a funny accent stop them immediately.
- DON'T speak too quickly … Even the people from England will find it hard to understand what you're saying.

35

- DO encourage your parents to come along and support you and the rest of the squad.

'Right, let's get a good warm-up in before the rest of the group gets here,' Kim says.

I carry my chair to the side of the hall and fold my hoodie on it, ANNA side up.

The tiny seed of a plan I had earlier starts to swirl around my head during my middle splits. Details begin to appear. Thinking about how it could work sends me a bit dizzy. I can hardly keep my balance during my side extensions; when I pull my left leg over my head I think I'm about to topple over. And these are easy for me. I change legs.

Kim stands in the middle of the hall staring hard at me. I hope she's not thinking about changing her mind. Evan's behind me, but I can tell that he's sniggering his head off. I hit the floor, feeling it's best all round if I concentrate on hamstring stretches instead. My hamstrings feel like a couple of rusty springs. Flippin' heck. OK, Anna, STOP devising plans while stretching your hamstrings or they'll snap.

After MadCrew is over it's mostly mums who do the pick-ups. Sometimes you see the odd dad glued to their phone, wishing they were in a man cave watching football. My dad used to do pick me up all the time until Greggs changed his shifts around. Shame, cos he loved having *dance chats* with other parents, and in the car he'd let me listen to Gold UK.

Doesn't matter what the weather is doing, Tanya's mum is never out of these enormous sunglasses. Her hair is always tied back on her head. Sometimes with a ponytail, sometimes with a bun. Today it's a bun. Always has bright red lips. And her fashion sense … wow! Let's just say she's not a George from Asda mum. Sometimes she wears gold hooped earrings. Not today though. Tanya's dead lucky.

'Hiya, Mrs Breen,' I say, but I really want to tell her how much I love her fashion choices.

'Hi, Anna love. Great news about Italy, isn't it?'

Tanya puffs out a blast of air.

'Yeah, it's amazing,' I say.

'And you girls will get to shop in the most incredible places when you're there. Lucky so-and-sos.' Mrs Breen flattens a palm over her hair. 'I might have to squeeze myself into Tanya's Samsonite.' I try hard not to look confused when she laughs at her own … joke?

'God sake, Mum,' Tanya whines. 'Can we just get in the car?'

'Maybe you two girls should get together for some practice,' Mrs Breen says directly to me.

'Erm …' I say.

37

'Mum!' Tanya growls. 'Can we just—'

'Where do you do your practising, Anna love?'

'Erm, usually in my bedroom, or down in the living room,' I say.

'Well, now that school's over for the summer,' Mrs Breen says. 'Tanya's not doing anything tomorrow.'

'Right,' I say, looking for some stones to kick.

'Are you doing anything important tomorrow, Anna?'

'Erm … I don't … erm … I'm not sure.'

'Perfect, I could drop her at yours.'

You'd swear that Tanya's bursting for the loo cos she's standing twisting her body like she's in some deep agony.

'It's fine if you want to,' I say. Gran and Papa always remind me to be kind at all times. Especially when someone is twisting themselves in front of you. 'It might be a good idea to try out some of the new stuff.'

My mind instantly jumps to worry mode. What if Mum and Dad start scrapping with each other? What if Tanya hears everything? I count the syllables on one hidden hand: hu–mil–i–a–tion.

'Probably wouldn't do us any harm,' Tanya says, as if I've just asked her if she wants to rob the charity shop. 'Maybe we should.'

'Perfect!' Mrs Breen says. 'Shall we say midday?'

'That's fine,' I go. 'Will I send you my address?'

'I know where you are,' Mrs Breen says.

Really?

How is it adults always know exactly where everyone lives?

Tanya mumbles a *See you tomorrow* to me and climbs into her mum's car. I say car, but it's more like a tank, it would gobble our wee dinky one up. Tanya told me it's got voice-activated Spotify. Fine, but does it have Gold UK?

'I think she must be nervous already,' Mrs Breen says to me, nodding her head towards Tanya inside the car.

'Must be.' I don't know where to look.

I see Mum at the other end of the car park. She's staring right at me, arms folded. No smiles. I give her a wave. Her arms don't break their fold.

'Don't think she sees me,' I tell Mrs Breen.

'OK, midday tomorrow then,' Mrs Breen says and jumps into her tank.

As they're driving away I give Tanya a tiny wave, but she doesn't respond. Mrs Breen's arms are flying about like a woman possessed. Someone's getting a voice-activated tongue-lashing.

I walk towards Mum, who's standing beside our wee Twingo in her Primark tracksuit, the grey fluffy one she puts on for watching telly. Her hair is dragged back off her face. No make-up. The natural look. Her skin glows like one of those porcelain dolls. She must've had those special tea bags on her eyes again. *My magic bags*, she calls them. Imagine her in Italy, she'd look so amazing. People's necks would be as sore as anything with all the turning and twisting going on. Wouldn't be surprised if someone kidnapped her, only for her to turn up days later strutting down a catwalk somewhere. She'd need to ditch the trackie though.

Mum sees me at last because suddenly her arms drop and she does a comedy scream. Not even Tanya's mum seemed as jazzed about it. She hugs me and kisses the top of my head. For some reason I thought she was angry at me. I hold on to her, gripping the fluffy trackie around her waist as tightly as I can. I breathe her through my nose, she smells like the flower shop in the precinct.

'I'm so chuffed for you, Anna.'

'It's good news, isn't it?'

'Good? It's great news. What an experience you'll have.'

Doesn't have to be just my experience. I don't say this out loud.

I briefly imagine that we're all in this big fancy restaurant somewhere in Italy. It smells of a boiling summer's day. Dad's practising his bad Italian on the waiter. Mum's dress is from one of the most incredible of places. When the pizzas come they look nothing like the ones we get at Macari's …

On the way home Mum lets me listen to Spin 108. Usually she moans constantly about all the songs they play. But this is clearly my day. And I'm going to blinking well have it.

'Mum.'

'What?'

'Can we have pizza for dinner tonight?'

'Takeaway?'

'Yeah, from Macari's. Can we?'

'Getting into the spirit already?'

'We can surprise Dad when he gets in from work,' I plead. 'Can we?'

'Of course we can.'

I'm chuffed, I can almost smell that cheese crust.

'Oh, by the way, Tanya Breen is coming round tomorrow.' Mum fires me a glance. 'So we can practise,' I tell her. For some reason she cheekily changes the radio station from the steering wheel. I don't mind. I do, but I don't as well.

'We need to pick up Anthony from your Gran and Papa's.'

- DON'T worry too much.
- DO hope by the time you get to Italy you'll have persuaded your mum and dad to come too.

41

Six

When we're looking through Macari's pizza menu Anto slaps his hand on the kitchen table twice when I read out *Diavolo*.

I warn him:

'It's got jalapenos *and* chilli flakes on it.'

He slaps twice.

'You sure?' I ask.

Slaps.

'Anthony, it's really spicy, remember,' Mum tells him.

'*Diavolo* actually means *Devil*, Anto,' I say.

Screams. A happy one.

'OK, but if you can't eat it, don't blame us,' Mum adds.

'It's not called the Devil for nothing, you know.'

Slaps.

I shake my head cos I know he's just trying to act the big

man; he thinks that by eating some spiced time bomb everyone will be impressed. It's showing off and nothing more. Sometimes there's just no talking to my brother.

'It's your choice, but just as long as you know, it's definitely going to blow the nut off you,' I say.

Whenever he smiles, which isn't that often, Anto's eyes could light up an entire shopping mall. We all love takeaways, but he could live off them.

Mum phones in the order, then comes back to deliver the bad news.

'They can't deliver until half seven,' she says.

See, Anto always gets his hair washed every Sunday night at half seven. But tonight it'll have to happen around half six. But Sunday at half six is when he listens to music on his Bluetooth headphones. So, major issue alert. This is what's called a conundrum.

Anto almost sprints upstairs. Issue occurring.

Mum puffs out her cheeks. 'I'll go up to him in a minute.'

'No, I'll go,' I tell her. 'He'll be fine with me.'

Mum doesn't put up a fight.

He's clicking bricks together when I enter his room. I knew that's what he'd be doing. Without looking at me, he holds up the brick structure as if he's a referee. Red bricks mean many things:

Stop.

Go away.

I'm not interested.

I don't want/like that.

Beat it.

And a good old-fashioned, NO.

It can also mean, I hate you. Or is that four reds with a black one in the middle? Sometimes it's hard to keep up.

'Anto, we can wash your hair before the pizzas arrive,' I suggest. 'It's no big deal.' I feel like slapping myself on the wrist. What am I saying? Of course it's a big deal. It's a deal with a capital BIG. 'It'll be just this once.' Might not be actually, I shouldn't have said that.

He rummages through the pile of Lego on the floor and rapidly clicks four brown bricks together before raising it high in the air. This means, I don't give two hoots what you think. (And that's me being really polite.)

'I'll wash it quickly. I promise.' Whenever Anto's upset and doesn't look at you, Dad always says, *No dice*. This is a no dice moment. 'If we do it at half six we'll still have plenty of time to wash your hair and eat pizza.' I see him scrounging around looking for yellows and blues.

'No, Anto. Don't even think about it.' He clicks them into place. 'Seriously, Anto.' Yellow, blue, yellow, blue. In that order.

'I'm not happy about this.' When he holds the yellow and blue up to me, my anger alarm blares. 'It was my idea

44

to get pizza. This is my day and you're just being a selfish wee brat. Not good.' I slam the door on the way out and sit on the top stair listening to the noises coming from his room; all that Lego being thrashed around inside as if it's raining plastic. Then it hits me, the idea of a lifetime. Sometimes I scare myself with these genius ideas I have.

When it stops raining bricks I gently knock on his door and peek my head around. He's lying on his soft floor mat, bum in the air. Lost count of the times I've been dying to run and give it a huge kick.

'I've a good idea, Anto.' He rocks his bum. 'Want to hear it?' The rocking speeds up. 'Anto? Do you want to hear it or not? Last chance. Three seconds and I'm heading down-stairs.' I hear him moaning like a wounded puppy. Heard it too many times to worry. 'One … I'm deadly serious … Two … right, I'm going … Th—'

He leaps from his mat and starts on the bricks again. He holds up four white. One of my favourites:

Yes.

OK.

Please, go ahead, I'm listening.

To help him listen he covers his ears with split fingers.

'What if we take my bedside clock into the bathroom and set the time to half seven?' He blinks twice. And thrusts the white bricks again.

'That way it can be half seven in the bathroom and another time on the outside. We don't even have to think about the time outside cos it'll always be seven thirty or after inside the bathroom, know what I mean?' I see him thinking about it. 'Does that sound OK?'

He grabs his coat hanger from the bed and taps his temple with it, then hooks it through his arm and leaves it dangling off his shoulder. This is a good sign.

'It's a decent idea, isn't it?' I say.

He starts digging through the Lego again. Black, white, black, white. We call this one the zebra, it's a non-angry way for him to say, hold your horses a minute.

He gets his Bluetooth headphones and hangs them around his neck. Oh, no, his Sunday playlist! I completely forgot about that. There goes my genius status. Anto's playlists aren't like mine, his are tightly connected to the timing of certain things he does. For example, when school term is on he only listens to The Beatles. Every single morning without fail.

- 'A Day in the Life' = Get up, wash face until the soap lathers.
- 'I Am the Walrus' = Brush teeth thoroughly.
- 'Hey Jude' = Get dressed as neatly as possible.
- 'Let It Be' = Fix hair. Not with fingers.

- 'The Long and Winding Road' = Eat half a mug of cereal.
- 'Back in the USSR' = Bag check and jacket.

From getting up until leaving the house it's about twenty-seven minutes in total. Always those songs. Always in that order. It continues in the car.

But now we're talking about his pre-hair-wash playlist.

'You can still listen to your Sunday playlist,' I remind him. He doesn't change his expression.

'You can do it, Anto. It'll be easy.' He looks at me as if I'm half daft. 'I'll let you know when to play the last three songs, and when they're finished all you need to do is come into the bathroom. You'll see the clock saying half seven. That's dead doable, isn't it?' He tightens his eyes. 'So, it'll be The Bee Gees, then Neil Diamond, and when Harry Styles finishes, you just go in and I'll wash your hair, OK?'

I can see that there's an information overload for him to deal with. He needs a whole bunch of time. I don't move, I stand at the door with my arms folded, staring down at him. I might be turning into Mum in my old age.

'The Bee Gees, then Neil Diamond and Harry Styles,' I say again.

47

Anto brings the coat hanger from his shoulder to his wrist and begins twirling it. YES! I'm so good at this big sister malarkey.

He holds up four white bricks. And it's official: I *am* a genius. Actually, it's Mum and Dad who are the geniuses for creating the brick-colour thing with him. Ages and ages it took. Actually, it's Anto who's the real genius for bringing it all to life.

For about twenty seconds I wait to see if he'll do my favourite brick combination. I'm almost urging him to make the four whites separated by one red, but my stupid brother crashes and burns. I know one day he'll hold the *I love you* bricks in front of my face. Not today though. For a split second I have a feeling that I can't wait for that Diavolo pizza to blow the nut off him.

I think we seriously need to start using the picture charts more, cos waiting for bricks to be clicked together can take you out of the emotion of the moment, while just pointing to a picture of what that feeling is would be much quicker. We'll get around to making new ones, but not today.

'Right, half seven in the bathroom, OK?' I wink at him. He keeps twirling.

Before I go downstairs Anto clicks together a few pink and purple bricks. Holds it high. They're the Congratulations colours.

I spread my arms out and say, 'K … K … K … K.' Anto shakes his head, but copies me by spreading his arms too. So we do a congratulations hug from a distance.

He's already topless when he stoats into the bathroom. I can hear Harry Styles blaring out from his headphones. When he sees half seven on the clock he takes off the headphones and kneels with his head dangling over the bath. I sling the *Welcome To Corfu* towel that Gran and Papa brought him from their Easter holiday over his bare shoulders. Every week more and more spots appear. Yuck! He's lucky he can't see my face.

'I'm going to put the water on now. But only on my hand,' I say.

He flinches as soon as he hears the water skoosh out the shower head. It's the same every time. I let it run until it's perfect, sticky-toffee-pudding temperature. I prefer it much warmer myself.

'Put out your hand and you can test it,' I tell him. He fans out his hand and I spray his palm and the gaps in his fingers. 'OK?' He bangs the bath twice. 'Right, I'm going to wet your hair now.' His whole body tenses up, including his eyelids. I feel so sorry for his poor eyes being squeezed like that.

'G … G … G … G,' is the sound he makes. It's hard to

know if he's freezing or boiling. You'd think he was in the Antarctic or Benidorm, such an exaggerator.

'Too cold? Too hot?'

He doesn't bang his hand, meaning it's just right. He's at it.

His soaking mop starts sticking to his face. He snots away any dribbles that dare go anywhere near his nose. From the pictures I've seen I'd say his hair is nearly as long as Jesus's. It would be so much easier for everyone if he'd just get the thing chopped. Obviously not at the barber's, but Mum could definitely do a top job on it. I secretly suspect he's trying his hardest to be Harry Styles. Yeah, in your dreams, Anto.

I'm careful not to touch his scalp too much in case a pain shoots right through him. See, Anto doesn't feel pain like anyone else our age does. For him it's like being jabbed with ten knitting needles every time I press my fingertips on to his skull, so I've got to massage the shampoo as if he's a two-week-old baby, otherwise he'll go berserk and rattle off every wall in the house. We've all had a chance of washing his hair: Dad thinks he's kneading a bit of dough, while Mum's nails are as good as cats' claws, and *there's no way these are getting cut after the amount I've spent on them.* So I got the job, thanks to having feather fingers. Even so, I've still got to be ten times gentler than gentle.

Head & Shoulders Supreme Nourish & Smooth is his favourite. Nothing to do with the soft, shiny finish, it's all about the shape of the bottle and the picture of the greeny-blue leaves on front. After dropping a giant dollop on him I hand him the bottle to play with while I'm shampooing. This technique of giving him the shampoo bottle is new, created by yours truly in order to buy more time, even if it's only an extra minute. See, washing Anto's hair has to be done at top speed cos you never know when he's had enough. And when he's had enough, he's had enough. I've lost count the number of times he's jumped up with suds still foamy in his hair. Worst is when the shampoo isn't out his eyes, his screams could break glass, no joke.

'Nearly finished,' I tell him.

'G ... G ... G ... G,' he bellows. That's just him at the wind-up. The temperature is perfect and I know it.

Afterwards he dries his own hair; loves nothing more than running the *Welcome To Corfu* towel over his head as if trying to get rid of a swarm of bees. Clown. And suddenly all pain sensitivity has miraculously disappeared.

And that's us done.

Oh, I forgot to say, everything about washing the hair has to be done with the light switched off. The sound of electricity in the bathroom drives him round the twist, apparently. I've never even heard it.

Seven

Dad comes in from work with a big bag of stuff. Mum calls them *leftovers*, *cast-offs*, *reheats* or *dregs*. But never to his face. I just call them goodies. Usually when Dad lays out his dregs on the table, it's a cue for Anto to come rushing downstairs and shove his nose in them. Like a police dog at a crime scene. I'm telling you, that brother of mine could smell a Jaffa Cake in the eye of a tornado.

'Right, let's see what Santa Greggs brought home today then,' Dad says with a huge beam on his face as he starts plonking each cast-off on to the worktop. 'Mmm, yum-yums,' he says, in his stupid Yoda voice. 'Who doesn't like yum-yums?'

I press my front teeth together.

'Oh, and look what we have here …' He's continuing with the Yoda thing. 'We've only gone and got four triple chocolate doughnuts.' I think he's shifted from Yoda to Gollum. Anto would love hearing this. He's up in his room, no doubt still towelling his hair.

'And the *pièce de résistance*.' Oh, my God, he's doing his French accent now. I'd be completely mortified if any of my pals had to hear this. 'We have our eight delicious sausage rolls.' His French actually seems half Spanish, half Russian. I'm staring at the sausage rolls, thinking: *What's happening?* It's not sausage-roll day. Something's wrong, I know it. I can feel it in my gut. Dad starts making random Spanish/Russian sounds, you'd swear a dying pig had just entered our house.

'Dad, can you not?' I plead.

'And for my wee Italian dancer, I got this.' He pulls out a Jammie Dodger shaped like a love heart. I think my eyes are about to pop out. Followed by my tongue. 'Dessert for after these,' he says, pointing at the sausage rolls. His voice returns to normal.

Mum appears in the kitchen and stares at the food on the worktop. I know she's thinking of huffing out the words *dregs* or *cast-offs*. The corners of her mouth curl up a bit and she does a tiny wee lick of her lips, but not to suggest she wants to tuck in.

'We've ordered pizzas, Tony,' Mum says.

'But I've brought—'

'They'll be here at half seven,' she says.

Dad's face drops; looks like someone's just smashed all his doughnuts with a hammer. Suddenly I feel bad cos pizza was my idea.

'We ordered you a Hawaiian,' I say. 'But we can change it if you'd prefer.'

His mouth opens.

'We can't,' Mum shoots in, as if it's all my fault. 'Too late.'

'We got Anto a spicy one,' I say. 'It'll be funny seeing his face explode.'

'Funny for who?' Mum's eyes burn through me.

'Hawaiian's fine,' Dad says. 'I'll put all this in the fridge.' He gathers up all the scraps from Greggs. 'Maybe we can have it tomorrow.'

Mum puffs out air and goes to get something from the cupboard. It's the same air sound that she does instead of saying, *How many times do I need to tell you, Anna?* She's opening drawers and cupboards with some force. Me and Dad give each other a look.

After the fridge Dad goes to get some glasses; if ever there was a man desperate to help set a table this was him.

'I've got it,' Mum says, almost shoving him out of the way.

'It's fine,' Dad says, reaching over her head. 'I'm here now.'

54

'I said I've got it, Tony.'

'And I said it's fine, Liz.'

Dad wins cos his reach is longer. Mum looks as though she'd like to chuck one of the tumblers he's holding directly at his head. She marches out of the kitchen. We listen to her thundering up the stairs. I hope Anto's head-phones are back on his head.

When Dad plops the four glasses in the middle of the table he does the exact same air puff as Mum's.

'Pizza, eh? That's a surprise,' he says.

'I just thought, you know, since I got into the Italy squad that we could all celebrate together.'

'So my chocolate doughnuts aren't good enough any more?'

'What? No!'

'Pizza over doughnuts, what's the world coming to?'

'I asked Mum and she said it would be OK.'

I feel as if I've made him sad. I'm starting to miss his Gollum/Yoda voice now.

'Aw well, I'll just have to chuck them in the bin.'

'Dad!'

'I'm joking, love. I think it's a brilliant idea.'

'You do?'

'Who doesn't like pizza?'

'Or celebrations.'

'Exactly. We'll have the goodies after we've finished the pizza.' He winks.

'It'll be like a family party,' I say.

Dad smiles, then lifts his neck up to the ceiling, which makes his Adam's apple look huge. I do this when I'm trying to balance tears on the surface of my eyes. Nothing worse than wet cheeks. It's much easier when I'm lying in bed. People say that me and Dad have the same colour and shape of eyes. Blue almonds. Sometimes I think that all the onions he chops at work are beginning to turn his a bit red though. And puffy. Onions are more dangerous than people think.

'Maybe we should've invited Gran and Papa too,' I say.

'They go to bed early on a Sunday,' he says. 'They'd need more notice. Maybe next time.'

'When can we do a next time?'

'Let's just get this time out of the way first, eh.'

'But, we'll see, right?'

'We'll see.'

Maybe I should just start planning loads and loads of family events. Ask Gran and Papa. Ask Tanya and her mum. We could have a pre-Italy BBQ with all the other mums and dads who are going. That way everyone gets to meet each other properly; much better fun than saying a quick hello outside the MadCrew hall. Mum could buy wine for everyone, and Dad could get some goodies from work.

Half seven on the dot and Anto appears at the kitchen table ready for his Diavolo. His hair's still a bit damp – there's no way Mum'll go near him with a hairdryer.

'Hey, son, hungry?' Dad says.

Anto stares at the kitchen door, breathing through his nose. I can tell he's still raging at Dad cos of what he heard on the stairs last night. I try giving him the eyes so he'll stop doing that bull breathing and wasting everything. He just speeds up.

'Anto!' I say.

'You're a brave man getting that spicy one,' Dad says.

Anto glances at the hanging light and starts tapping his finger off the table, slow and loud.

'It wouldn't be me. I'm getting the Hawaiian. Aloha!' Dad throws his hands up in the air, trying hard to bring the laughter. To quote Mum, *Give me strength*.

The taps get louder.

Everything's annoying me now and I'm not sure why. It's not as if I haven't seen or heard it a thousand times before. Some celebration this is turning out to be.

Tap.

Tap.

Tap.

'Dad,' I say, shaking my head. 'Get the light, will you?'

It's as if Dad's just started living in our house, he's completely doolally sometimes. He knows to turn down the big light when Anto's sitting with us.

'Sit where you are, I'll get it,' Mum says, trying to juggle four pizzas in one arm and dim the light with the other. I didn't even hear the door go. Anto stops tapping and claps his hands three times.

Already I can tell Dad's disappointed; he's piling up wee chunks of pineapple on the side of his box. Mum nibbles away at the tip of a triangle, while Anto thinks he's auditioning for *Man v. Food*.

'Best thing about pizza,' I say, 'is no washing-up at the end.'

'Mmm,' Mum says.

'Like, it's only the glasses and nothing else,' I add. 'How cool is that?'

Dad gets up and scrapes pineapple into the bin. Mum picks off a piece of pepperoni. Maybe I shouldn't have mentioned the glasses.

'So, did you find any more info about Italy?' Dad says. 'It's exciting, isn't it?'

'Yeah, amazing,' I say. 'I'm dead chuffed.'

'It's terrific. I'm proud of you, sweetheart,' Mum says.

'I'm proud too,' Dad says.

'Really proud,' Mum adds.

Oh no, my parents are having a *Who's the proudest?* contest.

Anto slaps his hand into the middle of a Diavolo triangle. Tomato sauce covers his fingers and palm. The last thing I need is for him to enter the contest too. OK, I get it, I get it, everyone is dead proud of me.

Kim's DO's and DON'Ts list is now playing at full speed over and over in my head.

'So we're getting an airplane and staying in a hotel,' I tell them.

'Kim emailed us with all the details,' Mum says. 'It's going to be great.'

'And it'll be competitions all weekend. Heats, quarters, semis, finals, solos, groups, trios. I don't think we'll make the finals though.'

'You never know,' Dad says. 'Got to dream big.'

Mum gives him a look that could melt steel. I hear Anto breathing heavily.

'The dream was to get there, Dad.'

'But now you're there, you should aim to win, no?'

I mean, I love him to bits, but what my Dad knows about urban street dance and hip hop is as much as I know about what makes the perfect puff pastry.

'Dad, we'll have to come up with four new routines.

And make them all different. I'd say we'll be lucky to even get through the heats.'

'Never say never,' he says.

'Give me strength,' Mum mutters under her breath. It's so soft that it's only me who hears it. Anto thuds the table. Two glasses jump.

I decide it's best just to dive in with some of the DO's and DON'Ts. Well, one DO.

'Mum, Dad,' I say with my sweet, soft voice; the one I use when I've something important to say. Both stop and look at me. Pizza slices grounded. My brother continues to munch, however. All I hear is his chewing in my ear.

'Anto!' I bellow. 'Can you eat like a normal person?'

All eyes are on him; spotlight shining directly on his face. I can tell how this is going to play out. We've all been in this movie loads of times before.

Anto slides his chair out so hard that it smacks off the wall. He only does this cos his brain and body aren't communicating properly; everything gets muddled up. His teacher told Mum and Dad, who then told me, that it's a bit like his inner computer has lost its Wi-Fi connection. His head's telling him that things are *buffering buffering*. Sometimes I think Dad's going to throw his laptop in the bin cos of buffering issues. So, imagine Anto's body being unable to upload what his brain is telling him. That's what I call buffering issues times a thousand.

He runs upstairs, slamming doors on the way.

'He's not even finished that,' Dad points to his half-eaten Diavolo.

'I told him not to order that spicy one,' Mum says.

We finish the rest of our pizza in silence. Or, as they say in Italy, *silenzio*.

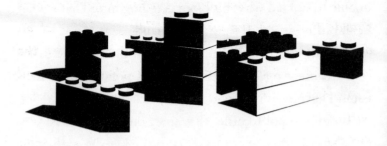

Eight

I'll tell you, eating with my family is exhausting. My head's heavy, so are my eyes. My pillow is soft, and it feels so good to be dozing in peace. I've still got bits of pizza wedged between my molars. Mum would be raging if she saw me attacking the jammed pizza with my tongue; she's put millions of hours into a thorough teeth-cleaning regime with us. Well, me really. Anto is a teeth-brushing law unto himself. Mum does hers for a whole two minutes with her fancy electric brush. Bought from Asda. A full two minutes! I mean, come on. I'm happy to fight for stuck pizza bits. It helps me sleep.

And sleep.

And sleep.

Well, that and the thoughts of Paris. Yes, Paris.

Zzzz.

Right, so, we're all in this big fancy Center Parcs outside Paris and the weather is like the inside of an oven. We're in one of the best chalets, overlooking the lake. It has a kitchen and French television. Mum and Dad's room has a shower and a toilet in it. I'm sharing with Anto, which is too weird to think about. I mean, I'm twelve, but for some reason I go with it cos it's only happening in my dreamy world. Mum and Dad spend half an hour rearranging our bedroom to make it feel similar to Anto's at home. Nothing under the window, wardrobe to the left of the door, bed flush against the wall, that sort of stuff. Bring in the *DIY SOS* team, or whoever; he still does caveman snores and makes an annoying clicking sound during the night. Wish they'd rearrange that.

We've a balcony in our room, but Anto doesn't go out on it in case it collapses, so it's all mine. My sanctuary. Every morning I go there before breakfast with my Judy Blume book and suck in the fresh air; France smells really different to Scotland.

Our suitcase was full of George stuff, even Dad's. Mum takes a picture of the three of us before we go to hire bikes and, honestly, we look like a family of rainbows. Dad says it's like we've been attacked by Picasso, which makes Mum convulse with laughter. I don't get the joke.

She laughs so much that she has to snuggle into Dad's neck in order to stop. I shrug towards Anto. Nothing back. I'd expect nothing else.

We don't get individual bikes cos Dad would probably say *this holiday has cost us a bomb already* and Anto can't be trusted, so he gets us this pedalling car thing that fits four. The two in the front (Dad and Anto) pedal like mad while the two in the back (me and Mum) relax, give directions and wave to French strangers. Dad shouts, *Quicker, quicker, faster,* and Anto goes as fast as his legs will take him. He screams his head off when we fly down a hill. A tiny hill. It's the best scream ever. He throws his arms in the air as if he's on a rollercoaster, hair fluttering behind him like a swooping crow.

When we come to a stop Anto takes Dad's hand and nuzzles it into his cheek. Mum and Dad look at each other and do the same smile that they have in their wedding photo.

Definitely the pedalling car was the way to go.

Next to the lake is a little park with picnic benches and swings. That's where we have our swanky packed lunch. All this foreign stuff and cheese that smells of farts. Mum and Dad have some wine. Anto loves throwing the ducks half-chewed bread. We sit on a blanket hoping he doesn't fall in. Someone (Mum) forgets to bring his armbands to lunch. When no one is looking he throws the ducks cherry tomatoes and olives, with the pits still in them. Honestly, can't take him anywhere.

Mum and Dad talk for ages about these French sausage rolls we bought. They chew, nibble and fondle them, checking to see if they're better than Greggs'. Mum says Dad thinks he's *Paul bleedin' Hollywood.* Dad says that he knows *a top-quality sausage roll when I see it ... like now!* Then he pounces on Mum and munches her neck, pretending it's an actual giant sausage roll. She's giggling her head off; he even does pig sounds. Pair of them make some racket. People look over. To say I'm embarrassed is the understatement of the holiday. If I wasn't scared of getting pelted with a cherry tomato I'd jump right in with the ducks.

The water park's changing rooms are beyond weird. Men *and* women change together. Can you imagine that? I am. *This is how they roll in France,* Dad tells us. Who knew? We all have to squeeze into this tiny family cubicle to get ready, which is another ... interesting moment. I'm the last to get into my costume cos there's no way I'm changing in front of Dad and Anto. I wait until they get into their trunks and leave. Dad looks like, well, a hairy sausage roll in his bright orange trunks. Mum could be a poster model in the Zara window. I tell

65

her she should definitely have a word with the Asda bosses.

The lazy river is beyond amazing. It floats and shifts you along with the current. Makes you feel as if you're gliding on wet air. Mum and Dad sail down it in each other's arms. Actually, Dad's holding her like a baby. She clings on to him like a human necklace. Just before we enter the rapids I see them kissing. A proper snog. Oh my God, the embarrassment never ends. Anto doesn't see them cos he's got a huge snorkel on and is much happier looking at people underwater. He wants to find money.

After the lazy river we wait for a go on the Kamikaze, the deadly water slide. *The fastest slide in France*, I bet the brochure in our chalet would've said. When we get to the top of the queue, Anto gets the jitterbugs and bottles it. If I knew he'd start screaming there's no way I'd have suggested it in the first place. Obviously this didn't really happen, but if it did I'd have taken him back down and we'd have decided to go on the slow, twisty slide with an inflatable ring instead; pretty sure that this is the gentlest slide in France. He insists on wearing his snorkel going down. A group of people with much better tans than me start sniggering but I don't say anything, then I feel bad for not saying anything. I don't know the French for *Can you stop laughing at my brother, please?* anyway. I get a massive wedgy. Mum and Dad go down a different slide altogether; it looks like a playground one, only bigger. They go down at the same time. Yawn. Mum sits in front of Dad. Double yawn. Both scream with their hands high in the air. What age do they think they are? They fall into the little pool at the bottom howling like a couple of banshees. Judy Blume says that parents will forever shame you. I know exactly what you mean, Judy.

On the last day of the holiday me and Dad attempt the Kamikaze. Now, I'm serious, don't talk to me about wedgies. It doesn't matter if they are real or imagined. Still makes me grimace.

'ANNA!'

Weeeeeeeeeee!

'ANNA!'

Kamiiiikkkkaaazzzeee!

'ANNA.' I open my eyes. Mum's roughly shaking my shoulder. 'Breakfast is on the table.' She's not wearing any swimwear.

'What?' I croak.

'Breakfast. Time to get up.'

I arch my back and stretch.

'OK.'

Mum leaves.

There's still pizza trapped in my teeth. A pre-breakfast starter. I lie thinking about how cool dreams are. That was the best holiday ever.

I'm about to hop out of bed when a light bulb flashes in my head. That's it! That's it! We're the happiest family on earth while on holiday, and we haven't been on holiday for yonk years, so Italy would be perfect. After all, it is the country of love with a capital LOVE. Or is that France? Whatever. It's the best idea I've had since my last one.

Right, that's exactly what we'll do; we'll all go to Italy and fall in love with it, and let Italy fall in love with us. Then Mum and Dad will fall in love with each other. One more time.

What can I say? I'm an ideas person.

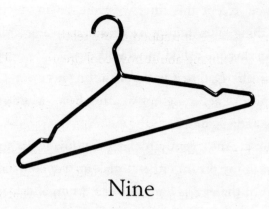

Nine

I get dressed and bound downstairs, ready to spring my idea upon them. Standing at the table I put on my bestest/happiest grin. Dad's scrolling through his phone, holding it far too close to his face. Mum's fingernail clicks off her screen. Anto's back is turned away from the table as he crunches into his toast. There's a boiled egg at my place, all alone like a baldy wee man.

'Morning!' I say, plonking myself down. Mum and Dad mutter *Morning* without looking up from their phones. It's a mystery to me why adults find Twitter and Instagram so interesting.

'I had this amazing dream last night,' I spout, hoping to unglue their screen eyes. PUT THE PHONES AWAY. I can't help feeling that the roles should be reversed here. 'Get this, it was kind of like Center Parcs where we went in France except this time we were staying in this wee chalet thing, plus there were tons more water slides and I went on this one called the Kamikaze—'

'Paris, eh!' Dad says without shifting his eyes.

'Be nice to get some hot weather here,' Mum says, still flicking and clicking.

I look at Anto, gently rocking and loving his toast. No interest in my dream either. I pick up a spoon and smash the top of the egg as hard as I can. Mum and Dad's eyes pop up. Finally! I just go for it:

'Kim asked us to ask our parents if they want to come and support us in Italy,' I say in a loud, excited voice. Dad glances at Mum. 'Anto too,' I say, softer. 'The whole family, in fact.' Mum stares at her nails. 'Like, come on, it's Italy. It'll be amazing, and dead hot, Mum.'

Dad coughs. Mum sips her tea.

'It's very short notice, Anna,' Mum says.

'I could probably get the time off, if that's what you'd like,' Dad says to her.

'It might be too expensive for us all to go,' Mum says, giving Dad some serious eye tonic.

'Please,' I say, stretching out the *eeeee* sound. 'It'll be brill.' I go too far with the *rrrrrr* sound.

'I'm not sure I can get that time off,' Mum says. 'That's our busiest period.'

'It's Asda,' Dad cuts in.

'Well, I haven't put in for those holidays, have I?' she snaps. 'Needed to have done that months ago.'

'So,' I say, feeling like doing an Anto with my egg. 'It's a no then?'

'I wouldn't say that,' Dad says. 'Not yet anyway.'

'Mum?'

She sighs heavily and pinches her eyes. 'I'll need to see, Anna.' You'd think I'd just asked her if I could have fifty quid to go on a shopping spree. I want to ask her what Rightmove is, but now's not the time.

My chest suddenly feels heavy; I tighten my lips, and swallow what seems like a giant gobstopper. I'm not going to cry, but I think I want to. This is the master plan. Italy is the superglue, the solution to everything, and they're not seeing it.

'It's just a no today,' Dad says, 'but it might be a yes tomorrow.'

'I bet all the other mums and dads will be going,' I spit.

Mum mutters something that I can't make out.

'What?'

'We can't make a decision like that after one conversation, Anna,' Mum says.

'So it's always going to be a no then?' I say.

Mum does her stern eyes at me. When her head is this still she means business.

'No, Anna. It is an I-will-think-about-it, OK?' She turns to Dad for back-up.

'Like your mum said, we'll think about it.'

'It's not fair, you never do anything for me.' I don't actually mean this but drastic action is required.

'Don't talk rubbish,' Mum says.

I know exactly what I'm doing and how to do it. I scrape the chair off the floor and jump up with the ferocity of an attacking cat. Anto makes one squealing sound. Very high pitched.

'I'm not talking rubbish. It's true. You never do anything for me or Anto.'

I don't run upstairs like he normally does, but I make sure that I stomp my Vans down hard on every step. There's another squeal before I head into my bedroom.

I'm lying on top of my duvet, with my Vans on. All the checkerboards are much dirtier these days but they're brilliant for gliding across the floor when breaking and popping. Kim said they're perfect too. Think we have to wear all black in Italy, so I'll have to get new ones. Mum'll be delighted. Thankfully George at Asda doesn't do all-black trainers. I've checked.

My door isn't fully closed, so sound can float in from downstairs. Or, even better, Mum and Dad's bedroom.

72

They're in there being really careful to speak in ultra-soft voices, but since we don't live in a mansion I can hear almost everything they say. Being mid-morning, Anto will probably have one of his playlists on, out of earshot. Honestly, Mum and Dad are the world's worst whisperers.

'She wants us to go, Liz.'

'Yeah, well, wait until tomorrow. She'll regret ever asking us.'

'But, did you not hear her? She's so excited.'

'Look, Tony, I don't feel like playing happy families. It's bad enough trying to do it here, never mind traipsing around Italy pretending everything's hunky-dory.'

'It's a terrific opportunity for her. I'd just like her to feel that she's being supported, that's all.'

'Supported? Don't. I'm in no mood for laughter.'

Mum puts on a pretend giggle, which kind of annoys me. OK, so being here in the house all the time isn't exactly happy for anyone, but it's Italy! Ice cream, sunshine, nice food and no umbrellas. That would make any family happy, wouldn't it? Even ours.

'We're still her parents, Liz. Whatever happens, that can't change.' Dad's voice gets closer, he must be heading towards the landing at the top of the stairs. Maybe he's going to the drawers at the bottom of the stairs where he keeps the big box of foreign cigarettes. The ones Gran and

Papa brought him back from Magaluf. I'll give it two minutes before I start sniffing Polo mints.

'And you know what?' Dad goes on. 'It'll be a shame if Anna's the only one there without any parents.'

'You'd know all about shame, wouldn't you?' Mum says.

'Listen, if you can't get the time off work, then maybe I could go?'

'What, on your own?' she says, doing that pretend giggle again.

'I wouldn't be on my own, I'd be with Anna.'

'And what about Anthony?'

'What about him?'

Then the third pretend giggle happens. Although this time she sounds a bit comedy witch.

'You think this is an opportunity to go on some jolly, don't you? To go for a wee saunter around Italy as if everything is perfect.'

'That's rubbish.'

'As if nothing's happened.'

'No, Liz, I'd be going to support our daughter.'

'Right enough, it's all about the family for you.' I hear their door creak open, as if it's groaning. 'Fine, away the two of you go then. Off you go, have a great time.' It sounds like Mum's talking to a dog. 'Say hello to all the other parents, won't you? Don't you worry about me and our Anthony. I'll look after him. Sure, it's what I've done for the past twelve years anyway.'

'That's not fair. I've worked with Anthony as much as you have, Liz, so don't give me that.'

I'm waiting for another pretend giggle, but it doesn't come. I think Mum is half in, half out of the room.

'You know who'll be going to Italy too, don't you?' Mum says.

'I'm not having that discussion.'

'Yeah, because you're gutless, that's why you don't want to have it.'

'I've told you everything about that.'

'Oh, that's big of you.' I hear more door groaning. 'Did I forget to thank you?'

'It's not news any more, Liz.'

'You don't tell me what is and what isn't news.'

It's as if the walls are talking to me. I want it to end. I need to be snuggled under my duvet. Curl up and dream about … oh, I don't know, ice cream and pizza dough. I want to be living in my own head and not someone else's. I want to be going over my dance routines until I fall asleep. Instead, I'm lying here balancing tears on the surface of my eyes again. They'll be even more like Dad's: all red and puffy. Two big onion eyes.

'So, I'll make arrangements for me and Anna to go then,' Dad says.

'You think I'm just going to say it's fine for you to waddle off to Italy and leave me and Anthony here? That's acceptable to you?'

'I thought you didn't want to come?'

'I don't, but that doesn't mean I'm going to be waiting here for the postcards to arrive.'

'Look, Liz—'

'You're not going.'

'Hey, wait a minute here—'

'Not without me and Anthony. That's for sure.'

Mum's fully back in the room again. In, out. In, out.

There's this long period when no one speaks. I'm trying to paint a picture of what's happening. Dad's stubbing out his menthol, then running his hands through his hair and stretching his neck from side to side. Mum's sitting on the edge of her bed filing her nails and blowing all the nail dust on to the carpet, which I'll probably have to clean up. I don't mind really. I like hoovering. We've got a Shark hoover with light-up eyes on the front. It makes Anto stomp and dance, in a good way though. Mum used her staff discount. Twenty-five per cent off, not to be sniffed at.

'Are we bringing Anthony?' Sometimes Dad opens his mouth and I just think: *Stop saying big eejit stuff all the time.*

'What, afraid he'll cramp your style, are you?'

'No, Liz.' Dad raises his voice. 'That's not what I meant.'

'Well, what did you mean then?'

'This is pointless,' Dad huffs. I can tell by the direction of his voice that he's looking at the ceiling now.

'That's the most honest thing you've said for years.'

'Of course Anthony can come, of course I want him to come.'

'Yeah, I can see the joy in your eyes.'

'Will you just stop, Liz. I'll email Kim tomorrow.'

Dad leaves and thunders downstairs. Mum follows with much less thunder.

I go to my door and listen. Sounds as if Mum's blowing out her calming candles. It's her *exasperated* sound. Dad's doing his as well. His *Oh, woe is me* sound. They remind me of the Big Bad Wolf huffing and puffing and blowing the house down. Only this time it's ours.

'Book two hotel rooms, not a family one. Two. Separate. Rooms.'

'Fine by me.'

'And I'll be sharing with Anna.'

I palm my eyes dry, pump my fist in the air. I might have dived on to my bed. I did. I'm so excited. Who needs dreams when you can have the real thing?

Ten

I hear Mrs Breen's tank way before seeing it. When I peek out of the blinds my heart starts pumping. Tanya's never been in my house before; what if she hates our furniture or eating Asda food? There's no trinkets from Dubai or Marbella cos no one's ever been there. I'm worried in case she'll tell everyone at MadCrew that our house is a bit on the minging side. And then there's Anto, the most important thing in the house. Although he's not a thing.

Mrs Molloy from across the road stops polishing her plants to have a good old nosy at their car. Maybe she thinks we've won the postcode lottery or the Pope has come to say howdy-doodles. Whenever Mrs Molloy sees Anto she always says the same thing: *Oh, that boy's getting bigger every time I set eyes on him,* in the most annoying voice ever. She thinks she's talking to an injured kitten.

Never says anything about me, and I'm the oldest. Thankfully Mum's on an afternoon Asda shift; she's not been a fan of Mrs Molloy ever since overhearing her say to Mrs Sheridan: *Oh, it's a right sin for that poor laddie.* Mum was properly raging – *I'll give her 'poor laddie', she should mind her own business. Nosy bleedin' Nora so she is.* Anyway, I'm glad she's working.

Tanya and her mum open their doors at the same time. Mrs Breen is wearing a fur bomber jacket, tight jeans and white trainers. And when I say tight I mean TIGHT. I don't think her hair has moved since I saw her in the MadCrew car park. I think Mrs Breen's hobby is practising different make-up styles on herself. I won't tell Tanya this, but I think her mum would make a tremendous *Made in Chelsea* star, if, that is, she didn't have a Scottish accent and actually lived in Chelsea.

Tanya is in her new hoodie and black leggings. Me too. I gulp some nerves down. And try to put some moisture on to my dry tongue. Just before they walk up the path, the tank's back door swings open. Eh? What? Who else is coming? Mr Breen? I screw up my eyes in anticipation. One leg hits the concrete. Leg number two quickly joins it; next an arm, followed by a body. Then, finally, a head with a hat pops out. I mean, I thought my heart was pumping fast before seeing this, but now it's supercharged. Evan

Flynn looks my house up and down as if he's standing outside one of Gran and Papa's *hotels from hell*. He's wearing his hoodie too. I'm so confused I want to lock myself in the bathroom. But I don't. I look in the mirror, quickly pat my hair and rush down the stairs in time to make the doorbell. Before opening the door I look behind me in case Anto's hovering at the top of the stairs. The last thing I knew, him and Dad were trying to build the Starship Something-or-Other in his room.

Mrs Breen is grinning from ear to ear. Her mouth is massive. Tanya and Evan just look as if they are entering Tesco.

'Hi, Mrs Breen – hi, Tanya,' I say, dead enthusiastic. 'Hello, Evan,' I say, working hard to hush the voice in my head that wants to scream: WHAT IN THE KING'S KNICKERS ARE YOU DOING HERE?

'All right, Anna,' Tanya says, looking right past me into the house. You could fit a watermelon in her mouth. OK, so we might not have three toilets and an open-plan kitchen with island, but it's not *that* bad. It's just a house. Normal and warm.

'Nice smell,' Evan says, twitching his nose. I'm not sure he's being sarcastic or referring to Mum's love of oil scent diffusers. She's forever bringing them home. I dare anyone not to at 25 per cent off. There's one in every room. Two in the living room. Sometimes Anto breaks the wee sticks that are in them. I'm not sure he likes the smell.

'Hi, Anna love,' Mrs Breen says.

I've never seen teeth as white as hers in all my life.

'Oh, hello there.' The voice comes from behind my shoulder. 'Are you going to invite our guests in, Anna, or are you just going to let them stand at the door?' Dad's found a giant juicy smile and stuck it to his face. It's the happiest I've seen him in ages.

'This is Tanya and Evan from MadCrew, and her mum.' I step to the side to let Tanya and Evan past. They don't move. 'We're going to do some practice upstairs.'

Dad shuffles forward.

'Well, I'm pleased to meet you,' he says, stretching out his hand. Tanya and Evan stare at it as if it's a loaded gun. I mean, who handshakes twelve-year-olds? Dads are so weird. I'm thinking this is the perfect moment for the ground to open up and suck me into its darkness. Mrs Breen kind of squishes through to take Dad's hand instead. The look on Tanya's face, you'd think she's inhaling turned milk. Evan's eyebrows almost hit the ceiling. Mrs Breen links her fingers in Dad's. All I'm saying is that Mum's nails are way more exciting.

'Where's Anto?' I ask Dad through gritted teeth.

'Don't worry, he's fine,' he says. 'Do you want to come in, guys?' he says to Tanya and Evan.

Mrs Breen shoves them through our door, squashing all three of us together in our tiny, square hallway. Bit embarrassing.

'I take it you're in the Italy squad too?' Dad asks them.

'Tanya and Evan are like the best dancers in MadCrew,' I say. 'Course they're going to Italy.'

'Evan's probably the best,' Tanya says.

'What do you mean, *probably*?' Evan tuts. 'I think we need to talk.'

Dad does a funny eye thing to Mrs Breen, who mouths, *I know*. I'm not stupid, I understand what they're getting at. I don't think Tanya's in love with Evan Flynn; she just wants to marry him, that's all.

'Well,' Dad says, 'do you three want to head upstairs and get some practice in?' But that's not him finished; he does something really excruciating: he wiggles his hips and pretends to be shaking maracas. Oh please, ground, I'm begging you, I'm on my knees here, open up and take me away from this torture. Mrs Breen laughs at Dad as though she's just heard the world's best joke. I've definitely missed something. He wouldn't be dad-dancing and shaking everyone's hand if Mum was here, that's for sure. Nor would he be smiling.

'Can I get you a coffee or tea or something?' Dad asks Mrs Breen. 'We've got doughnuts in the fridge.' His eyebrows flick up and down.

OH, SOMEBODY MAKE THIS END!

I don't want her to see our kitchen, or anywhere else for that matter. I do a quick glance up the stairs again. She taps her watch. It's an i-one with a pink strap. I bet it cost a bomb.

'I'm due at Toni and Guy at two,' she says. Dad looks at his as well. A black Swatch that Mum got him for Christmas two years ago. It makes a really annoying ticking sound. You can always hear it when we're eating our dinner. God knows how she sleeps in the same bed as him.

'It's only gone past twelve now,' he says. 'They're really nice doughnuts.'

Mrs Breen is in deep thinking mode, Tanya's looking straight at her through a huge forehead frown. Evan takes his hat off, runs his hand through his hair and puts the hat back on again. And the point of that is?

'Well, OK then,' Mrs Breen says. 'I'm sure I could fit in a quick coffee.'

She's kidding nobody, I know she's only after the doughnuts.

'Great.' Dad gestures her in. Now the five of us are standing in the hall like strangers in a lift.

'Right, sweetheart, I'll pick you guys up around three,' Mrs Breen says to Tanya.

'Whatever,' Tanya says.

'If that's OK with you, Mr—'

'Call me Tony,' Dad says, smiling strangely at Mrs Breen. 'Yeah, three's fine.'

Mrs Breen goes in for a kiss, but Tanya's having none of it; she dodges her mum's red lips as if dodging a stray firework.

'Sweet move,' Evan whispers to her.

'Want to get started, Anna?' Tanya says, desperate to get out of the hallway.

'Yeah, come on up,' I say, and the three of us bolt upstairs.

'Bye, sweetheart,' Mrs Breen shouts as Dad leads her into our kitchen. 'Have fun.'

At the top of the stairs Tanya does a NA-na-na-NA-na face. All that's missing is the thumb on nose and flickering fingers. 'I'm going to be a cool parent when I'm older,' she spits through her teeth. 'She's getting worse.'

'Your mum is super-cool, what are you talking about?' Evan says. 'I mean, have you had a gander at her trainers?'

'So …'

'So my mum thinks Matalan is just a cheaper version of Harvey Nicks. That's the level of cool we're talking here, Tanya,' he says.

'She does have an iWatch and a fur bomber jacket,' I add.

Tanya huffs. Frowns.

'Can we just practise?' she says.

I point to where my room is, and feel silly for doing it cos there's a sign that says ANNA'S ROOM on the door. That'll need to come down before I become thirteen.

Tanya and Evan stand in the middle of my room doing a full-circle scan. Checking out my bed, my desk, the posters on my wall and my books.

'Have you read all of them?' Tanya asks.

'Not all. Most. You can borrow something if you want.' I lift one of my Katherine Rundell books off the shelf. Mystery, adventure, intrigue. Who needs more? I show her the front cover. 'This is amazing, it kept me up all night. You'll love it. Here.' I hold it out and try giving it to her, but Tanya shakes her head and looks insulted.

'It's the summer holidays, Anna,' she says.

'And?'

'And it's bad enough at school.'

'Yeah, put that away before I get a migraine,' Evan says, waving his hand in my face.

I return Katherine Rundell to the shelf.

They slowly wander around picking up things, examining them before putting them back down again. Not always in the right place. Anto would have a canary.

'Is that your grandad?' Tanya says, pointing to one of my posters.

'I can see a wee resemblance around the eyes,' Evan says, shifting between me and the poster.

I don't want to laugh, but I can't help it. Not at them, just at the thought of Albert being my grandad. Imagine how spectacular those bedtime stories would be.

'No, that's Albert Einstein,' I tell them. They look like a pair of confused puppies, gazing up at the poster. 'He's this dead famous scientist with a really impressive mind, maybe the best that there's ever been.' Tanya moves closer to the poster and looks Albert right in the eye. 'My gran and papa bought me it,' I say. 'So it does remind me of my papa.'

'You're so weird,' Evan says.

I'm about to explain some of the cool things Albert Einstein did in life, but Dad's laughter booms from the kitchen and stops me. Mrs Breen giggles.

'Someone's having a good time,' Evan says.

'God, I wish she'd just beat it and go to the hairdresser's,' Tanya says.

'It's nice that they're getting on though,' I say.

'She'd talk to anyone,' Tanya says.

'Where's your mum?' Evan asks me.

'Work,' I say. 'She works in Asda. In the fashion section.'

'No,' Evan says, with an open hand close to my face. 'I'm

stopping you there. Asda does clothes. It does not do fashion.'

'Well, she's at work,' I say.

Evan goes to the window and peers out. 'Very convenient,' he mutters.

Tanya keeps checking out my room; I don't know why, hers is probably three times the size. With a big flatscreen and a laptop in it.

'Who's that?' she says.

Now she's pointing at a picture of me and Anto from last year when Mum and Dad took us to Legoland. Not the proper one in Denmark with the Lego tower; no, we went to one somewhere in England, which was heaving. Stressful with a capital FULL. In the picture I'm holding a Lego tennis racket and Anto is holding a Lego Darth Vader mask. We were all terrified in case he dropped it.

'That's my brother, Anto.'

Tanya leans towards the picture. 'He's cute.'

Of course Anto is cute. He's the spit of Mum so it's a no brainer. If he wasn't who he is he'd be doing what Dad had to do when he was a teenager: *fight them off with a big stick*. I go to tell them exactly that, but then I choose not to; not sure why I do that.

Tanya moves even closer to the picture. Evan follows.

'He is,' Tanya says. 'He's very cute.'

'Well, if he's your brother I'd say he is,' Evan says, glancing my way.

I feel someone has just cranked the Majorca dial right up past a hundred and twenty. I'm pretty sure Tanya's wanting to burn holes in the back of my head cos Evan Flynn paid me a compliment. Was it a compliment?

'We're twins,' I tell them. 'But I'm the oldest.'

'Twins?' she says. 'How come I've never seen him at school?'

'He goes to a different one.'

'That's weird. Why?'

For a wee second I don't know what to say, so I look down at my Vans. I notice Tanya's feet too.

'I've got a twin as well!' Evan pipes up.

'Really?' I say.

'You do not,' Tanya says. 'Don't listen to him.'

'Fine, she's a year older, but we're practically twins. It's the same thing really. What's eleven months? She's the reason I got into dancing.'

'Is she at our school?' I ask. 'Year above?'

'No, she lives down the Borders with my dad, but we still text and stuff, and talk to each other on WhatsApp all the time.'

'What's her name?' I ask.

'Chloe. She's amazing.'

'Nice name,' I say. 'Does that mean you live with your mum then?'

'Yeah, I got the short straw,' he says.

'Or your mum did,' Tanya spits.

Evan arches his neck and squeezes his eyes together like he's a character from a horror film.

'You have the Devil inside you, Tanya Breen,' he shoots at her, but in a comedy way. 'The Devil, I tell you.'

'Yeah, he says that he's missing you.'

They snigger and do a high five; I'd like to throw my hand into the mix too. Maybe another time.

'Cool trainers, Tanya,' I say instead.

She stands tall and sways from one toe to another as if she's wearing Dorothy's ruby slippers.

'Nike Air VaporMax,' she says, dead proud. 'My dad bought them for me yesterday. Told him I needed black ones for Italy.'

'And what, he just went out and bought them for you cos you asked him to?'

Tanya nods.

'Wow. I wish my dad would do stuff like that,' I say, almost salivating at the thought. 'He does bring us things from Greggs whenever we ask though.'

'Greggs?' Evan's face looks jumbled. 'Why Greggs?'

'That's where he works.'

'My neighbour goes there all the time,' Tanya says. 'My dad calls her the human caravan.'

'Well, it's nice of him to buy you the trainers.'

'I told him they had to be Nike Air VaporMax or not to bother.'

'No, they're definitely the ones to go with,' I say. 'They'll be amazing for Italy.'

No denying, they're quality trainers; way better than mine for our routines. I'd love a pair. But I also love my Vans, so it doesn't hurt me too much inside.

'Whenever my dad gets me stuff, my mum calls them his guilt gifts,' Evan says.

'Why?'

'Cos he can't be bothered driving up to see me now, so he just hits the Buy button on Amazon and his job is done.'

A million things are floating around in my head.

'Yeah, my dad hardly ever sees me now too,' Tanya says.

'Is that cos he works lots?' I ask.

'No, he just lives in another house. He only visits when he's got something for me.'

'Like trainers and things?' Evan says.

'Mum thinks that him buying me presents makes him feel better for not seeing me.'

I sit on my bed and look at them both.

'I'm sorry, guys,' I say.

'Why? I'm not,' Tanya goes.

'Yeah, don't be, Anna,' Evan adds.

'But not getting to see your dads must be hard.'

'You've never met my dad,' Evan says.

'It was way harder when he was staying with us,' Tanya says.

'How?'

'Him and Mum used to scream at each other all the time, nightmare so it was.'

'Tell me about it,' Evan says. 'Even now I can still hear some of their arguments from when I was a wee boy.'

'I can imagine,' I say. 'Still.'

'Still nothing,' Tanya butts in, 'When I get to see my dad now he's always happy and he's always got a present for me. It's perfect. OK, so maybe I only get to see him occasionally, but it's worth it, isn't it?'

'I don't know, is it?' I only ask cos I really don't know. I've no idea what the feeling is like to see either one of your parents occasionally, and I'm not sure I want to know. Imagine Anto living down the Borders? May as well be the other end of the world. No present could ever shorten that distance.

Tanya looks at Evan, then back at me.

'Anna, there was a fight every day in our house. I'm not joking. Mum was miserable. Dad was miserable. Even the walls were miserable.' Tanya puts the hood of her hoodie up, and tucks her hair in it. 'Now, the house is different. I mean, it's still the same house, but there's more space since Dad moved out. Everything's calmer.'

'Oh, I hear you. I hear you,' Evan says. 'Our house is practically a chapel these days. But it means I've more time to do this.' Evan stretches out his arms and does a perfect double pirouette on my carpet. I mean, on a *carpet*. 'He wasn't a fan of a dancing son.'

'Well, that's good then,' I add, without knowing why. All of a sudden I don't feel like practising. I'd rather spend the day curled up with a Malorie Blackman book. Or just moping around being twelve.

'What does your dad do, Tanya?' Evan asks.

'Not a hundred per cent sure. Mum says a bit of this and a bit of that.'

'No way,' he almost screams. 'That's what my dad does as well.'

They go for yet another high five. Parents separated. High fives like water. Great dancers. Talk about feeling left out.

'Is any of your dads coming to Italy?' I ask.

'No chance,' Tanya spits. 'If my mum and dad were on the same plane they'd cause a crash.'

'My mum would probably end up in an Italian jail if my dad was coming.'

We all laugh. I'm still figuring out whether Tanya and Evan are proper funny or not.

'But when everyone goes on holiday they usually get on well,' I say. 'It's the perfect time to leave all differences at home.' They both stare at me as if I haven't the foggiest idea of what I'm talking about. And they'd be right. But I do know all about *even the walls* being miserable.

'What about your parents?' Tanya asks me.

'Not sure yet. I think Dad's going to contact Kim and then maybe book something.'

The conversations yesterday are now really confusing me. The one with pizza was a giant NO. The other I overheard was more or less a big fat YES. Who knows what to think.

'Parents cramp your style,' Evan adds.

I don't think he's specifically talking about mine. At least, I hope he's not. He's hardly met them, there's no way he knows their dynamic. So nobody will be cramping anybody's style.

'They probably will come though,' I say. 'It'll be good if they did.'

'In my experience,' Evan says, 'it's all sugar and glitter one day, and the next your old man's bolted to the Borders with your sister.'

'Right.' I stare hard at the carpet cos I'm not sure if he's being serious or not.

'I read somewhere that, like, eighty-something per cent of people split up anyway,' he adds. 'So it's all the rage.'

'Where?' I pipe up, cos I'd love to read about that. 'Where did you read that?'

'It was on *Gogglebox*,' he says. 'And the subtitles were on, so it was the same as reading really.'

I've never seen *Gogglebox*, although I pretend that I have with a few knowing nods.

More sound from the kitchen. Dad must be on fire with his jokes, he can be really hilarious when he puts his mind to it. The sound of it is a bit like receiving a postcard from an old friend.

A crash comes from Anto's room that makes both Tanya and Evan jump.

'What the …' Tanya puts her hand on her chest exactly the same way Mum does this when she's watching *24 Hours in A&E*.

It's a familiar crash sound. Just Lego frustration. Or, as I suspect, frustration cos Dad's not playing with him. I'm so praying that he doesn't barge in.

'Oh, don't mind that,' I say. 'That's just my brother throwing Lego around his room.'

'So, he's the aggressive twin?' Evan asks.

'No, just gets frustrated with Lego sometimes,' I tell him. 'Plays it every day.'

94

Tanya's face twists, reminds me of one of her mum's hair scrunchies.

'Lego?' she says. 'As in the bricks?'

You can tell she's not got any brothers.

'It's his thing,' I say.

'But … I mean, is he not far too old for—' she mumbles.

'You're never too old for Lego,' Evan says, pointing his finger into Tanya's face. 'You're never too old to be young.'

I cough loudly, only to hide my laugh.

'Do you want to try some of the break routines that Kim wants us to do?' I shoot at them, hoping to knock them off the Lego issue. Which is not an issue, actually.

'Here?' Evan says, scanning my room again.

'Unless you'd rather do it downstairs?' I say.

'No, here's fine,' Tanya says. 'We've plenty of room.'

'Right, let's do it,' I say. 'Oh, we need some music before we start.'

'Do you have iTunes?' Tanya asks.

'No.'

'You use Spotify then?' Evan says.

'I usually just play my mum and dad's CDs.'

'Really?' Tanya says.

'Still works the same,' I say.

'God, what's it like living in the olden days, Anna?' Evan adds.

Tanya takes an iPhone out of her hoodie. Don't know if it's the new version or not. She twiddles through it.

'OK,' she says. 'You want Run-DMC or KRS-One?'

'Think we're breaking to Run-DMC in Italy, so best we stick to that,' Evan says.

'How about "Picture This" by Blondie?' I suggest.

They both nod their head.

More crashing. This time from downstairs. Not the same as Anto's crashing, it's our front door being yanked open. Tanya's mum leaving. We run and spy her from my bedroom window. You can guarantee that Anto will be smudged up to his window too. Unless he's having a post-Lego meltdown under his covers.

'Thanks, Tony,' Mrs Breen shouts from halfway down the path.

'Not a problem. Any time,' Dad shouts back.

'Remind that girl of mine that I'll be back around three.'

'Will do, but if you're not back by five we're keeping her.'

'That's fine by me,' Mrs Breen shouts. 'She's yours.'

I'm thinking that Mrs Molloy must be having an absolute field day at this, she'll be munching the Maltesers behind her curtains.

'Just go, will you?' Tanya urges. 'God sake.'

'Tell Toni and Guy I said hello,' Dad shouts.

'Ha ha, you're something else,' Mrs Breen says.

'Someone's having a flirty party,' Evan says.

'Shut up,' Tanya scowls.

Mrs Breen beeps the horn three times when driving away. Dad must've waited at the front door cos she waved and showed her teeth. She'd hardly be waving to the bricks, would she?

'Thank God she's gone,' Tanya says.

I'd never think that about my mum. My head's always saying *Thank God she's here*. The only time I'm on Tanya's wavelength is when we're in Asda and Mum's holding George stuff up to my body. When I was younger, she used to make me change on the shop floor. *Come on, hurry up, nobody's looking, Anna*. She'd get me to try on the boys' stuff for Anto cos we're roughly the same size.

'She's nice, your mum,' I say.

'You don't have to live with her.'

'No, but, she seems smiley.'

'You haven't seen her in the mornings, Anna.'

Evan breaks from the window and claps his hands together as if me and Tanya are a couple of dogs.

'OK, can we stop talking about mums and dads and twins and sisters please?' he says. 'It's killing the buzz.' Buzz? What buzz? 'Right, watch!' Evan removes his hoodie and chucks it in the corner.

I sit on the bed.

Evan tenses up his body and gestures for Tanya to come closer. They stand facing each other in the middle of the room. They start moving, first with a few Six Steps in perfect sync. Tip-top perfect in fact. After the Six Steps they do a few Crab Walks, which are complete wrist-killers. They finish on a textbook Baby Freeze. Amazing, given that the Baby Freeze on its own is beyond difficult. Try doing it with someone else. Nightmare hard. Tanya and Evan breeze through these as if they're skipping in the schoolyard. I'm a bit in awe, but also feeling like an old elephant on sleeping pills.

'That was incredible, guys,' I say. Tanya half smiles. 'Was it something new?'

'Kind of,' Evan says.

'I don't remember us doing it with Kim,' I say.

'That's because Kim doesn't have all the ideas, Anna,' Evan says, twisting his finger around his face. 'Some of us –' he points to himself – 'have the skills to choreograph our own routines as well, you know.'

'We created it together,' Tanya says. Evan gives her a fierce look. 'Didn't we?'

Evan's mouth opens a bit. He puts an arm on his hip. Why does everyone keep doing that in my world?

'So, what was it?' I ask.

'This, Anna Quinn,' Evan says, 'is the trio routine you,

me and Tanya are going to be doing in Italy.'

'Really?' I say, feeling honoured.

'Yes, really.'

I can't stop my jaw from dropping.

'What? You actually want me to be part of your trio?'

'You're the right height and size,' Tanya says. 'Maybe a bit bigger actually, but it's an age-category thing too.'

'You want to do it?' Evan asks.

'Yeah, we need an answer. We don't have loads of time,' she says.

'Of course I want to do it. I'd love to.'

How could I say no? That means when I get to Italy I'll be in a group dance each day, a solo AND I'll be doing the trio with the two best dancers in MadCrew as well. Oh, the pressure. Me and my hoodie are well up for it. I think Mum and Dad will have to put another notch on to their pride belts. They'll have to come to Italy now. This is a deal breaker, or maker. God, imagine if we won the trio …

'But just so you know, Anna –' Evan has his deadly serious face on – 'I'm not going to Italy to eat pizza and stand about watching guys on mopeds.'

'I know,' I say.

'I'm going there to win,' he says.

'Me too,' Tanya adds with less force.

'Yeah … me too,' I say. 'I want to win.'

'This is a step up, Anna.'

'A big step up,' Tanya says.

'We'll be going from intermediate to advanced level in a flash.' Evan does a lightning-flashing arm thing. 'You up for that?'

'I'm up for it, no problem,' I tell them.

'You need to work, work, work, Anna.' He chops his hand each time he says *work*. 'And practise, practise, practise.' More chops.

'I will work,' I say.

'No, work, work, work,' Tanya adds.

'I will work, work, work,' I say.

'And practise, practise, practise,' Evan says.

'And that too.'

'Great.' Evan claps his hands. 'Right, me and Tanya will show you what we have so far. If I were you I'd get some stretching in as this is a body bender.'

'You can put the music on now.' Tanya nods to where the CDs are.

'Are we going with the Blondie song for the trio?' I ask.

'Yeah, they won't know it in Italy, so that'll make us stand out right from the off,' he says. 'We'll sound as cool as.'

We all find a spot on my bedroom floor and do a bit more stretching. *Flexible body, flexible mind*, Kim tells us.

When stretching my back I try not to grimace, or show any pain while flexing my hamstrings like a couple of frayed elastic bands. At this rate I think I'll be retiring from competition dance by the time I'm fifteen. And then what? A life of getting shuffled between Mum and Dad every second weekend and the odd Wednesday. *Oh stop thinking that way, Anna.*

Tanya and Evan line up facing the window, with their backs to me. Legs apart. Hands down by their side and slightly out. Like two upside-down letter Vs.

'Music on six,' Evan shouts. 'And five, six, seven … MUSIC!'

I press PLAY.

'STOP!' They both turn to look at me. 'On six, Anna. On six,' he says. 'It's not brain science. A fish could do it.'

I bite down on my molars, desperately trying not to snigger. My mind is screaming, *But a fish has no hands, Evan! And, a fish can't count. What would a fish say anyway?*

'Sorry, I thought you were counting from one,' I go.

His eyes flicker. 'It's a standard five-to-eight four count.'

'Right, got it.'

I hear Tanya's huffing and hawing. When they get back into position I suddenly feel tense and nervous. And this is just me pressing a bloomin' PLAY button. What am I going to be like with a crowd, judges and all the other dancers looking at me?

'AND … five, six …'

This time I play a blinder.

They start moving on six … seven … EIGHT. Oh, they're good. No, better than good, they're fantastic. Their mirroring is mesmerising. I honestly haven't a clue who's leading. Their timing isn't on any of the Blondie lyrics either, which makes it doubly hard to achieve. I watch their every move like I'm following a bluebottle around a window. I'll have to copy these trio moves. I begin to feel slightly worried about my ability to be as good as them. Where do I fit in?

It was Mum's idea that I join MadCrew so I could *have something just for yourself.* It's not like I started breakdancing as soon as I could walk or anything like that.

'KEEP THAT SMILE BEAMING,' Evan shouts, while doing a couple of Dragging Ball moves. He stretches behind his back and drags that imaginary ball from a really low position. For a second it seems as if he's had to dislocate his shoulder in order to reach it. Tanya too. I mean, wow. Just wow.

Next they morph into a few forward and reverse Body Waves. And, honestly, they're like a couple of cobras with the way they're bending their backs. It's suddenly hot in my room. I need water.

'MAKE WAVES IN THE CALM SEA, TANYA.' Evan's very demanding, a total sergeant major out there. 'COME ON, TANYA, TURN THAT FLAT SEA INTO A BIG TSUNAMI.' I feel a wee bit sorry for her. 'AND REMEMBER TO KEEP THAT SMILE BEAMING.'

Tanya's beaming smile looks painful as they transition into some Robot Jerks before doing a couple of Reverse Turns and then directly into what I can only describe as a take on Beyoncé's 'Single Ladies' dance. Trust Evan Flynn.

'KEEP THAT SMILE BEAMING,' he keeps screaming. 'KEEP THAT SKIN GLEAMING.'

Oh my God, he actually does think he's Ariana Grande.

They finish with a massive double stomp on the very last beat of 'Picture This'. All I can do is stand, puff my cheeks out and press PAUSE on the CD player, but I really want to clap, whoop or do something to show my appreciation. They're certs to win the trio … Unfortunately they don't give trio titles to duos.

'So, what do you think?' Evan asks.

'Honestly?' I say.

'No, tell me a lie,' he spits. 'Yes, honestly. I wouldn't have asked otherwise.'

HONESTLY, he's such a numpty at times.

'I thought it was brilliant,' I tell him. 'So clever. So good.'

I was going to say *inspired*, but don't – he has to get his head out of my door soon.

'Really?' Tanya says.

'Really,' I say. She looks grateful. 'I thought you were both fantastic. You're definitely going to win.'

'We,' Tanya says.

'What?'

'*We* are definitely going to win, Anna,' she adds.

That gives me a warm glow inside. Maybe we can become BFFs after all. Stranger things have happened in life. Just ask my mum and dad. Twins! I'd liked to have been a fly on the wall when the doctor showed them the baby-scan picture with two heads in it.

'So, are you up for it?' Evan bites a fingernail and taps his foot.

'Course she's up for it,' Tanya adds. 'How could she not be?'

Hey, I'm still in the room, guys. I'm not the Elf on the Shelf you know.

'Cos if you're not up for it,' Evan goes, 'we'll have to ask Lucy Goldsmith.'

I feel my eyebrows raising, it's as if they've just staked my heart. Lucy Goldsmith! How could they even think about asking her instead of me?

'But we don't want to ask her,' Tanya goes.

'No, we definitely don't want to do that,' Evan says.

'You don't have to … I'm … eh … well up for it,' I mumble.

Evan smacks his hands together and twirls back on to the floor, straight into the upside-down V position. Tanya does the same. Maybe Tanya was right about him being Scotland's version of Bruno Tonioli. If nothing else he's got a twirl to die for. I shuffle slowly towards them. Me and Tanya stand each side of Evan. We're like his backing dancers.

'Right, Anna, we'll take it one step at a time,' he says. 'We'll do it stage by stage, then put it all together.'

'OK.' I have to wipe my sweaty hands on my leggings. 'Ready when you are.'

'A-F-A,' he shouts, which is one of Kim's favourites.

'A-F-A,' Tanya screams.

I'm thinking about poor Anto listening to all this commotion.

'Attention! Focus! Application!' Evan bawls.

I hold in my laugh and squint a look at Tanya; she's fully in the zone, breathing through the nose and out the mouth. It hits me: this is serious competitive dance. No fun. No enjoyment. Win. Win. Win. A-F-A.

There's no one to press PLAY now. Where is the fish when you need it?

The next song we want to dance to is by Run-DMC. Kim loves it. As soon as the music kicks in I know it's a mistake. Hip hop really upsets him. Must be the beat. I know it's not the swearing. I start counting in my head, knowing I'll never get to ten.

One: I stand in my dance position, one leg in front of the other.

Two: I start to move.

Three: In and out, increasing the pace.

Four: I don't get to five.

Tanya and Evan's faces kind of drop when they see him standing at the door, hands covering his ears. His coat hanger dangling from his wrist. I don't turn Run-DMC off. His eyes flicker around the room, anywhere to get away from their gaze. Tanya sidles up to me. Evan is glued to the carpet. Anto jumps on the spot three times while clapping his hands.

'OK, we'll turn the music down,' I say. 'Go back to your room.'

Tanya tugs at my hoodie, trying to slink behind me. Evan shuffles closer.

'Dad's downstairs, I think he's eating all the sausage rolls and doughnuts.' I give him the eyes, but I doubt he's noticed.

He opens his mouth and silent screams. If Tanya rips my hoodie, she better buy me a new one. With ANNA on the back as well. No way I'm going to Italy looking like a scrounger. She can ask her dad. Anto turns and scarpers back into his room. I notice Evan's mouth has drooped a bit. I keep my focus on the door.

'That's him,' I tell them.

'That's your brother?' Evan asks.

'The one and only.'

'So, that's your twin brother?' Tanya says, dead slow. I think she's a wee bit terrified. That happens sometimes.

'I mean …' she mumbles. 'What? … I mean … Why was he jumping like that, Anna?'

'Probably cos someone new is in the house,' I say.

'Us?' Evan asks.

'People he hasn't seen before. People who are different.'

'And what's up with us?' Tanya turns to face me, clearly out of her trance now. 'We're not *that* different.'

'Speak for yourself,' Evan says.

'No, I know,' I say. 'He's happy to see you.'

'Why was he covering his ears and carrying a coat hanger?' Tanya asks, as if it's a crime.

'Probably cos of the music,' I say. 'Maybe too loud for him. He's not a big fan of hip hop. He loves The Beatles.'

'He was really into that coat hanger,' Evan says.

I choose not to comment on the coat hanger. Where do you begin with that one?

Tanya shifts her weight on to her back feet and sways on her heels. Evan stretches his thighs.

'Just tell us to turn it down then,' Tanya says. 'You don't need to jump around clapping your hands as if you're a half-daft seal.'

I start counting in my head once more. This time I only get to four when Anto appears again, as I knew he would. This time he's holding up four green bricks. The 'Who, Why, What, When?' bricks.

'This is Tanya,' I tell him. 'And this is Evan.' He thrusts the bricks further. 'We're in MadCrew together. They're going to Italy too.'

I think Tanya's jaw has just smacked off the floor. Evan takes off his hat and fixes his hair. I feel Tanya's hand gripping on to my hoodie again.

'It's fine, we're just going to be doing some practising until three.'

He runs back to his own room. I don't move cos I know what's coming.

'Anna,' Tanya whispers. 'What's …'

Anto rushes back with his four white 'OK' bricks in his hand. He holds them aloft.

'What's he doing?' Tanya mutters.

'What's with the Lego?' Evan asks.

'It just means he's OK with us practising and you

being here, that's all,' I try to explain.

'Why can't he just say that?' Evan says. 'Instead of …'

I take a few tiny steps towards Anto.

'Amazing,' I say. 'Can we get on with it now?'

He pushes the white bricks up to my face.

'OK, I get it. I get it. Go now.' I add a bit of venom to my voice, but not too much. He squeezes his eyes, makes some clicking noises, then leaves. He bounces downstairs to see Dad, who's probably still salivating at his own jokes.

'Brothers are such a pain,' I say, turning to Tanya and Evan.

'What's wrong with him, Anna?' Tanya asks.

'Tanya!' Evan spits. 'You can't ask that.'

It's a fair enough question, I suppose … I'd be wondering the same if the roles were reversed.

'It's OK to ask,' I say. 'The answer is that there's nothing wrong with him.' I feel a strange sense in my stomach, like I want to scream at them, or lash out, or stamp on Tanya's trainers, or spit on Evan's hat. But I also want to hug my brother cos I'm so proud of him. Proud that he didn't lock himself away in his room and hide who he was. He faced the confusion 'He just finds it hard to communicate like you and me, that's all,' I say, cos it's the truth.

Tanya makes a sound that's halfway between a scoff and a snigger. It's the same sound Mum and Dad started doing to each other ages ago.

'No offence, but is nobody creeped out by this? The way he's standing there like a complete mong?' Tanya adds.

'He's a not a mong, Tanya. He's just not the same as you and me, that's all. It's no big deal.'

'Yeah, it's no big deal.' Evan backs me up.

'Too right he's not the same as me,' Tanya says under her breath.

'He is on the inside,' I say. 'He has a heart and lungs and a stomach and blood.' I didn't put on my nice voice while saying this.

'I just mean, why doesn't he speak?' she asks. 'That's really cheeky if you ask me.'

'Yeah, cheeky of *you*,' Evan says, doing his finger twist in her direction. I'm loving his support.

'Cos he doesn't,' I tell her.

'Doesn't or won't?' she goes.

'Can't. Not with words.'

Tanya's neck jerks back, I think her brain has just registered exactly what I've said. You know, what dogs do with their head when they're confused? That's her now. Without the cuteness though.

'What, he can't talk?' Evan asks.

'Not like you mean.'

'But he's twelve.'

'I know.'

'Is he like disabled or something?' Tanya says.

'No,' I reply sharply. 'He's none of those things, he's just Anto. We're twins.'

Tanya starts to wander around my room again, looking everything up and down in much more detail. All my stuff probably has a different meaning for her now. I'd bet if we were still at school she'd be telling everyone that *I'm* disabled cos I have loads of books in my room. That's just how some people are. Evan taps his hat off his thigh and sticks it back on his head. Backwards.

'No wonder he doesn't go to our school,' she says.

'Are you joking?' Evan says to Tanya. 'I'd be delighted if I was him. Our school is full of animals.'

'He goes to a school that helps him with his needs,' I say.

'A special school?' she asks.

'A school for special people. There's a difference, Tanya.'

'Is there?'

'A big one.'

'Tell you something, he'd get done in at our school for acting like that and not talking.'

'He wasn't acting, Tanya. That's how Anto communic-ates. He talks in a different way,' I tell her, but I know that's not true. Just a wee white lie that's part of our twin shield.

'Yeah, maybe he'll get a job on the radio,' she says. 'I can

111

just imagine it now.' And I see how in her head that she's trying to imagine it. She starts to laugh at her own joke.

Evan looks at me. He has *sorry* in his eyes. It's not his fault, he didn't create Tanya.

I've no desire to practise any more trio moves now. I wish it was already three o'clock.

Tanya runs her finger over the spines of my books. Yeah, in your dreams, Tanya. No way am I going to lend you one now. Evan maybe, but not you. No chance.

'So boring,' she mutters to herself.

'See the man in that poster up there, Tanya?' I nod up to Albert Einstein.

'Your grandad?'

'No, Albert Einstein.'

'Very hairy eyes,' Evan says.

'Well,' I say, closing my eyes the way Gran does when she's telling us how people were way friendlier when she was a girl. 'He didn't talk until he was older too. Not like Anto, but he wasn't the same as other people his age either.'

The three of us are staring up at the poster.

'And?' Tanya says.

'And, so, he was one of the brainiest people who ever lived.'

'I've never heard of him, Anna,' Evan adds. 'He can't be that brainy.'

'I'd say one of his brains is like hundreds of ours,' I tell them.

'You better hope your brother doesn't look like him when he's older,' Tanya says. 'Brainy or not, look at the nick of him.'

'My papa says that Albert Einstein and Anto have loads in common.'

'God, I don't know who to feel sorry for then.'

I turn sharply at Tanya. So does Evan. I don't give her too much evils in case she thinks we're ganging up on her.

'If Einstein was living now he'd be a millionaire. A multi-multi-billion millionaire,' I tell her.

'Why, cos he was dead brainy?'

'Exactly.'

'So if your brother is as brainy as that Albert guy, he might be a multi-billion millionaire too?' Evan asks.

'Might be.'

'How cool would that be?' he goes, nodding towards Tanya.

'Imagine all the trainers he'd buy me,' I say.

Tanya shakes her head.

'One problem though, Anna.'

'What?'

'Your brother is too retarded to be that brainy, so I reckon he'll be lucky if he makes it on to the dole.'

'Tanya Breen!' Evan says. 'Wash your mouth out this minute.'

'It's OK, Evan,' I say, staring hard at her. 'Tanya doesn't really mean what she's saying. She's just scared or confused like lots of people are.'

She looks at her knees. AND NOW I FEEL BAD.

I don't believe in physical violence to resolve problems. *Talk your problems through, never lift your hand in anger,* Mum always tells me. Cos when I was younger I'd want to punch Anto full-force in the face all the time. But that was then. Now I've the personality of a cucumber. But Tanya is pushing all my cucumber buttons. I really don't want to punch her or be cruel to her or make her miss her dad even more. But it's so hard not to say something that is sharper than an axe.

'I don't think I want to practise any more,' I tell them.

'We haven't done nearly enough,' Evan says.

'I think we should just wait downstairs until your mum picks you up. I don't want to be in my room any longer.' I head towards the door and pull it open. Evan and Tanya don't move. 'Can we go downstairs please?' Tanya just shrugs her shoulders and starts to move. Evan follows. 'We can watch some telly if you want.'

'You're so weird, Anna,' Tanya says, walking down each step. 'This whole house is weird.'

With the three of us wedged on my sofa I find it hard not to burst out crying. We wait for the *da-dum*. Tanya wants to pick, which I don't object to. Evan wants *Cheer.* A part of me hopes Anto would join us, I always hope this, but he stays away throughout the five episodes of *Modern Family.*

Eleven

That night I start with Google and Trip Advisor, even though Dad says Trip Advisor is *full of professional whingers*. But I've got to start my research somewhere, haven't I? I've got a pen, notepad and two highlighters. Green for MUST visit sights. Pink for WORTH a visit. The Colosseum and Trevi Fountain go into the green list along with the Spanish Steps and Piazza Navona, where it's almost impossible NOT to get an ice cream. Gran and Papa said the Vatican was *like walking straight into Heaven*. I mean, who wouldn't want that? Straight on to the green list it goes.

'Knock, knock!' Mum says without actually knocking the door. That's a polite way of just barging in.

'Mum, I didn't hear you come in,' I say, carefully flattening my palm over the list.

'Just wanted to ask how your dance practice with the Breen girl went?'

'It was OK. Evan came too.' Mum's face squints. 'He's the best dancer in MadCrew.'

'Is that right?'

'We're going to be a trio in Italy, you know,' I say, puffing up my chest.

'A trio!' she says, widening her eyes. 'I'd say you need lots of practice for that.'

'We did a wee bit, but not enough for my liking.'

'Did Anthony disturb you?'

'No. We just … did lots of chatting and I showed them my books and stuff. I asked Tanya if she'd like to borrow any of them.' Mum nods her head, as if she's not really listening. I thought she would be more impressed with my trio news.

'So you had a nice time then?'

'Erm … yeah … nice enough,' I say, sort of stuttering the words out. I always try not to show it on my face but I'm rubbish at hiding how I feel. May as well take a Sharpie and print it on my forehead.

'Did something happen?' Mum asks. I bite my lip. 'Anna, did something happen between you and the Breen girl?'

Think fast, Anna. If I tell Mum Tanya was a wee bit rude towards Anto she'll have her kidneys shoved in a blender.

117

And she can say adios to practising in this house ever again, or me being part of the trio.

'Anna,' Mum says more forcefully. 'Is there something I need to know about?'

'No, but …'

'But what?'

'It's nothing.'

'I'll be the judge of that.' For a second I think she's about to jump to her feet and do her stance. If I see that stance I'm spilling. 'Well?'

I think fast:

'It's just that she thought Albert Einstein was actually Papa. It's stupid,' I say. I didn't mean Tanya was stupid, only the fact that it's stupid that I'm making something out of nothing. I can tell by the lines on Mum's head that she doesn't believe me. Not one nugget.

'Albert Einstein?'

'Yeah, stupid really.'

She enters fully, has a wee glance at Albert and walks to the window. She mutters something under her breath. I can't be fully sure, and I wouldn't tell another soul cos, honestly, I'm not really one hundred per cent, but I think she said, *Yeah, stupid is right, just like her mother.* If Anto was here he'd back me up on it.

'Her mum seemed nice,' I say.

'She was in here?'

'Dad made her a cup of tea,' I tell her. 'Or maybe it was a coffee.'

'That's nice of him,' she says. Her face tells me that she doesn't believe this though. As she makes to leave, she stops. 'Don't stay up too late.'

'I'll just finish this,' I say, lifting my pen. For a split second I think she's about to grill me about what I'm writing, but she doesn't say a word. She closes my room door with a bit more force than normal.

I'm about to work on the pink list, but I just keep staring at a blank page in my notebook. I'm pretty sure I can hear the tinny music blasting from Anto's headphones. That can't be good for his ears. I'm not going to say a word, it's up to him if he wants to damage his brain. I try to concentrate; my mind is like a song being played backwards. I'm no longer seeing Rome, we're all somewhere else. No fighting, no stress, no fear. We're the perfect family glued with love. My eyes lose focus.

More tinny music comes through to me. My mind begins to play the song properly. When I let my eyelids drop I see us …

Right, so, we're all in this big fancy car. Everyone's done up to the nines. I'm wearing this floaty floral-print dress. My socks are pulled only halfway up my shins, so

119

they sag a bit, and I've a pair of black Nike Air trainers on. VaporMax ones. I tried the outfit with a hat but it wasted the look. *Oh my, are you really my daughter?* Mum says when she sees me, her hand covering her mouth. She hadn't seen me complete the look with the socks and trainers. She's delighted to have a daughter like me. I imagine myself looking just like this Instagrammer I saw. I didn't know the person, they just popped up, but they were the same age as me, so I thought: why not? I put on some strawberry lip gloss that I nick out of Mum's bag. Yuck! Sticky lips.

Mum's in a polka-dot minidress, with pleats and leather ankle boots. I want to do the hand-to-mouth thing and say, *Oh my, are you really my mum?* But I just grin and nod my head about twelve times. Sometimes girls don't need words. No joke, Mum looks like a model. The super kind. Dad's jaw slowly opens when he sees her. He eyes her all the way from ankle boot to the line in her middle parting. *Wow, you look incredible, Liz. So beautiful.* His voice sounds as if he's in the middle of a sunbeam. Sometimes they forget that I'm actually in the same room as them. I'm just about to cough: *And what about your daughter, Dad, eh?* But he beats me to it. *Both of you, you look absolutely stunning.* I've never seen Dad look prouder. In that moment it feels as though I've just gained six inches on to my height. It's one of the best feelings ever.

Dad looks really nice too. He's got neat, clean hair and an ironed shirt on. He's wearing the men's perfume that me and Anto got him for Christmas a couple of years ago. Well, Mum bought it for him and put, *Merry Xmas Dad, from Anthony and Anna xxx* on the name tag. I think he's poured half the bottle over himself right enough. Dads! From the back seat of the car I can see the Uber driver twitch his nose in the little mirror.

We're only taking the Uber car cos *we're having a few sherbets afterwards* and Dad doesn't want *to risk losing his licence*. It's massive inside, like a minibus. It's got holes for putting your cans of Coke and coffee in; there's also a section to plug your iPhones into. *Stop playing with the windows, Anna*, Mum whispers into my ear, but she's not angry cos she gives me a wee kiss on the cheek after telling me off. I feel her lipstick on my skin. I actually smell the strawberry off of it. She's sitting between me and Dad. I'm holding one of her hands and Dad the other. She's our model prisoner. *Know what? I'm feeling a little bit on edge*, she says. *Tell me about it*, I say, *I'm absolutely bricking it.* Dad's gazing out of the window in deep-thought mode. I nudge Mum and show her how Dad's trying to act all calm, as if he's not even thinking about it; she tries to imitate the look on his face and we have a girly laugh at his expense. He hasn't a clue. A tell-tale sign that Dad's close to the edge is when his leg bounces up and down. And now it's bouncing like a spring on a broken pogo stick.

Mum puts her hand on his knee. His hand moves on top of hers. *He'll be OK, I wouldn't worry too much, honey*, she says.

Dad looks at her, smiles. *I know he will ... It's just ... You know.*

I know.

Dad leans into Mum and gives her the gentlest peck on the cheek. Mum pulls him towards her and kisses him for longer than two seconds. I gaze at the mirror above the driver's head; I think he's feeling as awkward as I am, with a capital AWK. He keeps his eyes well and truly on the road.

Wouldn't it be amazing if I press the electronic window and push myself halfway out? Me, doing a huge YEE-HA! To the outside world. Dead loud, arms like an eagle's wings. I'd love to wave at everyone and let the wind gush through my hair and floaty dress.

When the car pulls up, Mum lets out a gust of air and says, *I don't know if I can handle this, my nerves are shattered.* Me and Dad laugh. *Calm down, Liz*, Dad says, taking her hand. *It's only Battle of the Bands at Airdrie Town Hall, it's not exactly Glastonbury we're going to.* The three of us stand at the entrance and look up at the Town Hall. The size of it. No joke, Airdrie Town Hall is massive. I've never seen anything like it in my life, not in the flesh anyway.

Still, Mum says, *it's singing in front of people, no matter where it is.*

We hand over our tickets and enter. There's millions of people floating around inside. The place is buzzing with excited, strange people and sweat. Anto probably feels that this is his tribe. Our seats are red velvet, very posh. That's cos we're family.

Dad?

Yeah.

Anto doesn't have a band.

He's a soloist.

So why do they call it Battle of the Bands if he isn't in a band then?

That's just what they call it.

One person and a guitar is the same as a band anyway, Mum says. *Right, Tony?*

Exactly.

I hope the crowd like him, I say.

I hope they don't laugh, Dad says.

Oh, my heart can't take much more of this, Mum says.

Dad yanks her in for a pre-show cuddle.

When it's Anto's turn to come out, my body starts to rumble. Mum squeezes my hand so tight that she actually cracks my knuckles. That woman has so much strength inside *and* out. Dad gets comfortable in his seat. The announcer man with long hair and a huge belly struts on stage; he waves at the crowd and tries to rile them up into a frenzy. Airdrie people are a different breed. *And now for our next battler, all the way from sunny Coatbridge, please give a big Airdrie Town Hall hand for the one and only Anthony Quinn!* Mum whoops. Dad whistles. She grips Dad's thigh. I close my eyes. And then he appears.

I'm like torn between being dead proud of my brother and having the biggest red neck known to man. Anto's hair is all slicked back, his jeans are from the new George skinny range and his shirt is the one Gran and Papa brought him back from their weekend in Blackpool. His guitar is slung over his shoulder. Dad leans over me and says to Mum, *What's happened to him? He looks like bloomin' Elvis.* Mum replies, *I know, but he looks amazing.*

When Anto starts walking the crowd cheer, especially some of the lassies standing down the front. There's a

124

voice inside me saying, *I'm begging you, Anto, please be good. At least be half decent. I've still got to go to school, you know.*

He approaches the mic, swings his guitar around to his stomach, and smiles. Oh my days! The lassies down the front absolutely love him, some are even blowing kisses. You'd think they were watching Harry Styles. Anto leans in. *Hi, Airdrie. I'm Anto Quinn and I'm from Coatbridge.* A few boos ring out, but fun boos. *I hope you like my tunes.* Anto starts playing the first of his two songs, it's a New Order one that Dad taught him. I look at Mum when he starts. I think she's about to burst out crying. I glance at Dad, he's got tears streaming down his face. The crowd are rocking. It's like a proper gig. With a proper singer. At the end of the song some of the lassies reach their hands out so Anto can lean down and touch them. 'OMG, Anto Quinn just brushed his fingers with mine!' Mum sees it all happening too; she shakes her head and mimes *I know.* Dad's somewhere in between bubbling and beaming.

Just gonna tone it down for the next tune, Anto says, and starts plucking his guitar. I don't believe it, some people have got their mobile lights on. *This one's from a band called The Beatles,* he screams into the mic. Some people clap. *You do know who The Beatles are, Airdrie, don't you?* Again some boos, but mostly I see people with huge grins. They love my brother. So do I. I wish I was up there with him. We could do a duet. Problem: I'm tone deaf and I don't play guitar. He sings a soft song called 'Blackbird' and the whole audience sway from side to side. His voice is like a mug of hot chocolate.

You should hear the cheer when he finishes; at one point I think the roof's about to cave in. Anto waves, blows a few kisses and reaches down to touch some fans' hands. Fans! *Enjoy the rest of your night, Airdrie. You've been absolutely magic,* he says, before slinging his guitar over his shoulder again, slicking back his hair and sauntering off stage.

How.

Cool.

Is.

My.

Brother?

When the guy with the huge belly comes on at the end to announce the winner we lean forward. All the contestants are lined up behind him. Anto was definitely the best.

He's a shoo-in, Dad says.

Oh don't, Tony, you'll jinx it, Mum says.

I hold hands with them like we're praying for a

miracle. As the announcer takes out the gold envelope from his back pocket, you can practically hear our nerves jangling.

Come on, my wee darling, Mum says.

Come on, wee man, Dad says.

Come on, wee bro, I say.

Airdrie Town Hall falls silent. The audience look like ghosts; the wait is killing us all.

I don't hear the names of who come second or third, all I know is that both of them made some serious noise. *All the singers and bands tonight have been fantastic but, guys, we can only have one winner*, the belly announcer says.

Oh, I can't take much more of this, Mum mutters.

And our winner is ... Our winner is ...

I want to scream, he's doing this on purpose. Trying to do that thing presenters on TV do when they wait ages between saying *And the winner is* and mentioning the actual winner's name. It's agony. Mum puts her hands into the prayer position.

And the winner is ... Drum roll, please.

Enough already!

The winner is ... Tanya Breen.

What? Eh?

Did he just say what I think he said?

No, it can't be.

Tanya Breen! Really?

I look for Anto on stage; his head is lowered.

Aw, well, Dad says, throwing his hands up in the air. *Better luck next time.*

Tanya Breen? Mum says. *Is she anything to do with …*

I can't believe that, I say. *It must be a fix. Has to be.*

Anto's guitar has disappeared. It's his coat hanger that's slung over his shoulder now. He's crouched down at the back of the stage while Tanya Breen takes the applause from the audience. She does a few Crab Walks and finishes with a Baby Freeze, which make the crowd go bananas.

I honestly don't understand.

Dad links his arm around Mum's waist. She drops her head on to his shoulder. He kisses her head. I'd say both are desperate to get on that stage and hug the life out of Anto. Who cares who won, right? For us, he's a winner every day of the week.

We'll stop off on the way home and get a couple of bags of chips, Mum suggests. *Anthony will like that.*

There's some sausage rolls in the fridge as well, Dad says.

We'll ask him what he wants to do. Poor wee soul.

You'll never guess what Tanya Breen does after her

Baby Freeze: she only goes to Anto's fans and reaches out her hand for them to slap. That's like adding insult to injury, isn't it? My heart's breaking for him.

Every time she slaps another hand I feel it thud my head. She keeps doing it.

Please stop!

Anto is rapping his coat hanger off the stage floor now.

Stop it!

Tanya Breen is now fist-bumping people.

STOP IT!

I can't watch this. I have to close my eyes. And when I do, Airdrie Town Hall becomes dead silent. So silent that all I can hear is the sound of Anto's coat hanger slowly hitting the stage floor.

STOP IT, ANTO!

I waken to a Minecraft onesie hovering over me. He's crashing his coat hanger off my head. Again and again. Not too sore, but still. My bones are racing. I'm a bit sweaty too.

'Stop it, Anto,' I say, rubbing my head.

He hits me once more.

'Stop it, I said.'

If only I had my very own Get out of my room bricks. Not a bad idea, maybe I should. My notepad is covered in pink-highlighted doodles. Daydream scrawling. I wish I could tell him how brilliant he was. Silence.

Then their voices rise up to fill my room. Wish I could tell him I'm feeling nervous.

He moves to the door and sounds out, 'Sh … Sh … Sh … Sh.' I sit up and put my hands into the calm-down position, hoping to drown out all other sounds. I get why Anto was clocking me on the head with his coat hanger. Obviously he's heard Mum and Dad going at it again, hasn't he? Their arguing must have rattled him. He's now tapping his temple with his finger. I know exactly what he's thinking and how he's feeling.

'Don't worry, Anto,' I whisper. His tapping speeds up. 'They're not going to separate us. That's not going to happen.' He makes a gagging sound. 'You really think I'll let that happen?'

I get out of the computer chair, go to him and try to blank out the voices from downstairs. Anto's tapping stops. I smile, not cos he's calmed a wee bit, but cos I can still picture him with his Elvis hairdo and hear all those daft girls going gaga for him. And that voice of his, it's so special. My smile turns into a laugh cos a few minutes ago he was on stage in his cool clothes and now he's standing in my room wearing his Minecraft onesie and beating a coat hanger off his thigh. Rock and roll, or what?

I drop the laugh and stretch out my arms.

'K … K … K … K?' I say. He looks bothered. I stop moving. 'It's OK, Anto. It'll never happen. We're not plugs.' He makes a confused face. I don't blame him. 'We can't be disconnected and left in the dark. We're twins. It's against the law or something.'

My arms are still wide.

'K … K … K … K?' I say. 'Last chance before I drop my arms.' He starts flicking his left wrist; which is still flicking as he's walking towards me.

His hug is the tightest he's ever hugged me. It lasts for about three seconds before stopping suddenly. But it's the best ever. Better than a fist bump or a hand slap any day. It feels amazing being the big sister of an international super-star. Every day is a VIP day.

Twelve

I wake cos of them. So does Anto. He ambles into my room tugging his hair. It's dark outside, not sure what time, but definitely past midnight. The streetlights from outside cast a warm amber glow around Anto, like he's a human star or something. No need to squeeze my eyes or shake my head, I know I'm not still dreaming.

We only catch the tail end of the conversation. They're shouting that much that we don't even need to sit at the top of the stairs.

'And you let that woman into my kitchen. Drinking from my cups. Eating from my fridge.'

'They were my doughnuts.'

'I can't believe that she was actually in my house?'

'It's my house too, Liz.'

Now I'm confused. Was there someone in here while

we were sleeping? Some woman that Mum clearly doesn't like. Especially doesn't like being in her kitchen.

'What woman?' I whisper to Anto. 'What's she going on about?'

He grits his teeth and bangs the back of his head against the door frame.

'Shhh,' I tell him.

'I know it's your house too, that's not the point, Tony. That's not what I'm saying. As usual, you're not listening to me.'

'Well, what are you saying?'

'I'm saying why was she here?'

'*Who?*' I mime to Anto. I feel my face scrunch up like a lizard's back. It's my befuddled expression.

'Since when have I needed your permission to offer someone a cup of coffee?' Dad screams.

Anto rushes across my room and picks up my new MadCrew hoodie from over the chair. He shows me the ANNA side.

'Ach, just get out my sight,' Mum says.

Anto throws the hoodie at me, but he doesn't need to. I understand now who Mum's talking about. I'd be such a rubbish detective. But then again she didn't go ballistic in the car home from MadCrew when I told her Tanya was coming round.

133

'Mrs Breen?' I say. 'Tanya's mum?' Anto doesn't need to go and assemble his four white bricks, I already know the answer's a big fat yes.

'But why is she so angry that Mrs Breen had been here this morning?' That's to myself. I put my hand out towards Anto. 'Give me that for a second?' He gives me what I want. This is definitely a much-needed coat-hanger moment. I don't hit myself with it the way he does, I just let it bobble up and down off my leg a few times, then give it back to him.

Maybe it's cos in her car you can speak to someone on the telephone without having to hold it up to your ear; or maybe it's cos Mrs Breen's ankles are always on show, or maybe it's cos Mrs Breen's dressed up to the nines all the time as if she's going to a swanky nightclub. I don't know, it's so hard to tell. What I do know is that some people are jealous of others for loads of crazy reasons: for the clothes they wear, the car they drive or the hairdo they have, but my mum's no need to be jealous of anyone cos she's more amazing than any car, coat or handbag. That's what I think anyway.

We don't move from the bedroom door. Not sure why, there's nothing being fed to us from below any more.

'Maybe we should get back to bed,' I suggest. Anto's not for moving, he just tugs at his onesie.

The slam of the front door makes us both flinch. I hope the wee glass panel hasn't smashed. We run to the window just in time to see Dad zooming away in the Twingo. Next thing, Mum's feet are booming up the stairs. I grab a Lauren Child book and go sit on my bed, I flop it open on page eighty-seven and pretend to be in my reading zone. Anto's hovering in the middle of my room like, well, Anto. Poor guy, he's standing there like a burglar who's been caught red-handed. Mum'll know we've heard something, she's not that daft, and neither are we.

She's sniffing into a hanky. Her skin doesn't seem as soft as it usually is. Mum's got the onion eyes in. That's us all had them now, except Anto. Obviously the strongest member of the Quinn family.

'Hi, guys, you OK up here?' she says. 'Why aren't you both sleeping?'

'Mum, you're crying,' I say.

'No, I've just been sneezing, I think I've got a head cold.'

Head cold?

It's summer, she can't have a head cold, can she? She blows into her hanky and Anto lets out a squeal. You'd swear it's a happy one, but, believe me, it's not.

'It's just me sneezing, Anthony. Think I must be allergic to something.' She dabs her poor eyes. 'It could be the pollen outside.'

135

I follow the speed of Anto's coat hanger as it goes on and off his chest. The figures on his onesie look as though they're moshing, that's how fast his body is moving.

'I'm fine, Anthony, love. Don't worry.' Mum goes to him, but he grunts and starts hitting the coat hanger off his forehead. Mum stops in her tracks. 'Look at me, Anthony,' she says. I'm thinking, *Schoolgirl error, Mum, schoolgirl error! Of course he's not going to look at you.* 'Anthony,' she says with more force. 'Look … at … me.' And, guess what? He does, he looks at her. My mum, the miracle worker. The Anto whisperer. 'I'm OK – OK?' She flattens her hands and presses them against her cheeks; this is her and Anto's way of cuddling. Anto puts one flat hand on his own cheek. Brilliant; so nobody is cuddling me. 'It always happens this time of year,' she adds. 'Bloomin' pollen is everywhere.'

I can't remember the pollen thing happening last year or the year before or the year before that. I've never seen Mum's eyes this bloated and sore-looking. I've always wanted hers, but today I'm happy with my blue almond ones.

'Is it not about time that you two got into bed?' she says, still cuddling Anto.

'Mum?'

'What?

'Why was Dad driving like a madman?' I ask.

136

'When?'

'He slammed the door and then sped off down the road. We saw him out the window, didn't we, Anto?'

Anto stops cuddling Mum. Clearly he wants answers, same as me.

'Oh, that.'

'Yeah, he could've knocked someone down.'

'Don't be silly.' She tuts.

'Mum, he could've ended up in jail.'

'Oh, don't be ridiculous, Anna.'

'But we saw him.' I slap my book on my bed to show how angry I am. I'm not kidding, I'm dead angry. I don't have the words to tell Mum what I'm thinking and feeling in this moment, so all I can do is smash my book down on my mattress. It doesn't make any angry sound so she fails to see how raging my rage is. I should just ask her the big question outright and be done with it. 'We saw the Twingo, Mum.'

'Oh, he was only trying to get to the shop before it closes.'

'It's after midnight.'

'The twenty-four-hour Tesco,' she says.

'Which doesn't close. That's why it's twenty—'

'Stop it, Anna!'

'No, I won't.'

'Stop it now.'

'I don't believe you.' I jab a fist down hard on to my thigh, which hurts. Anto squeals again. '*We* don't believe you.'

Mum comes to sit beside me, Anto flops on the floor in front of us with his legs crossed. The amber star has well faded around him. That used to be our storytime position when we were younger, when Mum or Dad would read to us from the bed. I'd say over eighty per cent of storytimes had to be abandoned after a few lines though. Still, nice memories. But now we want the proper story.

'It's complicated, sweetheart,' she says, and rubs my sore thigh. 'Dad was just a bit flustered, that's all.'

Anto starts rocking back and forth, staring at the carpet; this relaxes and calms him. You might think he's not listening, but he's so focused on what Mum's saying. He hangs on her every word as if they're being spilled out on the carpet right in front of him, then he can move them around and create his own meanings if he wants. That's exactly what I think he does. He doesn't need to look someone in the eye to know what's being said. Anto listens with his hands, hair, skin and bone.

'I hear you argue all the time,' I say. 'Anto as well.'

'Oh, darling.' She drops her head a bit. She's not about to cry, it's just dead awkward for us all. I want to say something, to ask her the big question, the BIG one, but I'm scared in case my throat cracks. I don't want to start crying. I want to be strong as an ox. He needs me to be his voice too, to ask the questions he has inside him, so I need to be calm and clever. There can't be any tears.

'I'm sorry you've had to hear some of that,' she says.

'But it's all the time now, Mum.'

She takes her hand off my leg. 'It's not all the time, Anna.' Mum's voice is a little sterner. I don't think she's up for crying any more. 'Don't exaggerate now.'

'What are you arguing about?'

'We're not arguing,' she says.

'Yes you are.'

Anto starts fanning his hand in front of his face, his coat hanger dangling from his wrist. Dad calls it his hand-fanning *doing the kaleidoscope* cos it lets him see different shapes and lights, and when light gets into him, Dad says, *he feels like he's swimming on the moon.*

'Anthony, don't worry,' she says. 'It's just how adults communicate with each other sometimes. It's adult chat.'

I know she's lying.

I know she's fighting to come up with the right words.

And I know that's NOT how adults communicate with each other, cos Gran and Papa never communicate with each other like that, and they're always going on bus tours around Scotland together.

'You know, after working all day, and being tired?' Mum adds.

'But we hear you, Mum. We hear you arguing. We heard you today. We heard Dad slamming the door and driving away like a robber. It's not how adults chat. Even I know that.'

Anto bounces to his feet and leaves.

'Anthony!'

Mum sighs, rubs her forehead and eyes. Takes in a huge deep breath and puffs it out again. I really don't want to ask her the big question, but I feel it's time.

'Mum,' I say. 'Are you and Dad—'

Anto bursts back into my room clutching a bag of bricks. He holds a yellow-red-yellow-red brick stack in front of Mum's face as though it's his crucifix against her vampire.

'It's not a lie, Anthony. It's the truth,' Mum says. 'I know you don't believe me, but it is the truth, son.'

He thrusts the brick stack back and forth, about four times. Mum has to flinch at one point.

'Anto, stop doing that,' I snap; I hate it when he's acting all aggressive. He quickly swaps over the red bricks for blue and does his best vampire-hunter move.

'No, she won't get out of the room,' I say. 'Cos it's my

room – not your room, is it? So if I want her to get out I'll tell her myself.'

'Would you two pack it in?' Mum says.

He's back rummaging around in his brick bag. Maybe it's time we created a new word chart with better pictures. Not today though. Then he throws up the two-brown-two-black combo. I mean, what have I done?

'No, Anto. I won't shut up.'

He pushes it so close that it almost hits me on the nose. 'YOU SHUT UP!' I scream at him.

Mum stands and does her classic hand-on-the-hip stance. She starts pointing the finger between both of us.

'I'm warning you. Pack it in now.'

'What have I done? It's him,' I say.

'It's both of you. Now, get back to bed,' Mum yells at us.

He's back in his bricks, clicking and assembling. Sniffing hard and grunting. A bit of snot hangs from his nose which he wipes clean with the sleeve of his onesie. God, sometimes I wish I had a sister. No, not sometimes, lots of times. Imagine the dance routines we could devise together. I know he's going for the four-red-and-one-black pattern. Honest to God!

'Don't bother, Anto. I hate you too.' I only say this cos I want to say it before he does.

'Anna!' Mum shouts. 'Apologise to him.'

'But … he was just about to—'

'Apologise now, I said.'

Anto shoots away before I get a chance to say sorry. Not that I would have anyway. Sometimes I've got to stand up for myself, especially when it's not my fault. Mum's onion eyes have suddenly turned into dagger eyes. It's not fair that he gets away with it all the time.

'Anna,' Mum says in her slow, deep, serious tone. 'You've upset your brother, now I suggest you go and apologise.'

I'VE UPSET HIM?

ME?

I bet he's already on his bed, making a duvet igloo for himself. And he'll stay there until I cajole him out of it. He'll be wedged deep in that igloo, disgusted with himself, worried that he's hurt me and that I'll never talk to him ever again. Twins know stuff like this. OK, maybe I will help him make a new chart then; he'll enjoy that. That's another Anto thing: staying angry with him will never help the situation. You have to take it, forget it and move on, all in the space of about forty seconds. This is what they call the rollercoaster effect. Well, Dad calls it that.

Maybe that's exactly what Mum and Dad need: a huge dose of rollercoasting.

'That wasn't my fault, Mum,' I say, pointing to Anto's room through the wall.

'I'm going to have a cup of tea and then go to bed,' she says. 'My head's splitting.'

There's so much noise in the house. I can't have Mum thinking I'm a complete pain and that all I do is give her splitting headaches. She needs to think I'm amazing. I mean, I've made it to Italy, and she told me how amazing I was cos of that.

'Mum,' I say as she's leaving my room.

She stops dead, but doesn't turn to face me. 'What is it?'

'What woman were you talking about earlier?'

She doesn't turn to face me. Her hand reaches up to the back of her head.

'Time for sleep now, Anna.'

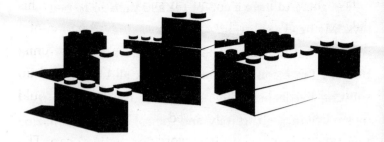

Thirteen

Next morning I hop into my hoodie, black leggings and checkerboard Vans, and then I go to him. It takes me about ten hours to get Anto out from his duvet igloo. Obviously that's me exaggerating. But it's never a case of him just doing something cos he's been asked.

'We can do a new chart if you want?' I ask him.

He grunts and groans like the baby he is.

'You can't stay under there all day, Anto, you'll suffocate.' Still in his igloo, he switches position on to his hands and knees so his bum's in the air. 'Or you might freeze to death.'

'G ... G ... G ... G.'

'Or a polar bear might get into your igloo and eat your heart out, or chew your head off.'

'G ... G ... G ... G.'

He wiggles his bum about; it sways slowly under his duvet. No way, he's actually doing an impersonation of a polar bear. I want to kill myself laughing, he's so funny sometimes. And he knows it too. He could be a stand-up comedian. Well, he couldn't really, but you know, he could do that if our roles were reversed.

'Come on, you need a new word and picture chart. The old ones you have are for ten-year-olds and under.'

I take some of the old ones from his shelf and place them out on the floor. Being super-careful not to touch any of his Lego that's scattered around. He's still in the middle of making an outer space something or other. Just looks like a bus to me.

'I mean, you know these,' I say, pointing to each mini-picture, even though he can't see what I'm doing. 'You know how to use the toilet and what a clock is. You definitely need some better ones, Anto.'

The polar bear stops moving.

'Come on.'

He's lying on his front, but still hiding under there. I think this could be a *No dice* moment.

'Some really good ones. Some ones that maybe only you and I know about.'

He pops his head out of the duvet, big, sweaty red face gawking down at me. Must have been the hottest igloo in

Scotland he was in. He's breathing heavily, but at least he's peaceful.

'Look!' I say, holding up some old charts that he doesn't use any more. 'You know *ball* and you know *watch television* and you know *I need a drink*. You're not a baby any more, Anto. It's time for some older ones.'

I stand up and morph into Mum, hand on hip and pout on my face.

'I mean, we're nearly teenagers now. Well, we've just turned twelve really, but everybody knows that time flies and next year we *will* be teenagers. It'll hit us in no time. New ones are definitely required, so you need to be ready. Agreed?'

He blinks twice. That's all I need. Anna Quinn is good to go.

'Right, get up and get out of that minging onesie!' He grunts at me. 'I'll go grab some colour pencils and paper from my room. I've still got that nice paper Gran and Papa got me when they went to that big museum in Edinburgh.'

Yeah, and they bought Anto a dinosaur T-shirt that said WEE REX on it, a pair of tartan socks and a T-Rex slap watch that he never wears. That was when he was going through his dinosaur phase. Think it only lasted three weeks. I wasn't jealous or anything cos none of those things are my kind of fashion, but still, it would've been good to have the option of wearing a WEE REX T-shirt, know what I mean?

When I return he's wearing his George tracksuit with the army design. He loves it cos he thinks he's a soldier on a battlefield. Sometimes I swear I hear him through the wall making gun noises and blowing things up with his mouth, but it's just my imagination running wild. It would be nice to bang on it and yell at him to SHUT UP, I'M TRYING TO READ. It's not on my most amazing wishlist or anything like that, it's just one of the silly things that I think about sometimes, that's all.

'That was quick,' I say. 'Did you change your pants?' He bats me away with a growl. Fair enough, but I mean, you know what boys are like, and Anto can be a complete ming-fest when he wants to be. Dad says that he *regularly sees his pants walking to the washing machine on their own.*

'Mum's in bed with a splitting headache so we need to be quiet, right.'

He squeals so loud that I think Mrs Molloy will be up like a flash peering behind her curtains.

'Anto! You did that on purpose. Shhh.'

His mouth is wide open. To someone who'd just met him it would look as if he's trying to bite chunks out of the ceiling, but actually he's peeing himself laughing. Not literally, that would be a disaster. His piercing squeal is only to take the mickey out of me and get me in trouble with Mum. He loves to see me suffer.

'Right, I wrote down a list of things we could put on your teenage chart. Just some things that I think might be important, especially these days. We can also add to the list whenever we want. There's some stuff that affects me as well.'

There's things on it that I know he won't agree to:

- Tidy up all the Lego in your room so no one sprains an ankle.
- Wear clothes that actually complement each other; it's not panto season.
- Put your smelly pants in the washing basket as soon as you take them off.
- Have a bath or shower ... or preferably both.
- Leave your coat hanger in your room when we're eating or have visitors.

I spread the sheets of paper with my lists on the floor. It's pink paper, but that's only cos Gran and Papa still think that's my favourite colour. I keep telling them that I'm not a girly girl. Anto paces up and down, coat hanger swaying beside him.

'We don't have to put everything on the chart,' I suggest. 'Maybe we could just start off with four or five?' He's pacing and listening. 'So, you just pick what you want and I'll make some nice phrases and pictures, then add them to the chart. Easy.'

It would be great to get it laminated. Can't exactly ask Mum or Dad to take it into their work to get it done, can we? Then they'd know.

He speeds up his pacing, hitting the coat hanger off the hand he's not holding it with.

'You'll need to come down and have a closer look,' I say. 'It's easy to read, I did big letters.' I wrote all my list in capital letters using a royal blue pen. That's his favourite.

'Actually, know what? It's probably best if I put the paper on your bed so it's easier for you.'

I lift up the sheet and place it on his unmade bed. I've hardly got it flattened out when he smacks the coat hanger into the middle of the paper. He doesn't rip it in two but almost. He'll still be able to read it, no bother. I Sellotape it back together as best as I can and try hard not to look annoyed.

'Probably safer to pick with your finger, Anto,' I say in my calmest voice possible. 'Maybe put the coat hanger over your shoulder.' He does, without making a fuss. I'm flabbergasted. This might not mean much, but it feels as if I've just shifted a mountain with my pinky.

'Perfect. Right, we're good to go.'

He takes a step towards the bed and quickly points. Then he springs back to his pacing.

'This one?' I ask.

He returns and points to the same one again. His pointing action is super-fast, blink and you'd miss it. I draw a big circle around MUM AND DAD ARE ARGUING, DO SOMETHING.

'I thought you'd choose that one.'

He cups his ears. I'm not sure if this is a joke or how he's feeling. But there's nobody making noise, so I think it's a joke. He seems happy anyway.

'OK, next one.'

Four times he goes back and forth to the list, and when he decides on what he wants, he does three rapid points. I circle MUM/DAD SEEM SAD, THEY NEED A CUDDLE.

'That's *you* who's doing the cuddling, by the way.' I grin. He lets out a screech. 'Don't worry, Anto. I'm on it.' He waves his hand in front of his face. 'They love cuddling me anyway.'

The next one that I have to circle is EXPLAIN TO ME WHAT'S GOING ON.

'I will, Anto, but, just so as you know, there's loads of times I haven't a clue what's going on either.'

He points to the next one about fifteen times. Obviously that's me exaggerating again. The paper rips completely in two. Not cos he meant it, cos he's eager that I put my circle around it. The Twingo pulling up outside our house doesn't stop him from pacing and pointing. At least it sounds like someone normal is behind the wheel this time.

Anto points again at the paper.

'Don't worry, Anto, that'll never happen.' He cups his ears once more when the front door clicks open. 'I won't let that happen.'

It's not a growl he's doing when he hears Dad's steps coming up the stairs. Almost like a mini-scream. A whine. Yes, that's it, he's whining. Anto knows exactly how many steps it takes from the bottom of the stairs to reach the door of his room. Twenty-one. I know by his face that he's counting. And when they get to around eighteen or nineteen he chucks the coat hanger at me. I get the message and manage to cover the paper with his pillow in the nick of time. I don't even get to do my circle.

'What are you two up to?' Dad says, squinting his head around the door. His eyes flick from Anto to me and back again. 'What's going on?'

'Nothing, me and Anto are just about to do some dancing.'

LEGO!

I meant to say *Lego*, not bloomin' *dancing*.

'Dancing?' Dad says, looking confused.

151

'I need to practise for Italy, I was going to show him some of my moves. I'm in a trio with Tanya and Evan.'

Anto screams. He loves seeing me squirm. Sometimes I'd like to punch him right on the sausage roll.

'Erm … OK, that sounds like fun,' Dad says. 'Where's your mum?'

'I haven't seen her this morning. She had a splitting headache last night. Maybe she's till lying down.'

Dad tightens his mouth and nods his head slightly. 'Headache, right.'

'I think it's all the pollen outside. She's allergic to it, I think.'

'I'll go and see how she's feeling. You two behave, and don't make too much noise, OK?' His teacher voice doesn't scare us.

When he leaves I do a *Phew!* Anto squeals at the ceiling. So good for not making any noise. I chuck his coat hanger back at him, hard … Not really, but wish I could. I gently hold it out for him to take, shooshing with a finger to my lips at the same time cos I can hear murmuring coming from Mum and Dad's bedroom. Not raised voices, soft. I can't make out any proper words, but they're definitely having a chat. Fingers crossed it's a nice wee blether. An all-is-forgiven one hopefully. I cross fingers on both hands as we listen closely to Dad's humming deep voice followed by Mum's silky one. Then silence. Lots of silence. Nothing apart from the bump of the coat hanger. I imagine – and hope – that they're kissing in the middle of the silences? My eyes swell and my head nods to Anto.

'Think they're kissing,' I murmur. Anto's full of listening and concentration; pacing and blinking. My face is heating up. Anto lets out one of his high-pitched yelps.

'Oh, shut up. I know they're not kissing,' I shoot at him. 'I'm not stupid, I was joking.' But I do wonder what was happening in the silence.

I'm about to yank the paper out and finish my circling when Dad pops his head around the door again.

'Come downstairs in twenty minutes,' he says, giant grin on his face. 'I've news.' Then he disappears.

'He's news,' I say to Anto. 'And he's smiling so it must be good news. What do you think? More doughnuts?'

Anto fans his face.

I slide the paper out from under the pillow and make my final circle. DON'T LET THEM SEPARATE US.

'Don't you worry, Anto. I will never let that happen. Ever.'

Anto doesn't wait for twenty minutes; he heads down after about forty-three seconds.

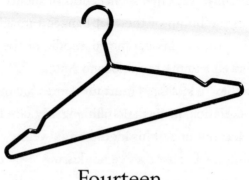

Fourteen

When I go downstairs after my twenty-minute warning, Mum's already there, lounging on the couch. The lines on her forehead are more noticeable; I'm thinking last night's headache is still hovering around. Also, daylight and headaches aren't the best of friends.

She doesn't smile when she sees me. The last thing she needs is the whole family in the same room together. Dad says the noise, sometimes, *would give a paracetamol a sore head, so it would*. Anto loves a family meeting, it turns him wild with excitement. I think Mum would rather be in her room with the lights out though.

I sit down and lift her legs on to my thighs. She's got dead bony feet, which I suppose is perfect for squeezing into some of the shoes she has. She'd give Schuh a run for their money. That's where I got my checkerboard Vans from. I'm pretty sure they sell the same Nikes that Tanya Breen has. Probably now's not the best time to raise the subject, but I'm thinking they'd make the perfect gift when I hit thirteen. I can ask for whatever I want when I'm a teenager; I just hope that there aren't two separate parties for us to go to, that's all. Although, two parties equals two presents. One normal and one guilt present, like Tanya and Evan get.

'Is your head better, Mum?'

'A little bit, sweetheart,' she says, and reaches over to run her fingers through my hair, fixing me a pattern with her long nails. Then rubs her hand over my back the same way she does when she's cleaning the kitchen worktops. It's nice until she starts fiddling, fixing and yanking at my vest top. 'Is that little bra comfortable on you, love?'

'M-u-m,' I say, stretching out the word and arching my back away from her. She's always on to me about stuff like that these days. It makes me go red, and anyway, there's the internet if I've any serious questions. Sometimes she asks me things when Dad's got his nose in the conversation too, which, I'm telling you, is worse than devastation.

'Was Anthony OK?'

'He was fine. Just did his igloo thing and then fell asleep.'

She sniggers through her nose; over the years Mum

must've been in more igloos – trying to fish Anto out – than the Eskimos.

'Where's Dad, by the way?'

'He's out there with your brother getting something from the car.'

Mum's jaw sags, it's such a tiny sag that only her daughter – ME – would've noticed. I rub her feet and try to connect my four fingers to her four twiggy foot bones. I go from ankle to toes about six times. I read in one of Mum's magazines that women love this. There were a lot of really big words in the magazine, but it's something to do with the feet being connected to the brain. Hopefully my fingers can soothe her splitting headache. Dad calls her magazines *a pile of prittle-prattle pish* whenever Mum's nose-deep in them. She always ignores him. But I like her magazines; they are full of good life tips and star signs and nice pictures of inside famous people's houses. Best part: she gets them with her staff discount. Result. I think Dad's just jealous cos all he gets is Greggs leftovers.

'Are you still angry with him for slamming the door last night?' I ask.

'Who, Dad?'

She takes her feet away from me and gets up. I hear her knees creak when getting to her feet. She goes to the window and bangs on it.

'Come on,' she shouts out at Dad and Anto. 'We're in here waiting.'

When they come back in, Anto's buzzing. Fanning his face. Smashing his coat hanger off his thigh. Making a load of noises.

'Someone's happy,' Dad says.

'Anthony, sit.' Mum scowls at him.

'He's not a dog, Mum.'

Just cos your head is splitting and you're shattered, you don't get to take it out on Anto. We're all guilty in this house of doing that. He's the easiest of targets cos he can't fire back. He flops on to the floor and rocks. Mum comes to sit beside me, and Dad stands in the middle of the living room like he's about to play charades. I wait until there is silence before saying what's on my mind.

'I had to nip out early to a very special shop before I missed the chance,' Dad says.

'What chance?' I ask. 'What shop?'

Dad goes to his bag and pulls out an envelope, one of the big bubble ones that you don't need to lick. He hands it to me. My heart starts to race, in a good way. I stare at Mum; she's looking as if she's just watching the news.

'Open it,' he says. 'Go on.'

Anto crashes his wrists together. God, I haven't seen him this excited since Gran and Papa brought him a pair of boxing gloves back from New York. And, I'm not joking, for a week he punched everything in sight. Everything.

The first thing I see when I open the envelope is a big, bright sun and a suntanned family with amazing teeth; looks roasting where they are. Behind the sun is the Sunways Travel logo written in thick red. The beach on the front cover is how you'd imagine Paradise to be. Even the man and woman's son has a sixpack; he's only ten. Their daughter's hair is the same colour as the sand. I'm betting they're American.

'No way,' I say, looking at Dad and then Mum. 'Are we going somewhere hot?' Both of them nod. 'Really?'

'We are,' Dad says. 'Incredibly hot.'

'Somewhere near the Bahamas?' I ask.

'Yeah, you wish, Anna,' Mum says.

I look at the brochure cover again, at the white, white beach and blue, blue sea. I can just picture myself lying on a lounger with an old Nancy Drew or new Rainbow Rowell book, someone bringing me a mocktail on the hour. Pineapple and passion fruit. It'd take me about three years to get a tan. Mum and Anto just need to look at the sun and it's as if someone's sprayed them brown. It's not fair how he got loads of the good parts.

'Open page thirty-nine,' Dad tells me.

I flick to the page and pull it open.

I want to squeal.

I want to cry.

I want to calm my heart down.

I want to hug my dad.

My mouth widens and I do a silent scream. Anto copies me. In actual fact it's me who's copying him. Mum's news-watching face changes to something much sweeter.

'No way,' I say. 'For the dance tournament?'

'We are going to Italia.' Dad does a silly fake Italian accent and makes these excruciatingly embarrassing gestures. Mum stares at him. I know she wants to laugh along, I know she does. It's written all over her face. And then something bizarre happens: they pass a smile to one another. Flippin' flip, they are as excited about Italy as I am! Told you Italy would solve everything. We're not even there yet, and it's already working its magic.

'Did you book this today?' I ask.

'About an hour ago,' he says.

I feel bad for giving him grief about his Twingo-driving now. The feeling goes away when I stare at the brochure again.

'And we're actually staying here?' I turn it around to show everyone the swanky hotel. It looks amazing with all the massive gold lights. The amount of flags outside the main entrance makes it seem as if the Olympics are staying there too. The hotel is about the length of our entire street. Best bit, it's got an infinity pool on the roof.

'Mocktails on the roof, Mum,' I spout.

'What on the roof?' she says.

'Wait.' Dad shuffles from one foot to the other and stares down at Mum on the couch. He's dropped his smile. Uh-oh; and she's got an offended look on her face now. Seen it a million times. Dad's licking his lips; he does that when he's thinking of the right thing to say. Funnily enough, so does his son.

'That's not where we're actually staying, Anna,' he says.

'It's not?' I say, trying not to look as disappointed as Mum. But of course I can't hide it. Anto screeches at the top of his lungs. He just loves it, doesn't he? I could kick him in the face from where I'm sitting. I'm telling you, sometimes it takes the strength of ten elephants to stop me.

'Of course it's not, Anna,' Mum adds. 'Do you think we're made of money?'

'No, but …' I try and hold the brochure up again.

'But we're staying very close to that hotel,' Dad says. 'Just around the corner really.'

'How close?' I say.

'Oh, well, the guy in Sunways said it was just a short walk.'

'How short?'

Dad's doing his lip-licking thing again. He tilts his head as if the answer is printed on the ceiling.

'Between one and two kilometres away,' he says. Mum lets out a little snide giggle. Dad glares at her; she shakes her head cos he *can never do anything right*. 'It's in the same area Kim suggested.'

'Many stars?' Mum asks.

'Yeah, many stars, Dad?'

He pulls out his phone and scrolls.

'It's, eh, three. Yeah, three stars.'

'Three stars?' Mum says. 'Does it have air conditioning?'

'It's three stars, Liz, of course it'll have air con.'

'Does it have an infinity pool?' I ask, which is a daft question cos there's NO three-star hotel in the world with an infinity pool. Be lucky to have a power shower. I know it's wrong, but hearing about those three stars has yanked the rug from under my happy feet.

Anto fans his face and yelps. I'm pretty sure he made a splashing sound. He's taking the pure mickey.

'Who says you're coming anyway?' I say to him. 'You'll be staying with Gran and Papa. They don't even have Netflix.' I stare down at him. 'So swim in that.' He responds by slamming his wrists against each other.

'Thanks for that, Anna,' Mum says. 'Well done.'

'But it's him,' I plead.

'How can it be him?' she says.

Under my breath I say, *'I wish he wasn't coming.'* But Mum hears it.

'Your dad has booked two rooms, so of course Anto is coming.'

It's like she's switched a kettle on and it's boiling away inside my head, and now it's needing to be poured into the cup. I leap from the couch, chuck the brochure near Mum's bony feet and stomp one of my Vans on the floor. My fists stay clenched by my sides.

'Well, I better not be sharing a room with him,' I shout.

'You'll do what you're told,' Dad adds.

'I'm twelve and I wear vest tops, so it's not happening.'

Anto fights with his body to stop it twisting and tensing up on him. I've caused it. It must be hurting him so bad, but I don't care … I do.

'And it's because you're twelve is exactly why you'll be doing what you're told,' Mum shouts at me.

I want to say something horrible to both of them. It's funny how they're like a wee gang now, backing up what the other says. It's not that when they're keeping us up all night arguing the heads off one another, is it? Actually, it's not funny.

'I'm going to my room,' I say.

'Yeah, before you get sent,' Mum says as I'm leaving.

Sometimes I'm on her side and other times I'm on Dad's. Always I'm on Anto's. Capital ALWAYS. But who's on mine?

I hear Anto's howls as I'm bounding up the stairs. Mum and Dad start up again as well.

Why did you say that?

Why did you do that?

Why did you have to stand there like a lost clown?

I can't seem to do anything right in your eyes!

When I reach my bed I yank the covers over my head and block out all noise. Now I have my very own igloo. See, it's not just you who can create one, Anto. I'm equally as clever. I can make my own special place in this house too.

I concentrate on trying to listen to the sound of my own breathing. See, I can do special breathing too, Anto.

I know he's down there with his hands cupped over his ears and swaying back and forth, raging cos I practically told him he's not welcome on my trip to Italy; may as well have told him that I didn't want him to be part of this family.

DON'T LET THEM SEPARATE US.

'Don't you worry, Anto. I will never let that happen. Ever.'

I know that's what he'll be thinking. Bet if he could, Albert Einstein would shake his head at my stupidity, my selfishness. *I'm sorry, Albert, I don't know why I said what I said.* I try hard not to be selfish, so hard to keep calm without hurting anyone.

My breathing is heavy, maybe it's the heat in here or the fact that I'm so angry. How can I be angry? Dad just booked the Italy hotel so I've no need to be. And, the major plan was to get us Italy bound so we can have the best family holiday on the planet; after which there'll be no need to split anything up. It's a strange feeling and I don't know the what, where or why of any of it. It's confusing, big time. One minute I'm doing nice word and picture charts with Anto, then I'm rubbing Mum's feet, then I'm slobbering at the brochure Dad gave me; and the next I'm under here wanting to throw all my books out of the window. How could it not be confusing? The only thing I can do is smother my face into the pillow and scream at the top of my lungs. It feels like there's a tiny line between what's amazing and what's heart-breaking. Different drinks mixed in the same glass.

After screaming, I play out what happened in my head: I should be jumping for joy now, downstairs planning a fancy dinner, planning all the cool things we'll be doing in Italy; me and Mum planning our outfits for day and night activities. Getting dead excited that my family will be together in a foreign country. A proper foreign country too. Italy! I want to hear Dad's idiot version of Italian; it should be a full-on laugh-fest downstairs, with me bang in the middle of it, cracking jokes and writing itinerary lists. Where I shouldn't be is in this dark and sweltering igloo, worried that I've made things horrible for everyone cos of my big gob.

So what if Tanya Breen gets to stay in a fancy-dan hotel. Who cares? Her life isn't my life. OK, so I don't know her like a twin or a BFF, but I'm pretty sure she'd rather have her dad at home over some swish hotel any day of the week. No infinity pool or big gold lights or a massive comfy bed can ever replace what I have. I'm not saying I would never like any of that stuff, but it's not important. Feeling bonded, that we've been stuck together with the world's strongest glue, is what's important; that nothing can tear us apart. No amount of presents could ever make things better.

There's pain at the back of my legs, like someone's jabbing hammers into them. My ribs seem to be squishing into my stomach and chest; think my body's trying to turn me into a human accordion, or something. My head should be throbbing, but it's not, it's tingling in the way that pins and needles tingle your soul. I have to stay under these covers cos the light will melt my eyes.

This is the first time this has happened, the first time my body has made a proper physical connection with his. The first time I've actually experienced that twin thing. And I want him here, underneath the covers with me, just the two of us, as if we're back inside Mum's belly. Back when we were swimming and swirling around together for months and months; getting on like two peas in a Mum pod. That's where I want to be. But most of all I want to say sorry to him for being the cruellest big sister ever. Mum and Dad also need a giant sorry for paying all that money to come support me in Italy, and all I paid them back with was a fist-clenched foot-stomp. And maybe Tanya Breen needs my sorry with a capital BIG – I'll let Evan Flynn off with a wee one – cos I allowed myself to get upset about their reaction to Anto. Thing is, if I go around getting narky at everyone who reacts to Anto the way they did, I'll be spending most of my life apologising to folk. And why? Just cos Tanya doesn't understand what's going on? It's wrong to blame people for failing to understand what they don't understand, isn't it? Sometimes when people don't understand something they get embarrassed, and some-times when people get embarrassed it brings out their rudeness. Mum has always told me that *expecting people to instantly switch on to what's happening is too much to hope for*. Maybe she's right. But I don't know how to protect him in any other way. I'm his voice, his feelings, his suit of armour. I'm his twin.

I said that I don't care. But I do care. I care every day. I wake up caring. I'm so sad that I've made him sad. And I'm sad too, cos Mum and Dad can't see our sadness.

Fifteen

Right, so, we're all in the top floor of this building where there's a big fancy dance studio. Four walls: two with mirrors, two with windows. Me and Mum gaze out of them. Look, you can see the Colosseum away in the distance, Anna. All the rooftops and huge church domes are orangey, yellowy and reddy; different heights and sizes, they're the most perfect rooftops for doing parkour. Long, straight streets scatter off in every direction, cars fight with scooters for road space. The beep-beeps never stop. People walk and talk at a hundred miles an hour. It's bonkers. There's not one cloud in the sky, not one. The only time I've seen this type of blue colour is in paintings and some of the picture books I read when I was really young. You could swim in it.

This studio has the works: spotlights on the ceiling that you can dim up and down; the hardwood floor is perfect for sliding and spinning. It's a breaker's dream. I'm sure that I could do about twenty-five backflips from one wall to the other. When you speak, your voice echoes. Dad and Anto love this fact, they're like a couple of babies shouting out random words to each other and whistling: the piercing one you can only get when you use your fingers. Anto's a really talented whistler. But, there's a time and place. You'd think they've never been in an echoey toilet before. Me and Mum chuck some eyes at each other.

Some place this, Dad says.

Did you bring it? Mum asks him. Me and Anto look at each other, confused. Dad goes into his pocket and shakes his latest iPhone model at her. *Downloaded on to my iTunes*, he says. He fiddles with the iPhone and places it on a chair across from where me and Anto are standing. He then sashays back over and holds out his hand towards Mum, the way ballroom dancers do. She reaches out her long, tanned arm and before you can say *arrivederci* she's twirling herself into his body. Into his *body*. Yuck! My eyes pop. I'm willing the wooden floor to crumble and take me with it. Or better, take them.

What's the deal? Anto mutters to me.

Stuffed if I know, I say. They don't move, just stand in the middle of the floor clutching each other, giggling like a couple of prom dates. This is any child's worst nightmare. Anto nudges me: *I swear to God, if those two embarrassments start dancing I'm jumping out of one of these windows.* I squint at him and say, *Of course they're going to dance, you think they're standing like that cos they're loved up?* Dad whisks Mum around in one crazy move and almost drops her to the floor, but he catches her just at the last second. When she's looking up at him, he leans down and pecks her lips.

I can't watch, Anto.

Tell me about it, sis. It's hard not to though.

The music starts blaring through the studio. Dad pulls Mum to a standing position and grabs her tight around the waist. Music fills the entire room; those new iPhones make some sound. We don't know the song, it's a woman with a cracking voice though. A lovey-dovey tune. They start moving around the studio with tons of grace. So smooth you'd swear they were wearing roller skates. Me and Anto look at each other and wind our necks in a bit.

They're good, he says, sounding confused.

I know, right.

No, I mean they're better than good.

I've got eyes, Anto.

Mum's wearing this bottle-green pleated midi skirt that floats and flutters on every turn and twist.

Her hair?

Oh my God, her hair!

Her movement is so elegant; she could be a professional. I'm deadly serious. And Dad, he's the darkest horse in Dark Town. Who knew those big hairy arms and legs of his could flow like water? He's easing Mum around that floor like a summer's breeze; every so often he turns into a gust of wind and does something extraordinary. My mouth opens. Who even are these people? My parents, that's who.

Are you watching this? Anto says.

No, I'm still thinking about my ice cream earlier.

You're an idiot.

We never once take our eyes off them. I watch their every step, spin and rotation.

This was our wedding song, Dad shouts over the music.

Before you two came along, Mum adds with a wink and a smile.

We don't know the song, but it's not some mortifying cheesy number or anything, if I had to guess I'd say it's a soul singer from way back. *Good tune,* Anto shouts to them. This is a couple who, before they were married, dreamed of having children — a boy and a girl — the perfect set-up. A boy and a girl who'll take the world by storm and make them proud. A boy and girl who'll bring nothing but joy to their lives. My mum and dad excited for all the pleasures that the future will bring them.

When the song finishes, Mum coils away from Dad, then rolls back into him again like a human boomerang. Dance over. They giggle into each other's arms. Mum strokes Dad's cheek.

The noise outside is louder, now that the music has stopped. Dad, still humming the song, solo dances over to get his new iPhone. Mum runs her fingers through her hair and shoogles it loose; she fixes her skirt and tucks in her vest top. When she comes over to us she takes Anto's face in her hands and gives him a massive smacker on both cheeks. Then it's my turn.

Wow, look at the sky, she says.

There's some orange through the blue now. The ivory domes are half shaded and the rooftops are darker, but still amazing; a million tiny mosaics in conversation. I'd love to run all over the top of them, ninja-style in my black gear. No one would see me in the low sun.

Imagine living here, I say.

Dad comes over and wraps his arms around us, one dangling over Mum and the other over Anto. They get to grab a hand each. I'm crushed up in the middle, which doesn't bother me. We stand gazing out at Rome as if someone's taking our picture. The smiling family full of the joys and delights. Say CHEESE.

The Colosseum doesn't seem so far away now, Anto says.

Why don't we go? Dad suggests.

Where? I ask.

The Colosseum.

Now?

It's a beautiful evening, it'll be nice, Mum says, and kisses Dad on the palm of his hand.

I'm starving, Anto says. Shock! Horror! All he's done since we got here is eat slices of pizza and stuff his face with ice cream. I mean, look at this beauty, and all he thinks about is his stomach. And gawping at Italian girls too. He thinks I haven't noticed. Twins, remember. I see everything.

You never know, Anto, they could have a Greggs up near the Colosseum, I say. Mum and Dad do a wee giggle.

Rap it, you, he says.

Anyone know the Italian for sausage roll? I say. We all giggle. Anto punches me on the arm. Not a sore one.

Come on, Mum says. *We can all grab an ice cream on the walk up.*

Another one? I say, dead excited cos, I mean, two ice creams in the same day and it's not even Christmas.

When in Italy, Dad says.

He leads Mum to the studio exit door by the hand.

Before we leave the studio I shout, *Hey, guys!* and do a massive slide into an amazing Baby Freeze, just for the fun of it. Everyone gives me a huge applause; they whoop and cheer and pat me on the back.

I hope you win this competition, Anto says.

You've got a fantastic chance, Mum says.

That's my girl, Dad adds.

Outside I feel so alive that I really could jump on those rooftops. It's been a perfect day walking around the sights of Rome with laughs and banter. And now there's more ice cream to be had. My mind is running over different flavours. On the way to the Colosseum I smack my lips. Lick them.

Smack them.

My mouth is so dry, the air is hot. Gorgeous but hot. Everything smells different.

Smack again. I'm parched. Hot. Very hot.

'ANNA.'

Smack my lips.

'Hey.'

Someone's pushing my shoulder; it makes my body

174

sway. *It better not be Anto or he's not getting a bite of my ice cream.*

'ANNA!'

I'm so dry.

'ANNA!'

Suddenly I'm lying looking up at the faded stars on my ceiling. Bye-bye, amazing sky. I'm back in the land of the pressure cooker.

'I need water,' I moan.

'You fell asleep under there.' Mum's perched on the side of my bed. 'You must be roasting.'

'I'm boiling.' I sit up and take off my hoodie. 'I need a drink,' I say. 'What time is it?'

'It's only gone six,' she says. 'You feeling all right?

What happened earlier floods back. I feel a tragic grey cloud hanging over me.

'Is he OK, Mum?'

'Anthony's fine, he's helping Dad wash the car.'

We both smile cos we know that Anto doesn't actually wash the car, he battles with the water hose. He'll be drenched. It's weird, cos he's not a massive fan of the shower or bath, but hand him a hose outside and he's in dreamland.

'Mum, I really didn't mean what I said.'

'I know you didn't, sweetheart.'

'I do want him to come, you know. To Italy.'

'We all do.'

'I don't know why I said those things.'

'Listen, Anna, we understand. I'm his mother and I still get frustrated with him for no reason. I'm always thinking about what's going on inside that head of his.'

'Me too.'

'And, because more often than not I don't know the answer to that, I sometimes take all my frustrations out on him.' She puts her hands like a shield to protect herself with. 'I know it's not fair.'

'I feel the same way at times, Mum.'

'And our frustration can turn to sadness too. I've seen it.'

'Sadness for him as well,' I say.

'Oh, definitely sadness for him.' She gets up and glances around my room, doing her inspection thing. I stand and stretch the sleep out of my body. Mum picks up one of my books without even looking at it, as though she's just wanting something to hold. 'But deep down, I know he's not a sad boy.'

'No, I know that. But he's still allowed to feel sad if he sees and hears stuff that makes him that way. Just like me.'

'Of course he is.'

'I mean, if I hit my leg on the door, I'm sad cos it's

painful. But if I hear stuff I don't want to hear, then that's a completely different painful altogether, which gets you right in here.' I point to my chest. 'The leg pain goes away, but see that pain inside? Well, that's much harder to shift.'

Mum tilts her head and gives me a soft look; it's her *I'm so proud of you* look … I think. I've a notion she wants to hug.

'And remember,' Mum says. 'Anthony's probably more frustrated because he can't express that in the same way you can.'

'I know he is,' I say, feeling a wee bit rubbish for him.

Mum touches the front cover of the book, Claire McFall's last novel; it was a belter, blew me away. She opens it up at a random page, then flicks to another, then another. Looks like she's searching for something. Whatever it is, she won't find it in a book, I can tell you that for nothing. Yeah, I think she might be lost.

'It would be nice to have a proper conversation with him though, wouldn't it?' she mumbles, then puts her hand on her chest and does a big inhale. 'God, I wish that every day. Every day! So does your dad,' she says very softly.

'But we do have conversation, Mum, it's just a different type of conversation, that's all.'

'I know it is, sweetheart. I know it is.' She replaces my book.

I don't want to bring up all that stuff about late-night fights or talk about the fear that me and Anto have, but I'm dying to know. Other times when I've wanted to ask the big questions, my legs have wobbled and my bottle has crashed into a billion pieces. But now I have a real need to know if what we've been listening to is true facts. Do they mean all the things they say to each other? If we're a real family we should all be talking together, not keeping secrets. That's what I think.

'I just want us all to be happy,' I say.

Mum lowers her head and gazes at me through the top of her eyes. Her grin is gentle and caring.

'I think someone needs a hug,' she says. I nod.

She approaches with outstretched arms. Before I can say anything else, I'm snuggling against her chest. 'It'll be great seeing you dance in another country.' I can't reply cos I'm chewing her jumper. 'Oh, that reminds me,' she says, releasing me into clean air. 'That Breen girl called the house phone.' Her mouth goes all crooked as if she's angry with me for something. 'Asked if you wanted to go to her house tomorrow.'

'Why didn't you come get me?'

'You were upset, and you were also sleeping. Sleeping

people generally can't talk on the phone, Anna.'

'She wants me to go to *her* house?'

'You can't be a trio if you don't practise.'

'Right,' I say, feeling a bit awkward for some reason. Should I say yes or no? Will Mum be offended if I go to her house cos it's in the posh part and probably much bigger than ours? I suppose it'll give me the chance for the sorrys to be chucked around. Maybe we can both apologise.

'Well, do you want to go or not?' Mum's voice has a sharp bite to it now. What happened to all the hugs and sweethearts?

'But how will I get there?'

'We can take you.'

'You don't all need to come. Can Dad not just drop me off?'

'What, and deprive Anthony of a car trip?'

If there's anything Anto loves more than the millions of other stuff he loves, it's a family car journey. Doesn't matter if it's to Gran and Papa's, Aldi's or the dump, he can't get enough of them. He'd go absolutely gaga over a road trip.

'OK, so, I guess I'll say yes then,' I say. 'Will I phone and tell her?'

'No need, we already said yes on your behalf.'

That night I fluff up Anto's pillow and leave four white bricks on it. As well as being the Yes bricks, they can be other things too. He'll know that I'm saying sorry. It might be time to do a new set which includes I'm really sorry. I also draw a big Diavolo pizza the size of his head and sit it under the four white bricks. I'm not the world's best drawer, but he'll get it. Below the pizza I write: *Can't wait to share a real Italian one of these with you, love you, eejit, your BIG sister. KKKK.*

Sixteen

'Isn't it a bit weird if we all rock up?' I say.

'I've already mentioned it to Anthony, and now he's desperate to come,' Mum says.

Anto likes to sit in the front seat and either play with the radio or the electric window switch. Mum gets scared when he sticks his head out of it like a dog, but to see his cheeks wobble and his face meet the fierce wind is a thing of wonder. His mind doesn't touch danger when he's feeling so alive, and the wind outside the Twingo does that for him. He soars above everything, including the weather; his hair could be a flapping kite above those clouds.

'You better all stay in the car when we arrive,' I say.

'Oh, don't worry, we will all be staying in the car,' Mum says. I see her knee jab into the back of Dad's driving seat.

We're hardly out of our estate and already we've been

on to four different radio stations. I can tell Dad isn't too chuffed that Mum and Anto are in the car too. But what can you do when your twin throws all his tantrums out of the pram whenever he wants to get a ride in the car? Deep down it was such a big deal for me, but I did my best not to make it into one, especially after my performance yesterday. Having the whole family drive me there is a wee bit embarrassing, but if Tanya Breen spies us sitting outside her house squeezed into our Twingo that'll stretch to being mortifying.

I sensed it was a mistake when Anto insisted – once we were all seatbelted up in the car – on smacking his head repeatedly cos he wanted something from the house. And when he wants something that badly and can't express what it is, *that's his MO*, as Dad says. It took us ages to understand what he wanted, then more ages when he went to look for what he wanted, and further ages when he decided he needed a pee after finding the thing that he wanted. My first thought was that he'd left his headphones in his room as he's got a specific playlist for car journeys, but cos it isn't *his* car journey, and not part of his routine, he doesn't need it. Dad sat in the car with one hand resting on his forehead. For the first two minutes of our journey we all had steam coming out of our nostrils while the bold Anto sat in the front seat, with the Diavolo pizza drawing

I gave him draped over his legs like a shawl, fiddling with the radio and window.

'We're always pandering to him,' Dad hisses, more to himself than anyone else.

'You're a parent, pandering to your children is part of the contract,' Mum kind of utters out the window.

'No one asked you to come,' Dad utters out of his window. 'I don't require a chaperone.'

Anto starts blowing raspberries. A happy thought comes to me.

'Dad?'

'What's up?'

'Will we be getting a hire car when we're in Italy?' I ask.

'Hire car?'

'Yeah.'

Dad lets off a fake laugh; it's loud, with only one giant *HA*!

'Oh, no, there won't be any hire cars, Anna,' he says. 'Sadly that's an indulgence that your mum wouldn't let us stretch to, so it'll have to be public transport all the way I'm afraid.'

'Aw, that's a shame,' I say. Mum gives me the daggers. What have I done?

Dad beeps the horn and waves at some randomer outside, who doesn't wave back. As we pass, I twist my head to see the randomer standing still, wondering who we are, thinking it's a Twingo mickey-taking beep.

'Hire car would've been nice all right,' Dad adds. 'But I presume we'll just have to slum it on public transport and accept getting ripped off by taxis whenever we want to go somewhere. It'll be a hoot with all our luggage in that heat.'

Mum goes to say something, but she stops herself at the last minute. My guess was that it had a *shut* and an *up* in it.

'What I'm really looking forward to, however,' Dad goes on, 'is exposing Anthony to the joys and stresses of it all. Now that, I can't wait for.'

Mum shifts her daggers from me to the back of Dad's head.

'It won't be so bad,' I say.

'No, you'll love it,' he says.

'Anna, tell your dad that you'll be travelling with Kim and the other dancers in a special coach.' Mum nudges me. 'And, if he'd have read the bumph she sent through properly, he'd have known that.'

Anto blows more raspberries. Longer and wetter ones. Some of his slobbers fall on to the Diavolo pizza drawing.

'Maybe we can do one of those red bus sightseeing tours,' I suggest, cos that's like mixing public transport with family fun. Everyone's happy! I know, I know, I'm a legend. 'You know, like the ones Gran and Papa do all the time?' They send us pictures whenever they're on the top deck of one of them. For some reason they think Anto is mad for buses, which is news to me. Mum's got snaps from Lisbon, Berlin, Budapest and Stockholm on her phone. 'We could send them a picture of us all on the Rome one.' Something tells me that I'm on my own with the red bus suggestion. 'Come on, they'd love that.'

'I think your gran and papa get a discount,' Mum says.

Dad does that one *HA!* laugh again. I'm not sure I like it. 'There's your answer, Anna. I think we'll be hoofing it around Rome.'

Mum sighs, and shakes her head. Her mouth is closed, but I know she's gritting her teeth; her jaw is very stiff.

'Anna,' she says, still gazing out of the window. 'Tell your dad that *he* can hoof it around Rome if he wants, and we'll get the red bus tour.'

I don't have time to say a word before Dad jumps in.

'Tell your mum she can get the red bus on her own.'

'Tell your dad it won't be just the red bus I'll be getting on my own,' she spits out.

Oh God, we're back to this again. I pull my legs up on the seat and hug them. A complete no-no, but who cares? Who's watching?

'Anna, tell your mum I hope some Italian shoves her under the bloody red bus,' Dad spits back.

'I'll shove you under a … bloody bus.' Mum tries hard not to swear, as if she's skidded towards the cliff's edge and stops just short of falling off.

'You'd love to,' Dad slurs.

'Don't tempt me.'

OK, so we're not going anywhere near buses. Red, blue or green ones.

Anto lets out a supremely long and soggy raspberry. I fear for the drawing on his lap.

'STOP THAT NOW!' Mum shouts.

'PACK THAT IN!' Dad screams.

It's like they've both read my mind. It's exactly what I would like to roar at the top of my tiny lungs to them.

When he starts punching the roof there's nothing we can do. I want to get out of the car, he wants to get out of the car, Mum probably wants to get out too, but we can't. We're all stuck in this moving Twingo prison until we reach Tanya's house. I need to drown out the noise and loosen the tightness in my tummy, so I do what he does and cover my ears. I then put my head between my knees, clench my toes and do everything in my power not to burst out crying. Mum rests her hand on my back, right across the ANNA on my hoodie.

'Put your head out,' Dad says. I'm not sure if he's speaking to me or Anto.

'Just lean it out a little bit, Anthony,' Mum adds. 'But keep your seat belt buckled.'

When I look up from my knees, Anto is resting his head half in, half out the car. His hair is waving over his face and he seems to be semi-smiling. There's no electric windows in the back so I roll mine down and do the same as him.

'Careful, Anna,' Mum says.

I breathe through my nose and let the wind wash my face; it's not too cold; it soothes, and helps blow any stray tears off my cheeks. Maybe one will drift and find the randomer still rooted to his spot. He'll think it's started raining. That would be funny.

Right, so, we're all in this big fancy hire car, on a top day out to the beach. Apart from Dad, everyone's got their head out of the window. Inhaling the sand. The sea. The smell. It's glorious. The car is wedged with music and towels and hats and packed lunches. Anto spies the sea first and lets out a huge cheer … and then …. and then … and then …

It's not working. Why isn't it working? What am I doing wrong? I'm trying to dream, to imagine, to invent, but nothing's happening. Here goes again:

Right, so we're all in this big fancy car that looks like a tank, we're in the middle of the Italian countryside …

187

NO! What's happening? Come on, Anna, get your head in the game! Deep breath. Eyes closed.

RIGHT, we're in this big fancy ...

Nope.

RIGHT, we're in a giant balloon ...

Behave yourself, will you? Why can't I think? An image of Anto flashes up. Why won't my head work? For me this has only been a few minutes, but for him it's every minute of every hour. Think about that.

Last time:

RIGHT, so we're all swimming on the moon ...

Useless and stupid. Back to reality for you, Anna.

Aw!

The tarmac and takeaway smells from outside gush up my nose, and I have to stop breathing for a bit. It's OK, it passes, I survive. Dad's driving has sped up, so the force of the wind makes my cheeks tremble. I can see Anto's face in the passenger wing mirror; his eyes are so massive, we're looking directly at each other. No words needed. Why didn't I get those eyes? I mean, we're twins, we're meant to be the same, aren't we? We're only meant to have tiny differences. But in those six minutes, between me being free and him still trapped inside, someone decided that he got the eyes while I got everything else. How unlucky is that? Or, how lucky is that? Still, sometimes, not always,

I'd like to swap us around for a day, or an hour even, to see what life is like out of his eyes.

I pucker up my lips and smack them towards him. Sometimes I do these fake kisses to annoy the life out of him. One time, years ago, I actually jumped on his bed and kissed his cheeks about fifty times. Mum said the reason he didn't resist was cos he was in shock and in so much pain. He did scream a wee bit, but it was all for show – he loved it. So all that stuff about him not being tactile or affectionate is *utter tripe*, as Gran and Papa would say. Anyway, I mostly do my sister-kissing from a safe distance, but this is the first time it's happened in the Twingo, or any car for that matter. He blinks twice and lets his eyes do all the smiling. If this would've happened in the house we'd be doing our 'K … K … K … K' thing.

Through the wing mirror's little square I'm trying to tell him that everything will be fine, and not to worry. If we had the new chart, I could maybe point to MUM/DAD SEEM SAD, THEY NEED A CUDDLE. But the rub is, I think we all need a cuddle, one big giant group hug. I'm so hoping that when we're in Italy that'll happen every morning and night … but only if they're not trying to throw each other under a *bloody* bus.

After a much needed chunk of silence, we drive down a wide road where none of the houses are connected to one another or look the same. Some are like the Lego houses Anto's made in the past: flat roofs, loads of windows and big square gardens. I'd wager that we're the only Twingo as far as the eye can see. Every other lamp post has a diamond sign with *This is a Neighbourhood Watch Area* written on it.

'Think this is the street,' Dad says, slowing down and leaning closer to the windscreen to get a better look at the houses.

'He *thinks* it's the street!' Mum mumbles to herself.

'These are massive,' I say, trying not to sound as if I'm jealous. Some of the front doors look more expensive than our entire house. Both me and Anto keep springing our heads left and right, cos this would be like our dream street.

'I wonder if any of these places have swimming pools,' I say. 'Do you think they do?' No one answers. 'Anto, if we lived here, you could have a whole room just for doing Lego. How cool would that be?' He fans his face. 'And we could have a room full of books with a couple of comfy chairs in it.' That would be my relaxation chamber. My igloo library.

'Careful what you wish for, Anna,' Mum says.

'Why?' I twist my face to show how confused I am. 'Imagine living here, Mum.'

She taps me on the leg and widens her eyes the way adults do when they think you haven't a clue what they're talking about.

Dad's driving like a kerb crawler, which is definitely the wrong thing to do with a car overflowing with out-of-towners. The Neighbourhood Watch will be having kittens over their walkie-talkies.

'What number is it again?' he asks.

Mum gives him a strange look.

'Would you ever stop.' It's Dad's turn to mumble. When he hits the steering wheel with the palm of his hand Anto starts footering about with the window and radio again. My internal kettle starts to bubble and boil.

'Is it impossible for us to be in the car and go from one place to another?' I go, wanting to dig my knee into the back of Dad's seat the way Mum did. It's as if I'm the mum and they are the terrible twins. 'What are you two going on about?' I ask, and like good parents, they ignore me. 'I don't get what you're saying.' I hear the tone in my voice getting higher and higher. I'm not going to cry again, I'm fine.

The radio volume goes up and down and up and down. Same with the passenger window. The car is roasting. My back is sweating.

'Just hurry up and drop her off, Tony, so I can get home.'

Anto cranks the volume to sky-high level. The sound attacks our eardrums. Without warning Dad hammers on the brakes and we all plunge forward.

'DON'T!'

'ANTHONY!'

And all my fears comes true. One of the Twingo windows is fully down and I'm in it with three screamers. Complete one hundred per cent mortification. I pray that Tanya or Mrs Breen haven't heard anything.

'This is it here,' Dad says.

'Right, I'll go to the door myself,' I say. 'Nobody needs to get out.'

I land on the pavement and fix my hoodie and hair. The smell of trees in this area is dead strong.

'I'll pick you up at five,' Dad shouts through the window.

'He means he'll beep the horn at five, Anna,' Mum shouts. 'So make sure you're looking out for him.'

'Fine.' I frown and pout. All I want to say is *Just go*. We don't need some big family chinwag while I'm on the pavement.

'Don't *fine* me.' Mum leans over Anto until she's half out of the car. 'Or you'll be whipped back inside here.' Anto groans at the weight on his back.

'Right, five, OK. I'll look out for him.'

'Good.' She sits back down in the back seat.

Anto rests his head on the door, relieved that she's off him. I lean down and whisper into his ear, 'On the way home close your eyes and think of cool things we can do in Italy that don't revolve around eating pizza.' I look into the car. 'Bye then.'

Dad could be a volcano minutes before erupting; Mum a tornado way off in the distance. They don't say *Bye then* back.

'Close your eyes,' I quickly whisper again to Anto.

I don't wave at the Twingo driving off. I take in a giant gust of tree air and puff it out loudly – like I've just puffed away the past twenty minutes of my life – as I saunter up Tanya's driveway trying to calm myself down. I hope she's forgotten about all the stuff that we said to each other at my house. Real friends have disagreements and heated discussions, then get over them. Plastic friends hold grudges. Tanya's not made of plastic. And neither am I. It'll be OK. It will, won't it? Hope so, cos I really want to show Evan and Tanya that I can be a top member of the trio. I want to show them that I have been practising my legs off when I get some time off from trying to keep the Quinn family boat afloat.

Seventeen

Cos Tanya Breen's front door is thicker than an oak tree, when I do my knock-knock I almost break my knuckles. Their house number has been specially screwed to the wall and juts out a bit. And get this, a light glows behind each number making it seem it's in 3D. How cool is that? The number 70 beaming for the postman, takeaway delivery guy and … for sheer show. Still, it's way better that our wonky painted 46.

The door unbolts and opens slowly.

'Aw, Anna.' Mrs Breen grins when she sees me. I don't think I've ever seen teeth as white as hers. 'So lovely to see you again.'

'Hi, Mrs Breen.' Her hair is sitting on her shoulders instead of being tied back on her head. I'm pretty sure it's darker as well. She tucks part of it behind her ear. Anto does the very same with his hair. Toni and Guy definitely *know their onions*, as Dad would say. I want to tell her how much I love her big, gold loopy earrings, but I'm too shy. I'm probably still a bit young to be talking to grown women about their jewellery anyway. I get a waft of her perfume. It tingles my nostrils.

'Come in, come in,' she says, opening the door further. 'Tanya and Evan are down in the basement. She's so excited that you could come over.'

'In the basement ... OK,' I say, thinking that only Americans had basements.

'We're just had a refurb on it.'

'Right,' I say, not exactly knowing what she's talking about.

'We've gone for a dance studio vibe on it, but it's also our home gym too.'

'Sounds good, Mrs Breen.' I gaze around the huge square hallway; my eyes take me up the bendy staircase to this bling-tastic chandelier hanging from the top of the house to just above our heads. Obviously I don't carry a tape measure around with me, but it's a much bigger house than the one in *Home Alone*.

'Stunning, isn't it?' Mrs Breen says. 'We got this imported from Italy.'

'Italy?'

'Turin, to be precise.'

We're both gazing above at the bling from Turin. I don't know what to say.

'She's my pride and joy.'

I want to say something nice. I want to tell her how much I love it, but I've never spoken about a chandelier in my life before; I don't have the words. I stupidly nod my head instead.

Actually I want to tell her how much I love her trainers, but there's no way I'm going there. When she sees me looking at them – and I swear it was only a two-second glance – she pivots on one foot like Cinderella after Prince Charming holds her by the heel.

'I know, these are my real pride and joy,' she says.

'Are those—'

'Balenciagas, yes. They're my new babies.'

Actually I thought they were Puma RS-X3 Wildcats, so I do my best unconfused look when she tells me that they're Balen-somethings. I notice that she's not wearing any socks again. Her ankle bone is perfectly round.

'Wish my mum and dad would get me a pair of those.' I instantly regret saying this.

'Well, I'm sure if you do all your chores and homework they just might.'

I was going to show her my checkerboard Vans, but I try

and hide them behind my legs as if I'm half an idiot. I feel like a hundred shades of awkward cos I don't know what else I can say about her house, her trainers or her chandelier. Also, I don't know where Turin is on the map. Bet Anto would get it in a heartbeat.

'Is the basement this way?' I point to the bendy staircase that's going to another level below.

'Yes, just straight down, and through the door at the bottom of the stairs. You'll hear the others.'

I can't wait to show them the work I've been doing on our trio dance.

'Bye then, Mrs Breen.' I make to go below.

'Was it your dad who dropped you off?' she asks when my foot is hovering over the first step down.

'Yeah,'

'Oh, he should've popped in, I'd have made him a coffee.'

'My brother was in the car so he had to get home.'

Mrs Breen takes a tiny step towards me and puts one hand on her chest. It's the very same hand-to-chest movement every time Gran says *Guess who died?* to Mum and Dad. Her face droops like Gran's too.

'Oh, I'm really sorry about that,' she says.

About what? Now I am fully confused. Is she sorry that Anto is my brother or sorry that she didn't get to make

197

Dad a coffee? I might be imagining it, but I'm pretty sure she wants to give me a hug. I don't know what to say.

'It's only cos he gets a bit car sick, that's all,' I lie.

She nods her head.

'Oh, I see.'

'Anto, not Dad,' I say, which makes her put her other hand across her chest and snigger.

Right, so I'm wrong, she doesn't want to give me a hug.

'Well, he might pop in for a quick cuppa when he comes to pick you up.' Her voice jumps a tone.

'I can ask him, but my mum and brother might be in the car.'

'Straight down and through the first door,' she says again, then spins on her Balenci-somethings and is gone before I can say thanks or smile or wave.

The staircase twists like a helter-skelter. Before I reach the bottom I hear music blasting out of the door. 'Last Nite' by a band called The Strokes that Kim plays for us.

There's no use in knocking so I open the door slowly and peek my head around. Tanya is in the middle of a full-blown routine, in her white MadCrew vest, purple leggings and new 'dad present' trainers; she makes it look dead easy, she's so talented. I notice she's wearing a bit of make-up. My dad would flip if I wore as much as a smidgeon on my face, so would Mum. Although she does enjoy a tea bag on the eyes

198

from time to time. You can see Tanya's red bra straps flopping off her shoulders. I prefer T-shirts myself. Evan is leaning on the back wall watching her. Arms folded, one leg against the wall. He's pouting in deep concentration.

Tanya sees me and immediately stops dancing. She nods to Evan, who turns the music off.

'Anna!' she says with a huge smile as though I've been lost at sea for fourteen years. 'You're here.'

'Hiya.'

'Where have you been, girl? We've been waiting ages,' Evan says, tapping his wrist. I think he's got a fake iWatch. 'I've got this new thing I want to try.'

'Am I late?' I can hear the nervous shake in my voice.

'No, not really,' he says, 'but yes, very.'

The basement is a proper dance studio/gym/yoga retreat/hangout/utter cool place. Thankfully only one wall has mirrors, I couldn't be doing with a 360-angle of myself. I take my hoodie off cos it's as close as you'll get to Majorca weather down here. I cover my vest top with my T-shirt.

'I was just telling Evan that I thought you did well on Monday,' Tanya says, giving me some seriously strange eye-movement codes. I haven't a clue what's she's on about, we've not spoken about what went on at my house. It's all so confusing: has the air been cleared or not? Is everything sweet between us? Can we be BFFs in the future? Who

knows. 'And that you've been practising like a crazy woman.'
More weird eye stuff. She better be careful in case her eyes
pop out of her head. I don't want to embarrass her by saying
I haven't been practising like a crazy woman and that's when
I get it. It's Evan Flynn we're talking about; Tanya has a
need to constantly impress him. I think some sweat is
beginning to streak through the make-up on her forehead.
I say nothing that will defeat her.

'Oh, right. Yeah, I've done loads of practice, Evan,' I say.

Evan walks towards me; well, kind of dances towards me.

'Just as well, missy. This trio isn't going to work if one of
its wheels are buckled, know what I mean?'

NO.

'Yes,' I say.

He then looks at us for what seems a month. He's
wearing his serious face, his sussing-us-out face. I'm pretty
sure it's cos we're in a proper dance studio. I'd say he's just
overcome with the power.

'Are we all ready to do some work?' he says.

'Yes,' Tanya goes.

'Yes,' I say.

I'm thinking, should we have said *sir* after our yeses?

'Right, let's do this,' Evan says, and stands in the middle
of the studio floor, facing the mirror. 'Let's put a tiara on
our trio then.'

He gestures for us to join him. I try not to giggle. Me and Tanya look at each other and shrug, which makes me feel much better; I think we're connecting again. Time to get the tiara out I guess.

Over two hours it took. There were tons of sideways glances, shaking heads, slapping hands against hips and about a million tuts, but I managed to get through the routine from start to finish without stopping. THREE TIMES. Even though the backs of my knees are aching, my thighs are throbbing, my neck is rattling, my toes are about to fall off and my ribs might need to be jigsawed back together again, I'm chuffed to bits with myself. We are a proper trio.

Anyone who tells you that dance isn't a sport, just look at me; my T-shirt is completely stuck to my body and is sucking itself into my stomach. This should be in the Olympics. I mean, if daft stuff like trampolining and horse skipping are, then why not dance? I put my hoodie on. We are all exhausted. All the spikes in Evan's hair have collapsed, although he does try his best to reshape them in the mirror. His hair is having a *No dice* moment, which seems to be getting on his wick. I don't want to highlight the state of Tanya's make-up. All I'm saying is that I won't be recommending that she puts on so much when we're in

Italy. It might put a dent in the judges' decision making. But real pals can tell each other anything, can't they? I'll have a ponder.

'More practice sessions and we'll be ready,' Evan says. 'We've got time to get this perfected.'

'And some when we get to Italy,' I say.

'Well, naturally, Anna. Naturally,' he says, turning to Tanya and circling his hand around her streaky face. 'I wouldn't wear any of that when you're dancing. Makes your face look like a cheap leather bag.'

'Cheap? This was from Harvey Nicks.'

'I don't care if it was from your granny's knicks.'

'It cost my mum a fortune.'

'Well, I'd ask her to get her money back, cos that –' he circles her face again – 'is not a good look on you.'

There's one thing giving advice, there's another being rude and cruel. *Be kind today, Anna,* Mum says almost every time I leave for school. I want to step in and say something to him, but I'm fed up with confrontation and angry voices. If there's going to be a future for us being friends then we have to be better than this.

'It's really hot in here. That's probably why,' I say, nodding at her face. They both give me a hard stare, each for different reasons. Think I might be making it much worse. I'll just shut up.

'It'll be roasting in Italy, Anna. She can't be looking like a melted candle when she's competing.'

Tanya looks down and defeated. A wee wounded sheep. She should stand up for herself, but she always acts super-weird when he's around. I'm thinking of calling a truce on bleating out rude and cruel things.

'Let's get some water.' Tanya walks towards the door. I look at Evan and shake my head a tiny bit. He opens his mouth and mimes, '*What?*' As if he doesn't know. *It's not brain science, Evan.* We follow her up the stairs to the main section. That's right, her house has sections.

There's a black marble island in her kitchen with glistening bits in it, looks like the darkest starry sky ever. I keep running my hand over them as if they're actual stars, or diamonds. Tanya gets us water from a special compartment in her fridge. And get this, there's a button that spits out as much ice as you want. Wait until I tell Anto. If we had one of these on our fridge there'd be an ice-bucket challenge every day of the week. Dad would need to put a lock on it.

We sit around the island on these high stools guzzling our water. It instantly cools my whole body. Evan does a mammoth belch. Disgusting. He's giving me some seriously strange looks.

'I'll say one thing about you, Anna,' he says. 'You're a fast learner. Isn't she, Tanya?'

'Rapid.'

I use my eyes to say thanks, but don't say anything.

'I can see how you've improved,' he says.

You'd think he was Nureyev the way he carries on. Gran and Papa sent me a postcard of the famous ballet dancer Rudolf Nureyev when they went to Moscow. *Stick in, Anna, and someday you'll be as good as Nureyev*, they wrote on it. Google told me, at one time he was the best in the whole world. I've still got the postcard pinned on my wall.

'Thanks,' I say.

There is a gigantic clock on the kitchen wall. Bigger than the Starbucks sign. Dad'll be here soon.

'So, Anna,' Evan says, leaning back and folding his arms. 'Tanya wants to apologise for thinking your brother is special.'

The look Tanya gives Evan is entirely between them. I don't want to get involved. But for a second her face is the same as someone after they've being punched in the guts. Tanya glances at me with these spongy eyes.

'You're right,' I say. 'He is special, but not in the way you think.'

Tanya half grins.

'Why doesn't he go to our school?' Evan asks.

'You can't ask that, Evan,' Tanya says, but I can tell she's secretly dying for me to spill the beans.

'It's OK,' I say. 'I don't mind talking about Anto.' They both sit up on their stools. 'I never mind.'

'Is it strange having a really good-looking brother?' Tanya says, widening her eyes and nodding her head before suddenly realising that she's just said something utterly daft. Her shoulders sink a little. Evan's head shakes like one of those dashboard dolls, as if he can't believe she would've said something so dippy.

'What? It's just a fact,' Tanya says.

'Tell us more about him, Anna,' Evan asks.

'Like what?' I say.

'Well, what does Anto do? Does he like dance? Does he have a girlfriend, or boyfriend?' Evan puts his hands up into a submission pose. 'What? It's the 2020s.'

He talks the way they do on *Hollyoaks*, which Mum doesn't allow me to put on. *If I see you watching that rubbish again, I'm taking that remote off you, Anna.*

'He doesn't have a girlfriend or anything else.' I frown.

'That's interesting,' he says. 'Really interesting.'

'Is it?' I say.

'Very,' he says.

Since I don't know anyone with a boyfriend or girlfriend I'm not sure why it would be *that* interesting. It's at the bottom rung of my ladder when it comes to all the interesting things I can think of.

'What school does he go to?' Tanya asks.

'I think I'd like to meet him again,' Evan interrupts before I can answer.

'He's coming to Italy, so you'll get a chance then.'

'Can't wait,' he says.

Tanya puts her hand up as if we're at school. I nod to her. Who knows, maybe I'll become a teacher when I'm older.

'Can I ask a question, Anna?'

'Sure.'

'And I'm not being cheeky, honest I'm not,' she says.

I sit up, waiting for the cheek to flow.

'No, it's fine, you can ask me anything,' I tell her.

Her tongue rests on her top lip, she stares without blinking. I get it, this is Tanya's DEEP thinking face.

'I want to ask this in the right way,' she starts, ''cos I know the last time, I stuck my big foot in my big mouth, and you know I didn't mean to do that, don't you?'

'I do, yes.'

'I didn't mean to be cheeky ... and I'm ... It's just—'

'It's OK,' I tell her.

'I guess I just want to know what's wrong with him, Anna?' she says. 'Er ... I mean ... why can't he talk and stuff?'

No, nothing cheeky about that question, Tanya. Nothing

cheeky at all. Duh! I take another drink of the icy water. It could be the best house water I've ever tasted. I'm not going to tell her that though. She's waiting on my answer. They both are. We all shuffle on the stools. Stools just don't cut it when it comes to comfort. Their eyes are burning holes in me. The massive clock says ten to five. I look her straight in the eye, concentrating hard on not blinking.

'Anto's autistic, Tanya,' I say.

'Oh,' she says, racking her brain. Evan's eyes start to juggle.

'His type of autism means that he doesn't speak.'

'What,' she says, looking mega-confused. 'He can't ever talk?'

'He makes sounds and stuff, but he doesn't talk like you and I do.'

'Autism,' Evan says, looking worried. 'Is that like an illness?'

'Honest to God, Evan,' Tanya snaps at him.

I laugh at Tanya being all sensitive and caring. Also, it's not Evan's fault he doesn't know.

'No, he doesn't have an illness,' I say. 'He's well able to understand everything people are saying, in fact, he's brainier than most people I know, Evan.' I smile at him a bit. 'Apart from not speaking, and showing some behaviours that *you* would probably think are odd, he's perfectly fine.'

'Like the coat hanger thing?' Tanya says.

'Yeah, like that.'

My face is getting redder. It's the first time I've really spoken about my brother and his coat hanger. Feels strange, as if I'm betraying him a wee bit.

'His mind is well able for anything,' I say, copying the phrase that Mum and Dad, the doctor, his teachers and Gran and Papa say about him. They can't all be wrong. That's cos they're not. Evan and Tanya look puzzled. *Look at Sudoku face*, Dad says when Mum has the very same expression. 'Imagine that all the conversation you're having with someone can only be heard by yourself,' I try and explain to them. Nothing. Blank faces. They're still in Sudokuland. 'Like, no matter what is said, you're the only one who can hear that conversation.' They sip their water, thinking the hardest they've ever thought. 'All I'm saying is that Anto has a mind. A real mind. Just like yours and mine.'

'Right,' Evan says.

'OK,' Tanya says.

'And sometimes he does things that he doesn't mean cos he's frustrated. Frustrated that no one can hear his conversation,' I say.

'Like what?' Evan asks, dead eager to get the full low-down.

'He'll throw a tantrum or maybe he'll hit himself or make some loud noises cos he can't control what his body does sometimes.'

'Wow, that's …' Evan stutters. 'That's … like … amazing or something.'

'I know,' Tanya adds.

'Other times when he's so frustrated he just goes for a lie-down.'

'So that's why he doesn't go to our school then?' Evan asks.

'He can't,' I say.

'How no?' Tanya presses further.

'Yeah, how no?' Evan asks.

What's wrong with these people? Why aren't they getting it?

'Listen,' I say, sounding like a proper teacher now. 'Imagine sitting in class and your body and voice are doing all these unusual things that you can't control, and everyone is either laughing or screaming at you to stop making noise and being so aggressive. You want to respond, you need to respond, you need to explain, but you can't do any of that cos you can't actually talk. You know what I mean?'

'Yeah.'

'Yeah.'

They don't!

'Well, that's Anto's world. Almost all the time.' I finish my water. Close to five o'clock now. 'He's a bit like the opposite to everyone else. He can't sit still and be quiet cos he feels so much better and calmer when his body is moving.'

'That's so rough,' Tanya says.

'God, I know. I'd hate that,' Evan goes.

'It is rough for him,' I say. 'See, for Anto, all the lights make a humming sound and all these sounds echo and boom around his body. Everything moves so fast that he struggles to keep up with it. It's like he's on a constant rollercoaster.'

'Poor guy, Anna,' Tanya says. 'I feel heartbroken for him now.'

'Don't be,' I say. 'Anto gets to experience the world in a very unique way. I consider him to be a silent speaker.' I picture him showing me his Lego bricks; chatting with his gestures, his eyes and expressions. That's our normal. 'You know, just because he doesn't use words doesn't mean he's got nothing to say.'

'Wow. Yeah. Right, Tanya,' Evan says. 'Totes agree, Anna.'

'I really am sorry how I was when I was at yours,' Tanya says. 'It's cos I didn't know, and it's always a bit scary when you don't know stuff. But I wouldn't be like that now cos of what you just told us.' She's got the same face when you've done something wrong at school and the teacher is all over you. 'Know what I mean?'

'I know what you mean, Tanya.'

'Same here,' Evan adds. 'I definitely want him to come to Italy.'

I run my hand over the twinkling stars and think of Italy; can't wait for how incredible it will be. I do feel better for properly talking about Anto to them. He's not some secret to be locked away in a box. Maybe in Italy Tanya and Evan will get to see his brilliance the way I see it. It'll be like they're going to experience two foreign countries where they haven't a clue what people are saying or thinking. In Italy and Antoland they'll learn an entirely new way of communicating. What spice to sprinkle upon them.

'You'll like him, he's nice,' I say.

Mrs Breen comes bouncing into the kitchen. Teeth galore. Eyes sparkling. It's almost five on the dot. She sits across from me at the island, plonks her new gold iPhone down, stretches out her hands. Her perfume is stronger than ever. She's got fresh make-up on and is now wearing a long skirt. Not that she needed to, but she's had a proper freshen-up. I don't get why people need to change forty-two times a day. She's kept the Balenga-thingies on though.

'Hi, Mrs Breen,' I say.

'Oh, call me Tash,' she says, flapping her hand at me. 'Mrs Breen makes me feel so old.'

''Sssake,' Tanya mutters.

'So, did you guys have a nice time?'

'Mum!' Tanya says, with a look that could bend spoons.

'You all seem as if you've put in a solid workout,' Mrs Breen says. 'That's what I like to see.'

'Honestly,' Tanya sighs. 'Gonna not?'

I'm thinking, *Gonna not what?*

Mrs Breen starts spinning her phone on the marble worktop, then tapping it with one of her nails. No one speaks. The clock clicks past five. I feel as though I'm intruding on something. Think Evan does too. It's like they want to continue an argument but can't until we've gone. When a car horn beeps from outside everyone kind of breathes their relief out. Our Twingo's beep is weak and timid, always reminds me of bleating goats, I'd know it anywhere. Mrs Breen jumps off as if it's the Disneyland bus come to whisk her away to a new world. She shoots for the door. I'm about to slide off my stool when her phone vibrates. Two emojis appear at the top of the screen: a yellow face blowing a love-heart kiss and a pair of juicy red lips. These are followed by the words *Thinking of U xxx. Wish these were real.* It's sent by someone called T2. I stare down at the phone. Who even has lips that red? And why can't people just say actual words to each other instead of sending daft images? It's like, *I can't think of anything interesting to say so here's a wee emoji instead.*

When I look up, Tanya is giving me this weird glare as if she's trying to read my mind, or share the story of what's happening in *her* mind. Maybe if we were BBFs I'd know what was going on, but I just find her expression top-heavy confusing. Does she think I want to nick the phone?

I hear the door being unbolted.

When Mrs Breen returns to the kitchen, she's a bit less smiley.

'Your mum's outside waiting for you, Anna.' She whips her phone from the counter then wanders into another room off the kitchen. We all watch her go. We all hear the slam of a door. Tanya groans. I jump down from the stool and take my glass to the sink. I'm polite that way in other people's houses.

'Would be good if you could divorce your parents,' Tanya says with a scowl. I'm not sure if this is directed at me or the ceiling.

'I think you can, you know,' Evan adds.

'How long have your mum and dad been married for?' Tanya asks me.

I look at Evan for … I don't know, support?

'Erm …' I put on my thinking face. 'It's close to fourteen years,' I say.

'So, thirteen then?' Tanya adds.

'About that,' I say, but in truth I don't know the exact timescale. I should do, however. I make a mental note to ask Mum later. Maybe the happy memory of gold rings and *I do*s will bring some sunshine back to the house.

The Twingo's horn squeaks again. I turn to Evan and Tanya. 'I'd better go. That was a good practice. I'm excited.'

'We'll do it again next week.' Tanya looks at Evan, who nods like he's in a trance.

'Definitely, next week it is.' And, as if by magic, he snaps out of it and points to both of us. 'You girls still have a mountain to climb. So, no slacking.'

'We could do some on our own, Anna,' Tanya says.

'Good idea,' Evan says. 'Taking responsibility. I like that.'

We both kind of tut at him.

'Yes, that would be good,' I tell her.

'I'll phone later and we can arrange something,' she says.

'Perfect.'

214

Mrs Breen returns to the kitchen twirling her phone in her hand. There's something about her that's less friendly.

'Come, Anna,' Mrs Breen says. 'I'll see you to the door.'

I wave my bye-byes to Tanya and Evan.

'Your mum's been beeping like mad out there.'

'I thought Dad was picking me up.'

'Well, that's for them to discuss.'

'Strange, I thought she had to work.' This is to myself.

'I'm sure Asda's fashion house won't collapse,' Mrs Breen says.

I can't be positive if this is a joke or not. I don't reply cos she's not looking at me, she's reading her iPhone. T2's text probably. Her face explodes with a silent delight. It's a good feeling knowing that I know what she doesn't.

The Twingo beeps again.

'Thanks, Mrs Breen,' I say as I'm about to leave.

Any time, Anna love.' She grins and rubs my shoulder. 'Tell your dad I said hello.'

'Will do.'

I've hardly got two feet outside when the door thuds behind me. That'll be it closed then. No waiting for me to walk down the path, no friendly banter between mums.

I'm hardly in the door when the phone rings. I pick up.

'Hi, it's Tanya.'

For some reason I become all nervous. Not sure why. 'Oh, hiya.'

Two things: one, she's desperate keen to get this trio into tip-top condition. Two, she really wants us to be better pals. I'm with her on the first but cagey on the second.

'Can we practise at yours tomorrow?' She's speaking as if she's just run up a steep hill strapped to a huge boulder. 'Around eleven?'

'Hold on,' I say, and put my hand over the mouth bit. 'Mum!' I shout into the living room. 'Can Tanya come here to practise tomorrow?' There's a pause you could drive a bus through.

'You're going to Gran and Papa's for dinner, remember,' she shouts.

'It'll be around eleven, I'll have loads of time for Gran and Papa's,' I shout.

'Fine,' Mum shouts.

'Yeah, that's fine, Tanya,' I say. 'Eleven is good.'

'OK, I'll get my mum to drop me off.'

I don't get the chance to say *See you the morra* or anything like that cos Tanya clicked off.

I replace the receiver and stand in our hallway thinking how senseless coming to mine is. I mean, she's got a quality dance studio at her place, and yet she's eager to practise in my bedroom, with a carpet on the floor and books everywhere? I can't help thinking that all this *Can we practise at yours tomorrow?* might be more about Anto, especially after our chat. I really hope she doesn't want to come round for an ogle session. He's not some zooed-up animal that tourists come to see. If that's what she's all about then I think it might be curtains for any potential best-pals act between us. And maybe even the trio.

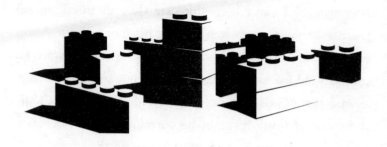

Eighteen

When I hear Tanya's mum's tank outside my hands start to sweat. I'm not that bad a dancer so there's really no need to get so nervous; it's not as if Tanya's pure amazing, by the way. My leg speed could be doing with some serious practice though. If I'm being brutally honest – without being brutal – I think Tanya was off her game a bit yesterday. Could have been her awkwardness about her being rude and cheeky, who knows. I wait at the door, but don't open it to welcome her. I'm not that excited.

Anto runs halfway down the stairs to get a nosy in.

'It's not for you, Anto,' I say. He's shaking his coat hanger so fast that there seems to be around fifteen of them in his hand. 'I'm not lying so you can go back up to your room.' I motion to run at him as you would a stray cat. But unlike a stray cat he doesn't shift. Why do brothers even exist?

'I'm telling Mum,' I warn him. He fans faster. Hits it off the NASA sign on his sweatshirt.

'Mum!' I shout. 'Anto's being a pain in the you-know-what.'

Mum's folding dish towels when she comes to the hall.

'What's going on?' she says.

'It's him,' I tell her. 'He's annoying me.'

'What's he doing?'

'Just being here. Tanya's about to come in and he's just standing there like some serial weirdo.'

The door goes.

'Mum, tell him,' I plead.

'Anthony, why don't you help me with the washing?'

Anto growls at her.

'Fine, well, go back to your room then,' she says. 'Anna's got a guest.'

Anto contorts his face. He stops rattling his coat hanger and lifts it up towards us, aims it high. I think he's raging that he's not invited to Gran and Papa's for dinner tonight. *It's hard enough looking after one at our age*, Gran says. We have to take it in turns.

The door goes again.

'Not for you,' I whisper-shout to him. He squeals, then scarpers. I've clearly annoyed him. He'll get over it.

'Hi, Tanya,' I say.

Mrs Breen speeds away without beeping or waving. When Tanya enters, Mum gives her a grin that appears forced. It's the one teachers give you when you pass them in the corridors.

'Hiya, hen,' Mum says.

'Hiya, Mrs Quinn,' Tanya says, looking at the floor. You'd think she was in the headmistress's office or something.

'Want to come up?' I say.

'OK.'

'If you girls need anything ...'

'We don't, Mum.'

'But—'

'Just make sure Anto doesn't interrupt us,' I say to her. Tanya doesn't know where to look, but I see her giving Mum a sweet(ish) smile, whose eyes seem tired ... and red. Now I feel bad for telling Mum to keep Anto away.

'OK,' Mum says, and folds the dish towel for about the thirtieth time. 'You girls enjoy yourself.'

My room has different lighting to the hallway; clearer and purer. It means that I can see Tanya's face better, and I'll tell you what, she's got the onion eyes. Two bulging bloodshot beauties. If there's one thing I know about, it's the post-cry puff-eye. This time she doesn't scan my room or make any sarky comments towards Albert.

She sits on my bed and rests her hands on her thighs.

Still and silent. By the looks of it I don't think she's in any mood to dance. She's also wearing jeans and a T-shirt with BLING ON NEXT YEAR written on it.

'You OK, Tanya?' I want to put my hand on her shoulder or maybe even sit next to her, but I stand above her instead. She looks up at me. Yes, definitely been crying. 'Did you have an argument with your mum?' I ask. She nods and covers her face. Time to act like a friend. I sit and put my arm around her. 'Tanya, what is it? You can tell me.' I'm very good with secrets (look at Mum and Dad) and with people's difficulties (ask Anto). I give her shoulders a wee rub. Sometimes that does the trick. In one of her books Judy Blume calls it *the human touch*.

Tanya removes her hands from her face and looks at me. I think the human touch worked wonders.

'Anna,' she slurs. 'Did you know?'

'Know what?' I say, removing my arm from her, creating space between us.

'Did you?' Tanya's voice is harsher. 'Or didn't you?' She sniffs and wipes her eyes. I turn my body towards her.

'I'm really not sure what you're talking about, Tanya. I don't know anything about anything,' I try to explain, but I'm really unsure what I'm trying to explain. My body is telling me to stand up and put a hand on my hip the way Mum does when she's waiting for an explanation. *Well?*

Well? I'm waiting. I do what my body tells me, and I'm above her again, hand on hip this time. 'You need to tell me what this is about.'

She reaches into her jeans pocket, pulls out her phone and starts thumb-scrolling like mad.

'I saw you looking at Mum's phone yesterday,' she says. I start blinking dead fast. 'In the kitchen.'

'I didn't ... I mean, I ... I only saw ... I didn't pick it up,' I say.

'But you saw the messages?'

My tongue strokes the top of my mouth. I swallow.

'I saw one message, I think, but I wasn't being nosy or anything like that, it pinged when I was sitting there. It was just a glance.' I hear myself pleading innocence to a crime I haven't committed. 'I didn't pick it up. I didn't touch the phone. You were there. You saw.'

'And what did you see?' she asks.

'Just a message and an emoji.'

'Kisses?'

'Red lips and a yellow-face kiss, that's all,' I tell her. 'Promise.'

'Did you see who sent it?'

Did I see who sent it? I don't exactly have a photographic memory. This is my house, my room, my bed, my rules, so why do I feel that I'm being accused of something? I think hard, not too hard cos I do actually remember.

'Someone called T2,' I say.

'And know who my mum is?' Tanya says.

I put my confused face on. 'Erm, Tash?'

'She's T1.'

'Makes sense,' I say.

'And when you and Evan left yesterday, I found out who T2 was though.'

'How?'

'I snooped in her phone.'

'Right.'

Tanya stands up and hands me her phone, which I take with my sweaty hand.

'Scroll left,' she says. 'There's three of them.' I stare at her before setting my eyes on the phone. It's one of those I-know-that-she-knows-that-I-know moments. I shut my eyes for about three seconds. Then open.

The first picture makes my body jerk back.

Scroll left.

The second makes my stomach swirl with sick.

Scroll left.

The third makes me want to curl up and die.

'That's him, isn't it?' Tanya says. 'That's your dad?'

'Yes, that's him,' I mutter, and manage to flop down on

my bed again. 'But I don't understand … why … why is he on your phone?'

'I took a picture of Mum's phone.'

'But I still—'

'Anna, your dad is T2. He's the one sending kisses and photos and heart emojis.'

'My dad?'

'Your dad. T2.'

I have no words. I stare at the floor and a thousand thoughts hit me. Anto being the main one.

'Are my dad and your mum …' I say to Tanya, 'you know … having an affair?'

'My mum's not married so she's not affairing with anyone, but your dad is.'

Is that how it works? Dad's the bad one? Well, he is, isn't he? Is there zero badness in Mrs Breen? Does her being a Mrs not count for anything? I'm far too young to understand how this works; I can't exactly ask Mum.

'Does your dad love my mum, Anna?'

NO! HE LOVES MUM. MY MUM. OUR ONE.

'I don't know. Maybe. I don't know.'

'Well, my mum can't love your dad,' Tanya says, as if it was all my fault.

'I don't want her to love him,' I say.

There's a thump. A loud one. My mind is in a different

zone, so I'm uncertain if it comes from a kick to my door or a boot to the wall. It's Anto's sound, that I do know. The noise makes Tanya jolt. Anto knowing about T1 and T2 would be a disaster movie.

'Don't take this the wrong way, Anna,' Tanya says, 'but I don't want a sister, and I definitely don't want a brother. Me and Mum are fine on our own.' There's no nastiness in her voice. If anything, I think fear is hiding inside her.

'Me neither, Tanya.' I jab my toe deep into the carpet, which kind of hurts. I bite the skin around my thumb and think: *Would having a sister who's a similar age be such a bad thing?* It would give me someone to talk to when I couldn't sleep, someone to share the load. 'Maybe you've made a mistake. Maybe it's just things adults send to each other. Maybe your mum and my dad are just friends. Maybe we're putting two and two together. Maybe … maybe it's all … it's all—'

'Anna,' Tanya spits, and puts up her hand. 'Mum calls him *babe* and he calls her *honey* and they send millions of kisses to each other and say things like *wish you were here* and *can't wait to see you again*. So there's no maybes about it.'

I let her words sink in. I keep seeing the three pictures of Dad on Tanya's phone; his big smiley face holding up a Greggs pie. With his daft baker's hat on. Hardly Mr Romance.

225

'Do you think your mum knows?' she asks.

Mum!

I can't hold it in any longer. The tears gush out of me. My jaw loosens and my face twists as I work hard to muffle the sound of crying. I don't think Tanya has read Judy Blume so she wouldn't be familiar with the *human touch* soothe thing. My nose runs and tears drop on to my hands. I wish she would've read Judy Blume. I need her right now; more than I need a dance partner.

I look up and Tanya's got tears streaming as well. I hold out my arms. I want her to fall into them; need her to fall into them. I stretch out further. She lands on me and we hug each other tight. Two of us tearing and terrified.

For a while we sit in silence with nothing but our own thoughts to chat with. Tanya breathes through her nose; it's heavy and noisy, but I don't say anything. I wonder if this is the reason why Mum has been like a simmering volcano with Dad. She must have known. She must have. If so, then I feel like a quality eejit for pressing her to come to Italy. *Yeah, Mum, it'll be great … me, you, Anto, Dad … and Mrs bloomin' Breen.* Quality eejit. In the space of two minutes I play out about fifty different scenarios, all of which make my stomach tumble and palms sweat. I notice that Tanya keeps rubbing her hands dry too.

'It'll be OK, Anna,' she sniffs.

'I hope so.'

'It will, you'll see.'

'I guess that's the practice off then?' I say.

She laughs. I laugh. We laugh.

'I can't be bothered,' she says. 'I'm going to just lie here until Mum picks me up, if that's OK?'

'That's fine,' I say. 'I'll do the same.'

'Why don't you read one of your stupid books to me.'

I know the very one that'll do the trick.

When Tanya leaves – or rather, when T1 comes to pick her up – I don't cry again. I quite easily could though. In a broken heartbeat I could. Cry for Mum. Cry for Christmas. Cry for all the never agains and no mores.

I'm face down in my fluffed-up pillow listening carefully to my breathing, which is heavy and angry. I think I can hear my brain swirling too; trying to bat away all the questions and thoughts that hurtle towards me. They come from every direction. Nothing takes priority, everything's fired from a sad-sludge gun:

When will I get to show my dance?

I'll never eat another pizza for as long as I live.

What will I say to Anto?

That's Italy well and truly kiboshed then.

I was so looking forward to visiting everything on my

green list too. Exotic ice cream, sandwiches on park benches and cobbled streets, sunburn on the nose. Normal family stuff. Just the four of us, the gang. The fam. I was even thinking that if Italy would've been a roaring success we could've gone on a beach holiday to Spain or Bulgaria. Everything's a total failure now.

I won't be able to look at Tanya's mum again, or even say her name.

Will I have to leave MadCrew?

Will Dad start buying me expensive things?

Poor Mum.

That's it, it's all done.

Trainers maybe, or a smartphone.

I'll have to decorate two Christmas trees now.

Evan will have kittens.

Did I see those pictures or was it trickery?

Do I need glasses?

There's no going back.

She's stylish and … well, he's not.

Will I have to go to a different school?

People do jump to conclusions.

Honestly, when was the last time I had an eye test?

Seriously, what will Christmas be like?

Will Mum start buying me special weekend gifts?

T1 loves T2.

Hollister?

If we have a choice of who to live with, I know who I'm picking.

Will Gran and Papa side with Dad cos he's their blue-eyed boy?

Can I still keep my ANNA hoodie?

I'll never leave Anto.

Never. Never. Never.

T2 loves T1.

I hate Dad.

Did Albert Einstein have a wife?

Does Dad have a brain?

Mum is five thousand times better looking than her.

Ten million.

ADOTW.

Any. Day. Of. The. Week.

I'll probably need to have my own coat hanger for this.

Am I right to think that Mum knows or suspects something?

Will we ever be on an airplane as a family?

That's me done with sausage rolls too.

I'll never get to win another trio.

No joke, Mum could be Italian or Spanish.

Albert Einstein would never have done this to his wife.

Should I just shut up and say nothing?

She wears those Balachinga things.

My Mum's a goddess.

Love is a lie.

Love lives on TV.

Love is just me and Anto.

Love is one great big dirty lie.

All because of her lies.

And his.

Tragic 1.

Terrible 2.

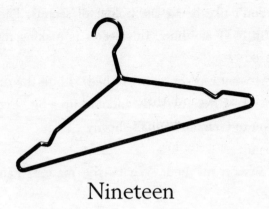

Nineteen

Anto's been making strange *whoop* sounds from his room but stops stone dead when Dad pulls the Twingo up outside the house. If he's laden with sausage rolls and other goodies I don't want them. I wish I was in a deep dream. When the car door slams I kick off my checkerboard Vans and sink under the covers.

Mum and Dad's muffled voices flow upstairs. They're chatting, not arguing. Probably matter-of-fact stuff; about what to have for dinner and what to watch on Netflix later. I've all the info in the world to lob an explosion into that conversation. So much info that it could blow the house down. I could bribe Dad into letting us watch *Squid Game*. I could bribe him into anything.

A few minutes later Mum pounds up the stairs. I feel so bad. So bad that I might projectile vomit all over the bed. I don't like being the holder of secrets. There's no power in it; if anything, this secret is making me weak and scared.

'Anna, what are you doing in bed?' I pull the duvet up to my neck, stiffen my body and curl up a bit. 'I've got to drive you to Gran and Papa's shortly.'

I groan.

She sits on my bed. 'What's the matter? Bad dance practice?'

Oh, please don't ask me that question, Mum. I don't want to talk about it. I want to sleep and let the whole thing disappear. And when it's gone forever I want us all to sit and plan our trip to Italy. My keeping-a-secret face is beyond rubbish.

'Nothing,' I say. 'I'm just not feeling up to going to Gran and Papa's, that's all.'

'But Gran's making lasagne and garlic bread.'

They went on some cooking holiday in Cornwall and, guess what? They learned how to make *authentic* lasagne. To be fair, it's a taste sensation, although the garlic bread is too spongy.

'You love lasagne, Anna.'

'My stomach got sore after practice.' I make an exaggerated groaning sound. *And the prize for Scotland's worst actor goes to …*

'Oh.' She puts the back of her hand on my cheek. 'Cramps?'

'Then my head started sweating and I felt a bit dizzy.'

'Oh, OK.'

'I didn't want to say anything to you or Dad.'

Mum rubs my head and smiles.

'I don't think your dad would understand,' she says. 'Do you need to go to the bathroom or anything?'

'No, I'm fine.'

'Well, get some rest here, and if you're up to it I'll drive you to Gran and Papa's in a wee while.'

'Do I have to go, Mum?' Actually I think it's probably best if I do. It'll give me a few hours of escape from the tension and Dad's phone.

'They're excited to see you, Anna. They haven't seen you since they got back from Estonia. Anyway, Anthony wants to come along for the ride. You know what he's like in the car.' We both flash our eyes upwards at the same time. 'He loves being in it with you.'

'OK, I'll go,' I say. Hopefully they've got me a present other than Cornwall lasagne.

'You'll feel better after you've been.'

I push out my bottom lip and raise my arms up for her to come in for a wee cuddle. It's a big one I'm after actually. She looks puzzled; I don't blame her, I haven't done the cuddle arms with her since I was about four and a half. I hold her with all my strength. She kisses the top of my head. Mum always smells the best. Much better than T1. Any. Day. Of. The. Week. Month. Year. Lifetime.

'It's going to be OK, Mum.'

'I know it is, sweetheart. Promise.'

'You mean that?'

'Of course I do.'

'How can you be so sure?'

'Trust me.'

She kisses me a final time, then goes back downstairs. *Of course I do. Trust me.* I've a feeling we were talking about two different things.

If I wipe it from my memory it might go away.

Will it?

Will it go away?

If I close my eyes, will I forget what I saw?

Will I?

I close them tight and hope for the best.

On the way to Gran and Papa's Anto doesn't do any form of communicating at all. He stares out of the window, twitching his head every now and then. He didn't kick up a fuss about me sitting in the front either. He doesn't even care that I'm playing UK Gold on the radio, cos my seat isn't being kicked. Something's up. Mum taps one finger off the steering wheel when a group called The Specials start singing on the radio.

'Feeling better?' she asks.

'Much,' I say. Lies. To add to all the others.

'Don't eat too much lasagne now.'

I turn down The Specials a bit.

'I can't wait to eat proper lasagne in Italy,' I go. Mum doesn't say anything, she sort of hums a yum. 'It'll be good eating nice food and stuff, won't it?'

Anto starts kneeing the back of my seat.

'Better than eating in any of these places.' Mum gestures to the rows of takeaway shops outside.

'If we like Italy we could maybe go back next year for a proper holiday,' I say. 'Somewhere by the sea.'

He kicks the seat again. Harder.

'Pack it in!' I turn and snap at him. He clenches his fists and grits his teeth.

'Guys, please.' Mum sounds tired.

I don't utter another word until we get to Gran and Papa's.

Mum doesn't get out of the car when Gran opens the door. Probably cos it's Dad's mum and not hers. Anto doesn't even bother getting up.

'I'll pick her up around eight,' Mum shouts from the car.

I'm not convinced Gran has heard. They do wave bye-bye to each other, which is something.

Gran pulls me to her chest, which is like falling on to a bouncy castle. The house smells of medicine, lasagne and garlic. Papa will be at the kitchen table awaiting his dinner, where else?

I'm barely in my seat when a huge plate of lasagne is plonked down in front of me. I nibble at it.

'You not hungry, hen?' Gran says, noticing me playing around with the food.

'Well, you've given her a mountain of it,' Papa says, winking at me. 'She's a wee sparrow of a thing.' He winks again. I smile.

'I'm a bit full, Gran,' I say, patting my belly.

'Well, I don't suppose you'll be wanting some of the chocolate we brought back from Estonia then?' she says.

'Don't be daft, woman,' Papa says to Gran. 'She'll be well able for it after I show her the holiday pictures.'

Papa fetches his laptop and sits beside me. His screen is dotted with files of cities and countries from around the world. He opens one called *Estonia* and starts clicking through the images.

'See that?' He points to one of the pictures. 'You don't get those skies in Scotland.'

It looks just like the one I dreamed about in Italy.

'Nice,' I say.

'And look at those cobbles,' he goes. 'Something else, isn't it?'

'Would you listen to yourself,' Gran pipes up. 'She doesn't want to be looking at pictures of cobbled streets.' She rubs my head. 'Sometimes I worry about him.'

'Aye, maybe,' Papa says. 'Right, wait until you see this.' He clicks off *Estonia* and opens the *Rome* file.

'Don't be showing her any more cobbles or skies, OK?' Gran warns Papa.

'Look, Anna,' Papa says. In the photo Gran is sitting on the edge of a bright blue fountain. She's wearing a summer dress and a big floppy hat. You can see her knees. 'Look how beautiful that woman is.'

'Oh, would you put a sock in it!' Gran tells him.

'It's nice, Gran,' I say. 'You look nice.'

'That's the world-famous Trevi Fountain,' Papa tells me. 'You need to go there when you're in Rome. It's a magical place.'

'Aye, it was nice,' Gran says. She flicks her eyebrow at Papa. Dead delicate, but I spied it.

The next photo is the two of them in front of the Trevi Fountain, arm in arm. For a long time they look at the picture. You'd think they were transporting themselves back to that exact time, to one of the best days in their lives. Gran touches her chest. Papa takes a breath and smiles to himself.

'We asked some wee Italian fella to take that for us,' Papa says. 'She thought he was going to run away with our camera.'

'Ach, don't listen to him, hen,' Gran says. 'Your papa thought he was going to run away with me.'

'Aye, he wished,' Papa says, and gives Gran a full-on toothy grin. I'm pretty sure she blushed. See, that's the power of Italy.

Papa shows me tons of Rome snaps along with some major tips on where we should go when we're there. He says if I like that Estonian chocolate, then I'm in for a real treat when I get to Rome. Maybe Mum and Dad can do their own picture at the Trevi Fountain. I can take it. Maybe things aren't as bad as I think. Everything can be mended, can't it.

Thing is, it's a magic fountain, you throw coins into it then make a wish. We could do that as a family. I definitely know what my wish would be.

Twenty

Eight o'clock on the dot and she's beeping like a mad woman. I kiss Gran and Papa and run out to the Twingo. I wave, acting all dead excited. I'll just pretend and hit her with how good the lasagne was and how the garlic bread wasn't as soggy as a soggy Weetabix; I also want to tell her about all the places Papa told me are a must (with a capital MUST) see in Rome.

I skip around the front of the car, and smile through the windscreen. Mum doesn't wave or smile or look remotely happy to see me. She's gripping the steering wheel as if her hands are glued to it. Her eyes are steel. My organs somersault. She's had the chat with Dad, bet it. Bet she's found his phone. Bet she's clocked his T2 nickname. She looks raging. I'd say she's had a visit from the onion-eyes people. So many tears in my world these days.

'I thought you might come in to see Gran and Papa?' I say, when I open the door.

'Just get in, Anna, we need to go.'

Mum's voice sounds exactly like a crackling radio. When I *just get in, Anna*, my fingers go straight for the music.

'Leave that and put your seat belt on,' she says. Yes, definitely a crackling radio.

There's not enough time to click my seat belt into place before the Twingo starts zooming past the houses in Gran and Papa's quiet street. A *This is a Crime Reduction Area: We Are Watching You* street. When I'm secure in my seat belt I glance behind me in case there's a blue light chasing us.

'Slow down, Mum.'

'We can't,' she says, making the car go even faster. I hold on to the sides of the seat. 'We have to get home quickly.'

'What's the rush?'

'Anthony is missing.' She runs her gear-changing hand through her hair. My heart begins racing as soon as the word *missing* comes out of her mouth.

'Missing? What do you mean, missing?' I ask.

'He's missing. We can't find him, Anna. That's what missing usually means?'

I made a mistake; her voice isn't a crackling radio. No. The sound she's making is fear. That's why her eyes are the way they are too.

'What happened?'

'We came home from dropping you off and he went upstairs—'

'And?'

'And that was the last time I saw him.'

'What do you mean?' I say, cos I'm genuinely confused. You don't just go upstairs in your own house and disappear. I know all his tricks, all the areas and spaces he can fit into. 'Did you look in his room?'

'Don't be stupid, Anna, of course I looked in his room.'

'Did Dad?'

'We've looked everywhere.'

I could sulk cos she called me stupid, but I have to forget that. Mum's through the roof with emotion and people through the roof with emotion say and do things they don't really mean. That's why people use the word *sorry* so often. Unless, that is, they've got a screw loose. Mum doesn't have a screw loose. I'm not stupid. So, let's all move on.

'He could be under his bed,' I say.

Anto sometimes squeezes under his bed when he really needs to get some peace and quiet; when he feels all his senses are being attacked. But Mum and Dad already know that. It's usually them he's trying to get peace and quiet from anyway.

'We've looked under the beds, in all the wardrobes and cupboards. Your dad also checked the loft. We've been everywhere in the house,' she says.

I bet they haven't. They don't know what I know. As soon as she told me he's missing I instantly knew why. He knows. He knows it all. All that crashing I heard from his room, that thud sound, was cos he heard me and Tanya talking. Anto always knows everything, he's got bionic ears or something.

'If he's not in the house I just hope he's not in any danger,' she whispers to herself.

That's all she needs to say for my vision to become narrower. The shops and other cars whizz past in a blur. Sound begins to *wha-wha-wha* in my ears. What if Anto might not be in our house? What if Anto might be alone on these streets? What if Anto is genuinely lost? Is it my fault for talking too loud? Or Tanya's for showing me her phone? I mean, she could have kept it to herself and said nothing; there would be no loss and no tears if she had. God sake, Tanya. Anto, running away isn't going to solve anything.

'I shouted up for him to come and eat something,' Mum says. 'He didn't answer.' Her chest heaves up and down.

'Did you find his coat hanger?'

'No, I think that's gone too.'

'When did this happen?'

'About an hour ago.'

AN HOUR AGO?

I picture Anto walking the streets; he'll be in utter terror and have no clue where he's going. He won't be able to ask anyone for directions or tell them he's lost or explain how desperate he is to get back home. Some gang will pick on him cos they think he's weird. They'll take his coat hanger and snap it in front of him. He'll squeal and bang his knuckles off his head; they'll howl with laughter. They'll definitely call him cruel stuff; something that'll hurt his gut. One of them might punch him in the face cos they can't deal with his difference. It'll confuse them and make them angrier.

'Mum, we've got to find him.'

'Your dad's out looking for him now.'

'If he's out there –' I point out of the window – 'he's not safe.'

Mum gives me a look as if to say, *Do you think I'm daft?*

At the traffic-lights stop in town we both scan the pavements and shop entrances. We're like a couple of frantic owls. Mother and daughter detectives.

'I can't remember what he was wearing,' she says.

Her voice is silky soft. It's the voice when you've done something wrong at school and the teacher catches you red-handed and all you can do is stare down at the desk when speaking.

I try to think back to when he was in the car earlier. I'm pretty sure he was wearing the sweatshirt that Gran and Papa got him from the time they went to that Science Museum in Dublin. I got a pencil case and three rubbers. Come on, I don't make that many mistakes.

'I think he might have been wearing his NASA sweatshirt,' I say.

Mum rubs her eyes and sighs.

'I can't think,' she says, still scanning the streets.

Outside I search for someone with a space rocket emblazoned across their chest ready to zoom past their face. Nothing. What twelve-year-old would be allowed to walk these streets alone?

Mum's jaw shudders, I think her eyes are about to glaze over. I'd like to hug her and tell her it'll be OK, that we'll find him in no time, that he'll be sleeping under a big pile of blankets somewhere or wedged between all the paint pots in the shed. I really would like to say, *You'll see, Mum, he'll be laughing at us all by bedtime*. But a huge part of me can't bring myself to hug her. Why? Cos, one, we're in a car and that's beyond dangerous, and two, cos I know exactly why Anto felt the need to bolt, and if I told her the truth she might crash the car. But no doubt he also had to escape the noise they were making and the fear they were hurling. But Mum needs a hug. In fact, she needs much more than that. If Anto could see her now, shaking, nervous and a wee bit weepy, he'd be so miserable. I know he'll hate himself when I tell him; he'll go bananas inside knowing the grief he's caused. If he knows other people are unhappy because of his actions, then it'll send him over the edge. It'll take him days to recover. He might still be recovering when we're in Italy. If we make it.

A car beeps at us from behind and we're off speeding again. Mum sucks in a huge intake of breath as though she's swallowing the massive lump that's been sitting in her throat.

'Maybe he's at Mrs Molloy's house,' I suggest.

'From across the road?'

'Yeah, she likes Anto.'

Mum shoots me a quick glance. It's full of sharp daggers.

'That woman doesn't like anyone,' she spits from the corner of her mouth.

'But she calls him sweet names and puts her hand on her chest,' I say, as if trying to persuade her. 'She could have offered him a cup of Coke of something. You never know.'

'Oh, please, Anna,' she mutters, then I hear her mumble *Nosy bloomin' Nora* under her breath. At least she didn't call me stupid again.

I don't get to play any song on the radio. Doesn't seem right, does it? I mean, it's hardly the first thing families of missing people turn to in times of distress, it is? *Right, someone stick Spin 108 on and we'll have a bop.* We don't speak another word until she pulls up to the house.

Dad rushes out to meet us as we're getting out of the car. His hair is all over the place and one side of his shirt is untucked from his jeans. He's like a wild man. A bad man. A horrible man. An affair man. I try not to show hatred on my face.

'Anything?' he asks Mum.

'Nothing, you?' she returns.

'Not a thing. I've been through the house again. No dice.'

'And what about the garden, the shed, the street? Have you been up and down the street, Tony? Have you?'

'I walked up that way,' Dad points in the direction of the glen. The word *glen* makes it sound majestic, like a place you'd go for family walks, where tourists come to visit. A place teeming with green dreams and glistening lakes. In reality it's a stretch of dying squelching fields with a rancid burn running through it. You only go to the glen if you're part of a drinking gang, got a death wish or you're homeless. Our family aren't any of those things.

'Did you go through the glen?' Mum asks.

'He won't have gone that far,' Dad says.

'And how do you know that, Tony? How do you know that?'

'He'd be too scared, is how I know it.'

'You're too scared, you mean.'

Dad looks at me for support, but he's not getting any. I don't support either of them, especially not him.

'If you want to nip down the glen, Liz, feel free,' he says, raising two hands in its direction. Mum's jaw clenches. Her upper body tenses. I spy some curtains twitching with the noisy voices, which means Anto is definitely not at Mrs Molloy's.

'Well, you could have at least phoned the police,' she says, before brushing past him and into the house.

'Yeah, right,' I say and I follow her inside.

Sitting beside her on the sofa I'm surprisingly calm. I think to myself, what would Nancy Drew do in this situation? She's found tons of missing people. Loads. And the two things she always does is remain cool under pressure and look for clues. Clue number one: he's got his coat hanger with him, which means he's a wee bit safe. Clue number two: he doesn't want to be found, so why would he head for places they're likely to look? Of course he's not lying right there under his bed or up in the loft. Anto is clever. I do have my suspicions of where he could be.

After about a minute Dad slams the front door shut.

'Anna, if your mum wants to phone the police, tell her to go ahead and phone them,' he says while tucking his shirt back into his jeans and fixing his hair. And that, as they say, is the straw that broke this camel's back. I see every shade of red there is. Mist. Rags. You name it, it comes into my view. I jump to my feet.

'Don't you get it?' I scream. 'That's why he's gone.'

'Anna, sit down,' Mum says, and tries to yank me back on to the couch.

'No, I won't sit down.' I pull my arm away from her grasp and take myself to the middle of the living-room floor. 'That's why Anto's run off or hiding somewhere,' I scream again. 'Cos of him.' I point at Dad. 'Cos he's been sending kisses to Mrs Breen's phone.' Mum gives Dad evil eyes, but I don't think it's for sending phone kisses, I think it's cos I know about them as well now. 'Tanya showed me messages she found on her mum's phone so there's no denying it.' Mum puts her face in her hands. 'And Anto knows as well, cos he heard us talking about it earlier,' I shout. 'Unlike some people,' I say, pointing towards Dad's face, 'he's not stupid.' Mum looks at Dad and her face falls; it's a mixture of pain, rage and sadness. I think she's *about to swing for him*, as Gran says. Dad's eyes have shame seeping from them. And so there bloomin' should be. 'OK,

248

so maybe he didn't hear anything and maybe he doesn't know, but all Anto sees is you fighting in front of him, and he's had enough. We've both had enough. That's why he's run off, isn't it?' They don't look at me, they don't look at anything other than the floor. 'He didn't have me to help him. He didn't have anyone. You're supposed to love him, and all you do is shout and bawl at each other. And it's probably cos of all those kisses you sent.'

'It's not exactly—' Dad tries to say.

'Did you know?' I ask Mum.

'Anna love.' Mum puts out her hand towards me. It's too late, my monster inside has escaped.

'No,' I tell her.

'Anna, calm—'

'Don't tell me to calm down. It's not fair. It's not fair on us. We haven't done anything wrong.' I stamp my foot on the carpet. 'And there's no way me or Anto are going to live with Mrs Breen either.' I feel as if I'm unloading everything I've been holding inside on to them. Spraying them with all my emotional bullets. I really want to say that I see us as one huge balloon, that me and Anto will always float together; if you split a balloon you basically destroy it with a capital BANG! Instead I say: 'And we're not getting split up either.'

'You happy now?' Mum says to Dad, who's started to breathe heavily. 'Eh, Tony? See what all this has done?'

'I can't say sorry any more than I already have,' Dad murmurs.

'No sorry will ever cover it,' Mum growls.

Dad and Mum sit and stare into their own thoughts, then at me. This is where I imagined they would be sitting when I thought about showing them my new routine. Not like this. Not with me trying to sniff tears away from my eyes.

'You don't care about us.'

'Sweetheart,' Dad says. 'You and Anthony are all we care about.' Mum nods in agreement. 'All we've ever cared about.'

'If you cared you wouldn't be saying that stuff about us night after night.'

'Oh, God.' Mum presses her palms to her eyes.

'We hear you all the time,' I say. 'We sit on the top stair and listen to everything.'

'Anna, it's not what you think,' Dad says.

'Well, what I hear is what I think.'

'You should've been sleeping,' Dad snaps, which then makes me snap.

'Don't you get it?' I scream. 'We're a huge balloon. Anto and me, we can't just be burst cos you say so.'

They look at each other with really confused faces, then at me again. I can't be bothered to even explain what I mean by the balloon thing.

'You might have got things round the wrong way,' Mum says.

'I haven't got anything wrong, Mum. How can you even say that?'

'I'm just saying—'

'I hear it. It's what I know, so it's what I think. You can't take it back with sorrys.' I put my focus on to Dad. 'You can't change the text messages.'

'I know that, Anna,' Dad says.

'You two are our world,' Mum says. 'We love you more than anything.' She's looking at Dad for protection, or support, or something they haven't found in each other since I don't know when.

'It's true, you're the only thing that matters,' Dad says, which makes Mum scowl a bit.

'Whatever happens,' she says, 'you two will always come first.'

Dad stares at his feet and simply nods his head. Mum gazes at her hands.

'I don't want you to come to Italy,' I snap, 'if all you'll be doing is grabbing on to each other's throat every minute when we're there. Or thinking about Mrs blinkin' Breen.'

Mum sighs loudly, like I've punched her shoulder. Suddenly I feel silly for saying that.

'I promise that won't happen,' Dad goes, while looking at Mum.

'And now, cos of all your fighting, Anto's missing.'

'We'll find him,' Dad says. 'He'll soon get hungry.' I think Mum wants to throttle him for saying that.

'I know where he might be,' I tell them. 'And so would you if you paid attention to him.'

I make to go out the living room and to where I'm pretty sure he'll be. Where I'm hoping he'll be. They both begin to follow.

'Don't bother following,' I say. 'If he's not where I think, you can phone the police. You'll know soon enough cos I'll be back down in thirty seconds if I can't find him.'

'Let me come with you, Anna?' Mum asks.

'He only needs me at the moment,' I tell her. 'It's a twin thing.'

'It's a twin thing,' Dad says to Mum.

'I guess it's a twin thing then,' she says, throwing her arms up to the ceiling and flopping back down on the couch as if she's not too bothered about the kissing texts. Dad flops too.

I'm not joking, he actually does need me.

More than ever.

See, it's a twin thing.

Twenty-One

Last January Mum said, *This is the worst winter I can remember*, and every time Dad went to leave the bins out or have a sneaky backdoor cigarette he'd come back in, wriggle his body and say, *Brrr, it's blinkin' brass monkeys out there*. The snow was so deep that they had to close my school, same with Anto's. I wasn't too happy about that cos I'm one of the three or four people in Scotland who actually like going to school. But some clever clogs thought it would be a *public health risk* to keep them open; maybe cos the level of snowball fights all over the country would've left the schools looking like war zones. I don't know. I'm not a clever clogs. Anyway, everyone took to the local parks for their snowball fights and turned them into war zones instead.

On Day Two of Snowmageddon Mum bought me and Anto these massive multicoloured snow suits from Asda.

The George Ski Range. With matching gloves. They were horrendous with a capital HORRENDOUS. Honestly, you could have fitted three people inside one of them and still had enough room to play hide-and-seek. Dad couldn't stop laughing when we tried them on. *You can't let them out in those things, Liz. They'll get arrested.* Mum's jaw twitched from holding in her laugh so much. It wasn't funny. Having your parents sniggering at you can leave you scarred for life, so the joke could've been on them. I only wore mine in the back garden when I helped Anto make a family of snowmen. Took us ages. He gave one of the wee snowmen his coat hanger for a few hours, dangled it off his twig arm. That's total snowman detail and dedication for you.

I mean, the daft suit did keep you warm and cosy, but still. All I remember is that Anto never wanted to take his off. He'd put it on as soon as he woke up and didn't remove it again until bedtime. When the hood was up all you could see were his two eyes peering out, it made him feel secure and hidden. He loved it. *He'll need to get that thing surgically removed when the snow melts*, Dad said. Getting him out of it was pure torture; ask Mum. They were so big that they didn't even fit into any of the wardrobes, they had to be shoved under my bed; we'll drag them back out when the next avalanche comes. Sure, they'll still fit us when we're all grown up.

Wearing my Nancy Drew hat, I think it's the ski-suit which holds all the clues to where Anto is. I just know it. My guess is that he's jammed under *my* bed wearing his now, with mine hiding him like a blanket; far from Mum and Dad's prying eyes.

'Anto,' I whisper when I step into my room. 'It's me, don't be scared.' I hold my breath for a few seconds and wait, listening for any swishing sounds. 'Mum and Dad are downstairs – don't worry, they won't come up. I told them to stay where they were. They're not going to disturb us, promise.'

He's been here. The bed is ruffled and my pillow is dented. I always fluff up my pillow. 'You must be roasting under there in all that gear.' Nothing. 'Dying for a drink of water?'

I listen some more. Not a sound. 'They aren't angry or annoyed with you,' I tell him. 'So there's no need to be scared or to hate yourself.'

He could be listening to The Beatles with his head-phones on. I'm not sure which of their songs would cover *Put on an oversized ski-suit and hide under my sister's bed* though. Knowing Anto, I'd guess it's something like 'She's Leaving Home'.

I hear the creak of a floorboard.

'I know why you're hiding, Anto. Mum and Dad do too.

I told them we've been listening to some of the things they've been saying. Said that they were bang out of order.'

I definitely hear another creak.

'I shouted at them – totally lost the head. You should have seen me in action. You'd have been fanning your face like it's nobody's business.'

I go and quickly rejig a few of my books on the shelf.

'I told them it wasn't fair on you or me.'

Not making a sound will be agony for him under there.

'I know you heard what me and Tanya were talking about this morning.'

I lean closer to the floor.

'You know about Dad and Mrs Breen, don't you?'

I wait for a sign, something. A grunt.

'I told Dad that I knew. I think Mum already knew.'

I carefully get on my knees, lean my head down to the floor and peek under my bed.

B-I-N-G-O.

One hundred per cent, that's him hibernating behind my ski-suit. You'd never know he was there right enough, it just looks like some shiny sack I've rammed under there. No wonder Mum and Dad didn't have a clue. This is why Anto has more determination than anyone I know, and that includes me and Nancy Drew. Keeping himself statue still for that length of time is a bit like someone else running a marathon, AFTER they've climbed Everest. It's so tough for his body not to be doing something. See, it's the moving and fidgeting that relaxes him. Not even Gran and Papa fully understand this. I know he's in that ski-suit scared out his wits, thinking his body is on fire. The unhappiest guy alive. That's why I sometimes wish he had the control over his body the way I have. But if he did, I guess we'd lose a massive part of him, and I don't want to lose him. Not now. Not ever.

I get on to my feet again and think of a speedy action plan. I can't just yank him out of there by the ankles, can I? That would cause explosions in his brain.

'I've done a brand-new dance routine for Italy,' I tell him. 'I was going to do a living-room takeover when I got back from Gran and Papa's and show you some of the moves I learned. No presents this time, but they say hi, by the way.'

I stop speaking, hoping the gap in my words will make him feel safe enough to come out.

'If you want I can show you some of them on your own, without Mum and Dad.'

When I fall on to my bed the floorboards creak more than once. There's a slight swishing sound too. He probably thinks the bed is going to squish him. It's a bold tactic, but if Nancy Drew does what people expect, then she's not going to get very far, is she? Always do the unexpected. That's how she discovered what the secret of Red Gate Farm was and who put the curse on the *Arctic Star*.

I fluff my pillow and place my hands behind my head. Albert Einstein's looking down at me, as if he's egging me on.

'Know what Mum said to me downstairs, Anto?' I say, hoping this will create a bit of movement in him; trying to wake up the swishing monster from the deep.

'She said, *You two are our world.* She did, and Dad nodded in agreement with her, and it made me feel a bit better inside.'

I make googly eyes to Albert Einstein; he just looks the same. Wonder what he was thinking of in the exact moment that photograph was taken.

The floor creaks again; I think the monster is on the move.

'Know what else Mum said?' I say, about to play the ace card. 'She said, *We love you more than anything.* Meaning both of us. It doesn't matter what Dad has done ... Well, it does ... but everyone makes mistakes, don't they? We're humans, that's what we do, we make mistakes and then spend large chunks of our life trying to mend those mistakes.' Did I hear a rustle? 'Everyone is worth a second and third chance.' I'm just saying this, not cos I believe it, cos I think if anyone will understand this more than anyone, it's Anto.

I hold my breath.

'Think of anything amazing in the world, Anto. Anything. Well, Mum and Dad love us more than that thing you're thinking about.'

I puff out my cheeks.

'That's good news, isn't it?'

I squeeze my face towards Albert. *Tell me what else to say, Albert, my big guns are all empty.*

'Anto, please come out, you'll roast to death under there. You'll be like a burnt sausage roll, and you know how much you hate those.'

You can't just ask him to do something and it'll be done at the click of a finger. See, Anto needs to go through his own process – that others don't even need to think about – when he's asked to do simple tasks. First he has to THINK about it. Then VISUALISE how he's going to do it. And finally he has to MOTIVATE himself to get his *arse in gear*, as Dad says, to do the task. This is one of those times.

'Please, Anto, for me.'

I feel like one of those snake charmers Gran and Papa saw when they went to Egypt, except I don't have the trumpet thing and Anto isn't a snake. I'm seriously considering climbing off my bed and dragging him out.

There's a bit of movement.

Something is shifting.

I drop my head over the side of the bed and see the coat hanger sliding out from underneath. His hand then pops out a few seconds later and nabs it. Next comes his noggin. No headphones. His body wriggles out like a caterpillar. Freedom! He sinks his face into the carpet and clutches his coat hanger, his lifejacket. That'll calm him.

'Anto,' I whisper.

He turns his body around and sees me looking down at him. His face is boiling, even his eyes seem as if they're sunburnt; his hair's matted and stuck to his head like loads of tiny dark rivers. I grin really wide. He blinks a long and tight one.

'S ... S ... S ... S.'

'No, Anto. You don't need to be sorry.'

He blinks again. Much longer this time. When he opens his eyes, two tears trundle towards each ear.

'S ... S ... S ... S.'

'You've nothing to be sorry for. Nothing.' I have a strong desire to reach down and fix those dark rivers on his face, smooth them away. Wipe his tear tracks as well.

'It's not our fault. I'd have done the same if I were you.'

I let my hair dangle down and tickle his face. He twitches his nose and does his baby moaning sound. I wiggle my head to annoy him some more. What? Sisters are supposed to annoy brothers to death. My hair is all over his face now. He's semi-laughing, semi-whining. I tickle again. His head shakes wildly, back and forth, back and forth. The shaking shifts down to his stomach and legs. In a flash his entire body is vibrating. It's making him feel much better. The pain is leaving his body. He's free again.

'I won't leave you in that position,' I tell him. 'Promise.' Now it's my turn to do a long and tight *sorry* blink.

'K … K … K … K.'

'I know, Anto. Me as well.'

'I think you better come out now or you'll boil to death. I'm not joking, you will.' I hop off the bed and he slowly gets to his feet.

It's so hard not to laugh at him standing in from of me, he's like the Michelin Man in that monstrosity. When he unzips and steps out of it, his NASA sweatshirt is practically sticking to his stomach. Anto falls to his knees and shoves the suit back under my bed, crawling further under as if he's returning it to the deep.

'Hey.'

When he appears again he's clutching our new picture chart to his chest. He lays it on the bed, grabs his coat hanger and taps it on top of the MUM AND DAD ARE ARGUING, DO SOMETHING bit.

He hasn't got his bricks. We need a better system. We always need a better system. We'll always be needing a better system. Every other day requires a new one now.

'G … G … G … G …'

He keeps tapping.

'I did, Anto. I did do something. I told Dad I knew about his messages to Mrs Breen.'

'G … G … G … G …'

'I told you that I got dead angry with them,' I say. 'You probably heard me.'

He blinks twice.

'Right, so, I told them that we could hear them all the time and it wasn't fair on us.'

He taps again.

'God sake, Anto, I told you, I *did* do something.'

'G … G … G … G.'

'Why are you getting annoyed with me?'

He swings his coat hanger around his wrist as if he's a proper gunslinger. *I'm sure that boy was a cowboy in a previous life*, Papa says whenever he does that. Sometimes Papa pretends to shoot an imaginary gun at him, then press his chest as if he's got a poorly heart. Anto thinks Papa's half daft most of the time, I can tell.

He stops swinging and taps the chart at the EXPLAIN TO ME WHAT'S GOING ON phrase.

'I have.'

He hits it hard.

'I *am* explaining. Just listen and stop being cheeky.'

'S … S … S … S.'

He blinks a sorry too.

'I also told them that we haven't done anything wrong and that they were using you and me to put the fear into each other.'

We lock eyes and he holds it, which is so unusual. I'm not sure if he's proud of me.

'They didn't like hearing that bit.' His head jerks up and down. I hate when he does this, I keep thinking he's going to damage his neck bones.

'Then I said we feel as though they don't care about us. But that's not true cos we now know they love us more than anything in the world.'

He stops his head jerking.

'G … G … G … G.'

'We do know this, Anto. I told you, they do love us more than anything in the world.'

He starts pacing. All that time spent hiding under my bed. I mean. He needs to move.

'After I told Mum about Dad's messing around they still said that you and me were all they ever cared about. You and me, Anto. No one else.'

He's tapping his temples; I've always thought that this helps with gluing information into his head. Or he just enjoys how it feels. I've tried it sometimes, but I don't imagine it's the same.

'I told them we've been sitting on the stairs listening to them.' Anto fans his face, I think mainly to get some air into it, as opposed to the light and colours in my room hurting him.

'So we probably can't do that any more cos they know what our game is now.'

He makes a kind of growling noise at me.

'It's not my fault, Anto,' I say, raising my voice at him. 'I *was* angry with them – well, Dad – for making you run away and hide. What would you've wanted me to say?'

His fists clench and unclench. His noise level goes up. I wish he'd just go and get his bricks cos this isn't the way I like to chat with him, especially when he's that peeved off.

'Married people argue from time to time, Anto,' I say, using my soft tone. I step closer. 'Mum told me that. It doesn't mean that *our* life should be a disaster cos theirs is.'

I'm sure I hear some rumblings from downstairs, think Mum and Dad might be getting ready to get the war back on. Or maybe they are snooping on us.

'I mean, my friend Evan's life is completely amazing and his mum and dad aren't married any more. I don't think they even talk to one another now. But he's got tons of talent and loads of cool pairs of trainers.'

Anto starts his violent head twitching again, brushes past me and drums the coat hanger off the picture chart. I lose count how many times, but it's more than twelve. He practically puts a hole in the middle of DON'T LET THEM SEPARATE US.

'I've told you before, that's not going to happen. Ever. So believe me, OK?'

He doesn't answer. Wipes away some of the wet mop from his face. If ever there was a person in need of a haircut.

'We're twins. You can't separate twins.'

'K ... K ... K ... K.'

'And I'm the oldest, so if I say it's not going to happen, then it's not going to happen.'

He hits his head four times with the coat hanger. I feel bad for lying to him, I hope he doesn't see it in my eyes. I've zero say in the matter.

I don't know what else to tell him, what to say. I do my usual.

'It's all going to be fine, Anto.'

He rattles me with his coat hanger, right on the forehead.

'Hey!'

And goes for it again.

'That was sore.' I put my hand up to stop him. He keeps coming so I jump away from him to prevent a secondary war. I wander around my room the way Tanya did when she was here. Poor Tanya. I should give her a ring, she's got no one to talk to. At least me and Anto can protect each other.

He looks the saddest I've ever seen him. His sadness always brings mine out too. But on top of this I'm angry as well. Livid angry. Gran and Papa went to this famous volcano in Italy once and they sent us a video of this bright orange lava bubbling deep in the ground, it was ready to explode at any time. Well, that's what I'm now thinking about. Like, that lava is flowing inside me, rising and falling. Rising. Falling. Ever since Tanya broke the news it's been happening. I'm now ready to explode. With a capital EXPLODE.

'OK, it's not going to be fine, Anto,' I bawl. 'It's going to be anything but fine. In fact it's going to be worse than fine. Everything's terrible and it's only going to get even more terrible. For you and me. Just all one big mess.'

No more words can come out; I plonk myself down in the middle of the room; I need to let the lava flood out of me. And it does: I sob and sob and sob. It won't stop. I don't want it to stop. Anto bounces up and starts pacing around smashing the coat hanger off his body every three or four seconds. Then he leaves. With my bare arm I try wiping my eyes and nose dry. No use.

Anto returns and hunkers down beside me. He's holding four white bricks. I know he's sorry but he doesn't need to be sorry for anything. He gently kicks me on the leg, which is more like a boot, his way of being affectionate. I look up at him; his arms are outstretched.

'K … K … K … K.' His head nods wildly.

I smile through the tears.

'K … K … K … K,' he says again.

His arms flinch. I stretch out mine, thinking we're about to do our pretend cuddle, but Anto falls into my body and grips me tight. He badly needs a wash and his hair is manky, but, still, it feels special to have his trust. To have this connection. To be his sister. Big sister. He screeches, screams and squeezes as if he's trying his hardest to wring all of the pain out of my body. It kind of works.

You can't separate twins. No way. Not in our house.

We rock for a bit. But Anto's muscles are steel, it's impossible to take much more. I release myself and leave him to roll on the ground. I wipe my face again and look down at him: a wee picture of sadness.

'Anto,' I say, trying to get him to focus. 'Anto, look at me,' I demand. His eyes circle the room. 'I think Mum and

Dad are going to split up,' I say louder. He fans his face. I take an exasperated breath. 'Or maybe even divorce.' It blurts out of me like I've no control. 'I think Dad might be in love with Tanya's mum.'

The room narrows.

He blinks fast and hard.

I need to speak to someone, and Anto's the best person to speak to cos he won't bombard me with questions or queries. I then put a sock in it as I don't want to make his world any more rotten than it is. No reason to talk about who'll live with who, will Italy still happen, and all that jazz.

He's about to react when something smashes from downstairs. A glass or plate against the kitchen floor. We've got fake marble tiles, perfect for breaking things into a trillion pieces. Not great for the clean-up. The smash makes us freeze. Well, as much as Anto can freeze. I put my finger to my lips shooshing him; tiptoe and open my room door, cos it's important that we hear this stuff.

There's noise. Smothered voices. Coughing. Or maybe that's just what angry crying sounds like? Mum shouts something to Dad. I can't tell you what exactly cos it has two swear words in it. Massive swear words. Anto stands. The poison below is drawing us closer and closer.

'Come on,' I say to Anto.

And here we are, back on the top of the stairs again. Mum and Dad have returned to the living room. Their voices are calm. Angry. Teary. Crackly. But calm. As if they've run out of anger. Anto is palming his forehead.

'Shhh,' I whisper and dig my fingers into his knee. In a nice way.

'This is pushing all my buttons. It's stressing me out,' Mum says.

'I'm so sorry, Liz.'

I hear Dad huffing and puffing and blowing our family to smithereens.

'How should I react?' she asks him. 'What should I do?'

'I don't know. I honestly don't know.'

There's silence for about ten seconds.

'I just want things to go back to how they were before, Liz.' Dad sounds as if he's speaking from the inside of a bag. He's obviously got his face in his hands, or plastered between his thighs. I don't feel sorry for him.

'Did you ever stop to even consider those two, Tony? I mean, what did you expect to happen?'

'I wasn't thinking properly, that's the problem.'

'Don't you get it? There was never going to be any romantic sunsets, no happy-ever-afters. Especially with that one.' I'm guessing she means Mrs Breen.

'I see that now. I see that clearer than ever.'

'This was your reality. This was where you belonged.'
Mum's voice soothes like a mug of green tea. 'And you let
it go.'

'It still can be,' Dad pleads.

I can just see her standing over him, berating him. Poor
Dad.

NO. NO. NO. Poor Dad nothing. T2 deserves it all.

'Well, we'll have to see about that,' Mum puffs. 'I'm
tired. Exhausted. I'd better go get them.

'I'll come too,' Dad says.

'It'll be OK, Anto,' I whisper. 'We're not going anywhere.'
His head slows a bit, but nothing major. 'We're staying
right here. We're going to swim on that bloomin' moon
together one day.'

And then we hear something weird. It starts like a little
puppy, then develops into Gran and Papa's Italian volcano.
Dad starts wailing heavily into his hands. The louder he
cries the more scared I become.

'I'm sorry, Liz. I'm so sorry,' he weeps, spits and sniffs.

When Anto rests his head on my shoulder I want to
start crying with Dad. However scary it is hearing him
howl, he's still our dad, and always will be. You can't
separate love either.

I've never seen Anto this peaceful before. He's been
lying on my bed for over half an hour, barely moving.

Hugging his coat hanger and staring at my wall. Usually he'd have smashed something up or damaged himself. I guess sometimes you've got to play at being the lion in order to unleash the lamb you really are. Still, all I've been looking at is his backside.

My bedroom door swings open. Mum and Dad are here. I try covering the chart we've made, but I think they've spied it already. Mum jolts when she sees Anto lying there. She probably thought it was someone else's son when she entered.

Anto fans his face and blinks at them.

'He's so sorry,' I say. 'Don't be angry with him.'

'We're not angry,' Dad says.

'Of course we're not,' Mum adds. 'We're just relieved he's safe.' She raises her hand and widens all her fingers. Mum looks sad when Anto doesn't respond. Instead, he starts hitting the chart again. Mum and Dad step further into the room and look down at the chart.

'We made it together,' I say.

'When?' Mum says, without taking her eyes off all the phrases.

'The other day,' I say.

'Why?' Dad asks, reading and re-reading and wondering.

'To help him with things that are going on in his head, to answer some questions he has. To communicate better,' I say.

Mum touches her chest, Dad strokes his chin. They look at each other. Anto crouches down on his hunkers, near my legs. Patting him on the head would be a disaster.

They can look sad and disappointed all they want, but they've no idea what's going on in our hearts or how scary it is to think that one day you'll wake up with half of your life gone and the other half living a mile down the road. They've no idea what these images look like. They aren't twins, so they haven't a clue what it's like to live with a part of you missing. Me and Anto want to stand, run, touch, grab forever; we need all our parts.

'Guys,' Dad says with a soppy voice, 'Why don't we all go downstairs and I'll phone for pizza.'

'Good idea,' Mum adds.

Yeah, that's going to solve everybody's problems, isn't it? Throw some pepperoni at the issue. A sprinkling of mozzarella and we're all good to go. Brilliant! Dad's about to run off with my pal's mum, and our solution to fix everything is chow down on some pizza slices.

'I've just had lasagne at Gran and Papa's,' I say. 'I don't want anything else, but you go for your life.'

Anto cups his ears. Like me, he's not interested in pizza. Or eating. All we want is for them to stop us panicking about the future. They have the power to do that.

'I could nip to the shop and grab Anthony some sausage

rolls if he'd prefer,' Dad offers. We all wait for Anto's reaction. I've a feeling that Dad is scraping the bottom of a very shallow barrel for stuff to offer. Anto squeezes his ears. 'No dice,' Dad says, looking at Mum for guidance.

'Anthony, maybe you and me can go and pick a couple of pizzas up,' Mum suggests. 'In the car.' Anto removes his hands from his ears and pushes his shoulders back. 'You'd like that, wouldn't you?' God, it's like she just entered him at Crufts. And why isn't Mum livid about Dad's kissy texts?

'Great idea!' Dad claps his hands.

Anto jumps to his feet.

What, that's it? That's all it takes? The promise of a fifteen-minute car ride into town and some pizza? Really?

Hey!

I'm here as well. Can anybody see me?

I feel like waving my arms around and swatting thin air too. Cupping my ears. Fanning my face. Smacking my head with a coat hanger. Diving under the bed and whisking myself away to an imaginary island.

'Coming?' Mum says to Anto, nodding him along as if he's some kind of Cockapoodlelabradoodlecavaskoodle breed. He follows her out of the door with his tongue practically wagging.

'See you in a wee while,' Mum says, touching my shoulder.

I give her a look that she loves giving me: head bent low, eyes shooting upwards through her brow.

'Drive carefully,' Dad says.

I begin tidying the word and picture chart that's covering my bed, folding it as neatly as I can. The front door slams shut and we hear the crunch of feet, the huff of the engine and rolling of the wheels. I listen until there's nothing else to listen to. Then it's just me, Dad and this awful awkward silence, so horrible that it attacks my chest. Big deep breaths help. The silence sets off a mini-explosion in my head; this is exactly how I'd imagine it to be like: me staying with Dad cos *he's* (Anto) *a problem for you*, and Anto with Mum cos *he* (Anto) *humiliates you in front of your friends*. Our family meeting for a few hours each week. Hellos. Hugs. Takeaways. More hugs. Goodbyes. Same the following week. And the one after that.

And the one after that.

And the one after that.

And the one after that.

And the one after that.

And the one after that.

And the one after that.

Then someone will skip a week, and another one.

And another one.

And another one.

And another one.

And another one.

And another one.

Then once a month.

Once a year.

Then whenever.

This little episode is our trial run.

I finish folding, fluff up my pillow, and slip down on to the floor, my back against the bed.

'How could you, Dad?' The words just gush out of me. Dad bows his head, sticks his hands in his pockets and sniffs hard. 'I don't understand. How could you?'

'It's complicated, Anna,' he manages to say.

'I'm twelve, I'm not a baby any more,' I spit at him. 'You haven't answered my question.'

His knees make a loud clicking sound when he sits down beside me. He makes a painful grunting noise when he adjusts his legs. Dad's body is like a rusty paperclip being unbent.

'I'm sorry you found those messages, Anna.'

'I feel sad for Mum.'

'Your mum already knew.'

For some reason I'm not shocked at this. I had my suspicions. She didn't exactly fly off the handle when I told her earlier.

'Are you going to marry Mrs Breen?'

Dad sniggers, which makes me want to punch him in the throat.

'No, of course not—'

'Then why are you sending love texts to each other then?'

Dad runs his hands over his face; he's got flour stuck to a couple of his nails. If this is what a person in love looks like, then I never want to be in love.

'Look, Anna, I love your mum, I'll always love your mum. We have you guys, that'll always connect us, but sometimes people just grow apart. There's no single reason for that happening.'

'There is a single reason. You and Mrs Breen. That's the single reason.'

'No.' Dad shakes his head. 'That's not the reason we grew apart.' He sucks in a gulp of air in preparation of starting a new sentence. 'Me and Tash … eh, Mrs Breen, are a symptom of me and your mum drifting away from each other.'

'So it's Mum's fault?'

'No, that's not what I'm saying, love.'

'I don't understand.'

'I'm saying that me and Mum find it hard to be in each other's company – you know that, right?'

'Right.'

'It's been that way for a long time now, for far too long for both of us.'

'That's why you always argue?'

'Which isn't good for you and Anthony, nor for me and your mum.' He looks at me and cups his hand around my kneecap. 'It's not good for our family.'

'So fix it, don't go off with another woman. Fix it.'

'We are trying, love. We really are.'

'How?'

'We're speaking to each other. And maybe we have spoken to someone else.'

Dad looks up behind him and nods to the picture of Albert.

'Someone like him,' he says.

'Albert Einstein?'

'Well, obviously not him, but someone who had a brain like his. Someone who tried to understand why we were fighting and arguing all the time.'

'Well, they were obviously rubbish at it,' I say.

His snort makes me grin.

'In the extreme.' He chuckles.

I enjoy it when people laugh at my jokes; maybe I could be a stand-up when I'm older. Although I do know we shouldn't be laughing at tragedy. This is no laughing matter.

'Are you and Mum going to divorce?' I say, putting a stop to the laughter.

'Don't talk that way, Anna.'

'We need to know.'

'Me and your mum have lots to discuss.'

'But if you want to be with Mrs Breen you'll have to divorce.'

'No one is even talking about this, Anna.'

'Are you going to move out? Into her giant house?'

Dad rubs his forehead, then squeezes his eyes with his thumb and finger.

'I think we're all a bit tired by this. Let's stop,' he says. 'For now?'

'Me and Anto have a right to know these things.'

'And you will.'

'When?'

'Look, Anna, we have more to talk about, but I promise, you and Anthony will be the first to know anything, OK?'

'Right.'

He crawls on to his feet and extends his creaky body. I mean, if Mrs Breen could see him now, she'd run a bloomin' mile in her Balenci-whatevers.

'I'm going to go down and set the table,' he says. 'You want to help?'

'I'd rather stay up here,' I say.

He grins, but nothing smiley comes out of his eyes, it's almost a wordless sorry. He tugs hard on the door. I know where he's going. If Mum detects the tiniest whiff of menthol she'll run the riot act over him. *You want to pack that filth in, Tony. It's hardly a great example you're setting.*

He's barely down the stairs when I can smell the reek of menthol seeping through the walls. It would put you off Polo mints for life. Mum's definitely going to go hoo-ha with a capital HOO-HA if she knows he's been smoking in the house. Information is power.

I can just see Dad flicking his cigarette far into the garden. Smoke shooting out of his mouth; his head tilting high into the sky without a care in the world. Disgusting. Vile. Horrible. There's no capital letters that could come close to describing the way I'm feeling. If pushed, I'd settle on NUMB.

Numb. Numb. Numb.

I remain on the floor and fight the urge not to cry. My bedroom's revolving; all sound, light and movement start confronting my body. Swirling around my head. I don't know what to do. It's as if my heart is trying to escape from my chest. Is this how Anto feels most days? I take deep breaths through the nose, as the experts tell you to do. *Find a spot on the wall and blend into it …* or something like that. *Dive into your imagination* … or something like that.

I dive head first …

Right, so, we're going to these big fancy botanic gardens somewhere near Edinburgh. We all pile into Dad's new Range Rover Discovery. Me and Anto don't have to fight over the armrest in the back seat cos there's room for about seven elbows on it. You could play snooker on that thing, Dad says. This car's more like a hotel on wheels. Le Château Quinn. There's even a place to plug in two new iPhone Pros. Makes sense; now that Dad's the area manager of twelve Greggs shops, he needs something comfortable to drive around in.

The hills in the distance are coated in snow; the world's biggest ice-cream cones. It feels snuggly being warm inside looking out at white landscape. The heating in this car is mind-blowing, it's in the seats AND the door handles AND the humongous armrest. Those Range Rover Discovery people have thought of everything.

Dad has one hand on the gearstick, his other barely touches the bottom of the steering wheel. It's practically self-driving. Mum's tilting her head slightly and staring out of her window; she seems somewhere else, in a cuddly dream perhaps. Anto's tapping his knee, I bet he's making up raps, his lips are doing those tiny singing movements. Yup, totally making up raps. Numpty.

Me? I'm just sitting in luxury, taking it all in.

'Beautiful, isn't it?' Mum says to Dad. They smile.

'Not as much as you,' he says.

She places her hand on top of his.

Anto nudges me and pretends to vomit. Obviously his rapping is over and he's escaped from whatever hood he's been in. Boys just don't get it, do they? I punch him on the thigh.

He yelps.

'Be nice,' I say.

'That's one I owe you.' He pushes my shoulder.

'Hey,' Dad says. 'Leave your sister alone, Anthony.'

'But it was her.'

I fake laugh and pretend to vomit too. All over him.

Anto lets me know again how he's going to bury me in the snow when we get there.

Dad's got a little section in his giant armrest for 'travel goodies'. A tub of chocolate peanuts, which are so addictive it's borderline abuse, and some special chewing gum. The special gum is for weak people to take when they're trying to pack in the cigarettes. Those are Dad's new addiction. He pops them at the same rate I pop peanuts.

'You're doing so well, Tony,' Mum tells him. 'I'm proud of you.' She turns to us. 'We're all proud of Dad, aren't we, guys?'

'I'd be prouder if he gave us a handful of chocolate peanuts,' Anto says.

That makes me laugh. He makes me laugh. I mean, he does hold the world record for being a pain, but he's by far the funniest person I know. Don't worry, I'll never tell him that. His head is already too big as it is. All the girls in my year are so jealous of me cos they *pure can't believe that you get to live with Anthony Quinn.* I'm sure if they saw his performance at our dinner table they'd soon change their tune. *That laddie is like a pig in a trough,* Papa has been known to have said on more than one occasion.

We have to drive through a canopy of snowy trees to get to the entrance of the Botanics. It's about a mile long. The canopy plunges the inside of our car into darkness.

'Oooh, this is the best ghost train ever,' Dad says; he actually thinks this'll scare me.

I don't reply.

There's silence for about half a mile cos it's so magical. I gobble up the beauty.

'Wow,' Mum says.

'I know,' Dad responds. 'Talk about romantic.'

'It's like a winter Disneyland,' I say.

'Except it's in Scotland and in a few days' time everything will have turned into the mud sludge of hell,' Anto says, killing everyone's vibe.

Dad zooms out of the canopy.

'You know he's never going to get a girlfriend,' I say to Mum and Dad. 'Don't you?'

'He's gorgeous, look at him,' Mum says. 'The girls will be queueing up.'

'Yeah, to get away from him,' I say. 'He'll be living with you two well into his fifties.'

'He can stay with us as long as he wants,' Mum says. 'And so can you, Anna.'

'Eh, no thanks,' I say.

Dad pulls up and clicks everything off. No more heating. 'Right, everyone out,' he says.

It's freezing. No joke, Scotland in deep winter is like a torture chamber.

'Right, let's get those ski-suits on,' Mum says to me and Anto.

Dad opens the boot, pulls out our suits and hands one to each of us. My face drops like an anchor. I scan a 360 to see if there's anyone I recognise. Anyone who could take a cheeky snap and stick it on Instagram or TikTok; under the title *Botanic Balloon Girl.*

'Look, Anna,' Mum says. 'I'm not going to force you to wear it, but you'll be miserable and cold if you don't, while we'll be all snug building our snow family. Is that what you want?'

'Come on,' Dad says. 'Check out Anthony, he loves his suit.'

Anto's in it already. Hood up. Gloves on. What a wally! He's moulding a giant snowball in his hands. Or a weapon.

'Anto, don't even think ...'

He smacks me on the head.

'That's for the leg punch in the car!' He laughs.

'Mum! Dad!'

They're both laughing too.

'Just get the suit on and join us in that big patch over there.'

Dad points to an untouched section in the gardens. There's not as much as a deer's hoof print in it. The ideal place to build our snow family. Seems a shame to spoil its gorgeousness with our snowmen tracks. I get into my ski-suit and watch the three of them scarper, starting the destruction. Not wanting to miss out on any fun, I rush to get the suit on. They're running and chucking handfuls of snow at each other. The giggles get quieter the further they run.

Mum falls.

Dad falls on top of her.

Mum screams.

Anto piles on top of Dad.

Dad howls.

I'm putting my gloves on while sprinting to catch up; I badly need to get myself on top of that pile-on.

'I can't breathe,' Mum shouts through her laughter.

I'm nearly there, willing them to stay in that exact position.

'My ribs!' Dad bellows, sounding like Papa when he's getting off a chair.

I'm trying to run as fast as I can through the snow; I don't even feel the freezing cold in my face. My technique is amazing. I'm faster than any wind. At this speed I'd have definitely won the sixty-metre sprint at our school sports day. Lucy Goldsmith would've been eating my dust.

'Get off,' Mum shouts.

'Right, come on, enough,' Dad shouts.

Anto sees me tearing towards the pile of bodies. He's got a cracking grin on his face. He knows what I'm about to do. He knows what I'm thinking. I know what he's thinking too. Of course I do. And, like a salmon or Wonder Woman, I leap high into the air and dive towards them. Everything slows down in that moment. Mum's mouth opens. Dad's face is full of fear. Anto looks like a clown.

BOOM!

I'm on the top of the pile for about a second before it collapses. We're all rolling around the snow giggling our heads off. Covering ourselves with layers of cold, white glitter. We don't care. These ski-suits are amazing. Best thing Mum has ever got us from Asda. Go, George!

Mum and Dad wrap their arms around each other and tumble around and around, giggling like a couple on a third date. Me and Anto get up, wipe snow from our bodies and scoop up more snow into our hands. We stop dead to look at our embarrassing parents. Mum and Dad have got themselves into a full-on clench kiss ON THE GROUND.

Our staring goes on for far too long, so I flick Anto's hand and the snowball he's holding smashes into his face. I run. He chases.

'Help! Help!'

'This time you're getting it. I'm going to kill you,' Anto shouts after me.

Mum and Dad are on their feet again, and now we're all chasing each other randomly until our lungs can't take it any longer. Ring-a-ring-o'-roses ... We all sink on to the snow. I can't tell you how good these ski-suits are.

While me and Mum do snow angels, Dad and Anto start rolling the bodies for our snow family; cos, you know, that's such a man's job. But me and Mum get to do the most important part: faces. We search for some body buttons, eyes and nose stones, and twig arms.

Dad takes loads of pictures on his new iPhone Pro; they look proper professional. I'd say at least two of them will make the mantelpiece.

Afterwards we walk through the rest of the gardens. Mum and Dad, arm in arm, are about ten metres in front; snuggling and chatting close to each other's ear. Sometimes they laugh together, sometimes separately. But always loud. If you could draw a picture of the word *romantic* on a big canvas, this is what you'd draw. Then a strange thing happens: Anto links his arm into mine, which is the opposite of romantic. If you could draw puke …

'It's cold, sis, you better keep near.'

'Yeah, it is cold,' I say, and pull myself closer to him. 'Let's keep each other warm.'

'Sure, who else is going to keep us warm?' he says.

Walking through those gardens I actually feel my heart heating up; feel the balmy blood rush around my body again. It's hard to explain, but it's as if someone has covered the four of us with a massive security blanket. Still, the cold always finds its way in, always finds a wee nook to creep through. And it's gone incredibly cold. Now I feel as if I'm in the coldest day ever.

So cold.

Freezing cold.

Shivering cold.

Baltic cold.

I'm shaking all over, my legs, chest, mind. My iced-up blood.

It's my trembling body that shakes me back to life. I smell pizza. How many pizzas did they buy? I'm full, do I even want pizza? Do I even want to go to Italy? *Know what your problem is, Anna?* Mum says to me sometimes. *You can't make up your mind if you need a pee or a haircut.* I'm beginning to understand what she means now.

There's no point in getting a book, my concentration level is a mix between googoo and gaga. After his pizza maybe I could ask Anto if he wants to do some Lego; it'll give me an opportunity to tell him about my chat with Dad. On second thoughts, best not to.

I bet T1 is lying in her blingy bed right now, looking up at her blingy ceiling, thinking blingy thoughts about T2.

Wondering what trainers to wear, what emojis to use, how many *XXX*s to send and what kitchen island they'll choose when they're living together. If she could only see how T2 stinks of cigarettes and munches pizza, she'd soon change her mind.

My limbs are heavy. I need a pee. I need a haircut. I say a wee prayer to the god of families and hope for the best. But hope makes me feel stuck.

Twenty-Two

When I get downstairs it's late. Anto's already at the table gobbling pizza; munching so loud it's beyond annoying. I know he's doing it on purpose to punish me for my late show. His chewing is filled with so much anger.

'Anto, you're not eating a microphone you know,' I say. He smacks his head twice, I know everything he wants to say to me. I leave him to gorge on his pizza.

I go to enter the living room and stop myself. I can see Mum standing at the window nursing a mug of something as if she's cuddling a kitten. Dad's there too, staring at the fireplace, obviously not wanting to look at her. There's a hush that seems to be oozing from the walls, under the doors and through the letter box. Thank God we've no visitors. You can taste tension; smell the stink of stillness in the air. It's not nice. I kick my checkerboard Vans off the floor, pull my hoodie over my head, and go in. Dad's elbows rest on his knees, his hands almost praying under his chin. He doesn't look at me. Mum moves to the arm of the chair and crosses her legs. Her skin whiter than I've ever seen before. Her lips a worrying shade of grey. Both have red eyes. You don't need to be Nancy Drew to work out that a living-room tear-fest has taken place. They're both struggling. I don't say a word. Have they made up? Has Dad made promises to stop whatever he was doing? I think I hear my name being mentioned.

Should I say something? Leave? Sit down?

'Hi, sweetheart,' Mum says, glancing at me. 'Did you get some pizza?'

'Stomach still full of lasagne,' I say.

Mum puts her mug down and folds her arms. Dad leans back. They share a look that doesn't have any pain in it.

'You were talking about us there, weren't you?' I ask them.

Dad sniggers a wee bit.

'We're always talking about you two,' he says.

'Good or bad?' I ask.

Mum's turn to do a wee snigger.

'Good, it's always good,' she says.

'Liar!' I snap, and feel ashamed I directed it at her. I want to say sorry, but I can't get the word out of my mouth. I stare at Dad instead.

'We were just trying to sort a few things out, Anna,' he says.

'About where me and Anto will go?' I murmur.

'That's not something either of you need to worry about,' Mum adds. 'We were discussing what the future will look like.'

'Well, what does it look like then?' I press them. I want an answer that includes the phrases *Christmas dinners*, *lots of laughter* and *party games*.

'It's late, Anna,' Dad says.

I stand my ground. I'm not angry or anything, I just want a straight answer.

We all look towards the living-room door. Anto's behind it. We can hear him sucking his teeth. What a shocking spy he'd make.

'We were talking about Italy, if you must know,' Mum says, which is not what I was expecting.

'Really?'

'Among other things,' she says.

Anto bangs the door. OK, I get it, I'm to do all his questioning now.

'Are we still going to Italy?' I ask.

'We're discussing it,' Dad says.

Mum's eyes change when she looks at him.

'Along with a multitude of other stuff,' she says to him.

Anto batters the door again, louder.

'Right, I think you two better get to bed,' Dad says.

'Your dad's right,' Mum adds.

I don't move. I have to speak for both of us; that's a heavy load to carry.

'Will you be here tomorrow, Dad?' I ask.

More looks between them. I think my question makes them sad.

'Of course I'll be here tomorrow,' he says.

'What about the next day and the day after that?' I go.

Anto slaps the door as if he's applauding.

Mum's chest rises. 'Anna, it's very late. Of course your dad will be here tomorrow and the next day. As I said, we've got lots of things to talk about.'

'Why don't you take your brother upstairs and we'll talk more tomorrow,' Dad says. 'How does that sound?'

Not great.

'OK,' I say.

I pull my hood down and shift my eyes between them, searching for a weakness or signs of lying. Too late in the day for that.

Pillow fluffed to the size of a small cloud, I flop on to it. I'm desperate to sleep. I try and try, but it never comes. I wish I could close my eyes and dream of normal things.

Those dreams that bring me peace when I wake up. Now I'd like a dream without Mum, Dad or Anto in it. With people I don't know. They say that you can't dream of a face you've never seen before though. Who are *they* anyway?

I fully expect a war to be taking place, but all I hear from downstairs is silence. A peaceful one? Who knows.

It's well after midnight and I'm lying staring at the ceiling. A funny sensation hits me: I miss the arguing. Sometimes hush is worse than noise. They should be planning how to make things work. Nothing ever gets fixed in silence, does it?

I know Dad said that *we'll talk more tomorrow*. But I can't just lie all night waiting for tomorrow to happen. They don't honestly expect me to wait that long, do they? This is like the worst version of Christmas Eve ever: unable to sleep for the excitement.

I sit up, rub my eyes and swing my feet on to the carpet. Should I go down barefoot or slide some slippers on? I put on a pair of dirty socks and tiptoe so as not to creak the floor in case Anto gets a whiff of it.

They're both holding a glass of wine. Separate chairs. No telly. No talking. Dad sees me first.

'Anna, what are you doing up?' he says, looking at his watch as if that'll make a difference.

'I couldn't sleep,' I say.

I step into the living room and quietly close the door behind me.

'I can't wait until tomorrow,' I say. 'I need to know now.'

They sip their wine at the same time as if they've been practising. There's a slight nod between them.

'Sit down,' Mum says. 'And we'll have a little chat.'

My heart flip-flops as I sit.

Mum doesn't even wait a few beats or take any more sips before diving right in.

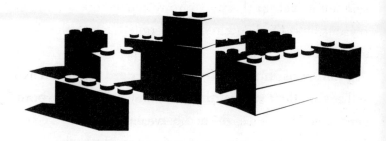

Twenty-Three

Flashes of the *little chat* with Mum and Dad jangle around every wall in my room. Well, I say *little chat*, but it felt more like being in the aftermath of a car crash when you're lying upside down in a ditch and all you can hear are faraway voices on the radio.

It's strange to be back in bed thinking: *Did that actually happen? Was I even there? When it was all laid out, did everything make sense? Does it now?* My brain's working overtime with these questions. I'm not shaking, my palms aren't sweating and my stomach isn't swirling.

It all comes slowly into view again: images of everyone's expression; tears splashing to the ground and making dark stains on clothes. Snippets of the conversation will be with me for life, shadowing me everywhere. Parts of what was said are as dull as the stars on my ceiling, other parts as crystal clear as T1's kitchen counters.

Your dad and I have decided to split up.

I yank my duvet up. Pull it all the way over my head. No more tears, but I still don't want Albert Einstein to see my puffy eyes. He must think I'm weak and useless. Can't have Nancy Drew believing I'm floppy and fragile.

We've talked a lot about it, and it's best if we separate.

Too late to worry what others think; this bloomin' lump in my throat isn't going away. I start sniffing. I'm hot. I'm far too hot. I'm doing that duvet thing again: forcing it down to below my hips. Maybe I should get up and pee … or cut my hair.

It's got nothing to do with either of you; none of this is of your making.

I listened to them ripping us apart, but really wanted to ask: Are we still going to Italy? Are we? Are we?

My skull and eyeballs have stopped popping. I can't imagine how Anto's feeling. Is he asleep now? Should I go to him? Nudge him? Cough into his face? I try an ear to his wall for the sound of clicking Lego. Not a sausage. No more sausage rolls. He'll be OK. Plenty of shade. He's sleeping soundly now. I think we're going to be OK, you know.

We'll still be a family, just a different one.

297

Actually I'm now thinking that Anto's two worlds might be light and lighter. Mum and Dad, basically. No more sitting at the top of the stairs listening to the battles below or smacking coat hangers off of me. It'll be my job to bring some light too. No problem, I'm the perfect BIG sister for that job. I just need to start seeing it myself, cos as soon as they said the words *split up* and *separate* it was as if the glow inside me was dimmed to murky mode. But that was then. You can't live in a tunnel forever, you need to follow whatever wee chinks of sun you see.

Dad will be within walking distance. Sure, he's not going to be trains, planes and automobiles away from us or Greggs, is he? I might suggest that he brings me and Anto with him when he's checking out new places. I could give him some design ideas. It'll be a few weeks anyway so I can start planning colour schemes.

We'll all just have to learn a new routine.

When Anto burst in, hammering his chart – always at the same bit: DON'T LET THEM SEPARATE US – Mum tried to comfort him with outstretched, fanned hands and soft tones. Completely useless. I could see he was too far gone. I regretted ever making that numpty chart.

No dice.

Dad told him to cup his ears and breathe through his nose, even demonstrating what he meant. Mum did something similar. Whatever they tried didn't work; nothing could stop him thundering that chart.

Of course we're not going to separate you, sweetheart.

It was true. He couldn't hear it though. He got to the *little chat* fifteen minutes late.

No, you two come as a pair. You can't split up a pair.

I felt like my body was being squeezed inside a vice. I just sat there, deep in the swamp, until the vice loosened and released me. I was no longer stuck. We'll never be apart. No more swamps. Light and lighter.

Your dad will be round here all the time.

Anto paced. He didn't know where to go. He ran into the kitchen, and back again, then into the hall, up a few stairs, down a few stairs. He did the full house circuit over and over. We all watched. Not a word was said, until Dad sliced through the silence.

Don't panic, he probably wants to be on his own.

I'm sick of hearing this; the last thing Anto wants is to be on his own. Human beings don't want to be on their own; he just doesn't want to cause trouble or get on anyone's nerves, that's all. He never wants to be on his own, yet he's always being left that way. There's a difference. I didn't hound Dad for getting this wrong, cos sometimes we all get it wrong.

When I get a nice place you can both come stay with me a

few nights a week. Obviously I'll need to sort out different shifts at Greggs, but that should be no problem.

After Dad said this, the worst moment came: Anto broke his coat hanger off his thigh. Snapped it in two. When the pieces fell I knew he instantly regretted it. I saw it in his face; he paused, did about forty blinks, then a silent scream, standing with his mouth wide open and eyes clamped shut. It was one of the loudest silent things I'd ever heard in my life. I cupped my ears. Beyond terrifying, so it was. I hate loud silent things. Nobody knew what to do or how to calm him down. We gawked at the fallen pieces on the carpet.

Your dad and I will always love you.

You can't just tape it back together again or replace it with another, that's not how these things work. That coat hanger got to touch his head, his shoulder, his knee, his hip, his palm, his wrist, his cheek, his stomach, his elbow. It got to share his bed, enter his igloos, snuggle up to his breathing, watch his eyes flicker during dreams. It had all these priv-ileges that no one else in the world had. It was part of Anto's every day, and now it's lying destroyed on our living-room floor like the death of a friendship. The best he's ever had.

Your mum and I will always love you, and always be there for you.

That's right, people, my brother's best friend is a coat hanger. Which sadly has now been obliterated. That was the moment when it hurt the most, seeing his best friend dying against his thigh. Cos I liked it too; it was my friend as well. But new beginnings mean new friends, for both of us.

You two are our life.

I hear the details of their split-up, separation, or whatever you want to call it. I hear every word, every sentence, and I get to place them in their correct order. I hear nothing about T1 or any other Ts. Anto *feels* the details, feels them in a series of images floating in front of his eyes. They could be red or purple balloons, sprinkles of multicoloured dust or flashes of fast cars. Maybe each word hovers over him as if he's looking into a giant kaleidoscope. I don't know, do I? Sometimes it smothers him, eats him whole. What a life! It would be torture to feel the level of his loneliness. But a part of me would love to see the beauty of it. He needs to know that we can swim on that moon, but it's up to us to make it happen.

You don't need to be afraid of any of this.

I couldn't help feeling it was my fault. That I was somehow to blame. If I hadn't wanted to join MadCrew, none of this would've happened. T1 wouldn't exist at this moment. There would be no late-night fights, no smashing of plates, cups or coat hangers and no Mum finding out. At the time I had a choice between Taekwondo and dancing. I chose MadCrew. If only I'd have chosen Taekwondo.

We'll always protect you.

Crying makes people feel tired, it takes some amount of energy. Crying for hours on end is exhausting. It stops you wanting food in your stomach and gives you the sorest headaches ever. I wonder if everyone is awake at this time, staring at their ceilings too. I have a Susin Nielsen book, which has been gathering dust on my To Read pile. If I dive into that it'll take my mind on the different journey it needs. But I have no eyes for reading. It's probably best if I try and sleep away these thoughts. For the time being anyway.

After a car crash there's a recovery truck. Italy was something I never expected to hear about. Thing is, I wasn't even thinking of that country, wasn't going to bring the subject up ever again, cos I believed it was a dead fish. It would've been easier trying to put a bubble in your pocket than start a chat about it. How could I pipe up with *Let's all play happy families in Italy* after hearing that the big split was just around the corner? But what they said yanked the rug from right under me. A real swimming-on-the-moon moment. I think the word I'm looking for is bittersweet with a capital BITTERSWEET:

We're still going to go to Italy.
Really? Altogether, as a family?
We want to support you, Anna.
That'll never change, sweetheart.
Support both of you.
You mean that?
Of course we do.

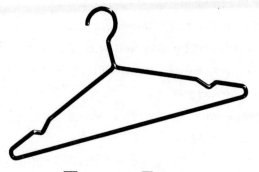

Twenty-Four

Anto looks as calm as I've ever seen him. He's sitting on his bedroom floor surrounded by stacks and stacks of Lego bricks. His words. His prompts. His conversations. All laid out in front of him. He seems very still. I'm confused. Why is he so still and so relaxed? Surely he should be chucking himself around the space. You think you know someone, eh? I'm putting this down to the devastating shock he's experienced.

I creep to his door, thinking he'll not hear me. Of course he does. He always knows when I'm in his air. But I'm glad he's in mine too. It looks like he's had a decent sleep, his bloodshot eyes have disappeared. After waking up at stupid time, and staring at my ceiling for a bit, I closed mine again for what I thought was about ten seconds. However, when I opened them it was suddenly after midday. That's what I call a strange ten seconds. Almost six hours. Six hours of not thinking about it.

I'm waiting to be attacked with the two yellow, two blue, Get Out of My Room bricks, but he doesn't do anything.

'We have to make some more of those,' I tell him, nodding to the Lego.

It's true, we need an organised plan to create new words. Get everything alphabetised. Maybe do a coloured dictionary. NO. Better: an index. Yes, a proper index. We'll need two copies. One for here and one for somewhere else. When I think about that notion, it hits me again. It's the same pattern: goes away for a bit, then recharges before returning to hit me even harder. Yes, we'll need two of everything now. Mammoth amounts of Lego. Onesies. Headphones. Brain-melt thinking how long that list will be, and that's before we even get to my stuff. But, if me and Anto need two of everything, does that mean Mum and Dad will need only one? One pillow, one bedside lamp, one bottle of wine? It's all a bit of a head-wrecker.

Without lifting his head, Anto holds up four white bricks.

'Why are you sorry?' I think he's sorry for the tantrum, for thinking he broke everyone's spirit. Or maybe he doesn't know why he's sorry. He just is. I know what that feels like.

'They both said it, Anto. They told me when we spoke about it. None of this has anything to do with us. I believe them cos it's true.'

His head twitches; not too violently though.

'And it hasn't. We didn't make this happen. Adults did. Mum and Dad are adults. Sometimes they do it to themselves.'

'K … K … K … K.'

He turns two yellow and two red bricks upside down, yellow at the top.

'I'm glad you think it's true as well. Cos it is. It's a hundred per cent true. All of it.'

He then rustles around for the next set. The zebra-crossing bricks.

'Yes, I think it is the end for them. Not for us, it'll never be the end for us.'

I walk further into the room and crouch down. Not too close.

'OK?'

He holds up the four white again.

'Good.'

I want to say something about the coat hanger, but it's best not to restart that fire. I considered bringing him one of mine. The one I hang my ANNA hoodie up with, it's got big bits for the shoulders. He might appreciate that more if he knows what it had been used for. But I guess when a friend dies you can't just replace them the next day with a different one. He'll choose another when he's ready, and the desire to have something connect with his body is overpowering. Or maybe he won't. Maybe that'll be part of the past. The before.

I get up and circle his room. Typical boy's. A bit messy and smelly with a capital SMELLY. Socks and pants and underarms mainly. I fix his duvet and puff his pillow. I find some long, stray hairs on it. That bloomin' hair of his.

'You need to do something about that, by the way.' I hold up the hair to him and point to his own fuzzy mop. When he flashes me the Get Out of My Room bricks it's hard not to laugh, but I do. Laughing makes me feel lighter already. I make an inner pact to laugh more often. Every hour of every day. I know I can't fix Mum and Dad, but surely I can stop me and Anto from breaking. See, we're steel, and you can't break steel.

'It's OK, I'm going. I'm going.' I put my hands up and snigger.

I turn before I leave.

'When we get to Italy, you and me are going to go bananas,' I tell him. 'Bananas in a good way.'

Twenty-Five

I'm so tired. The only part of my body that doesn't ache is my hair. I'm not even joking about that.

'Right, ladies.' Evan smacks his hands together. 'Do we want to go through it one last time?'

We're all sweating buckets, the MadCrew hall is slightly cooler than a sauna. This is Evan's idea. My new trainers, which were supposed to be christened in Italy, are well worn in now.

'I don't think we need to, Evan,' Tanya puffs. 'I think we have it.'

'I agree,' I say.

Evan wipes his brow, flicks his hair, then flattens down his eyebrows.

'You better believe it we have it. You two are amazing.' When he says this I fight the urge not to swallow a sunbeam. This is Evan Flynn we're talking about here, and he's telling me that I'm amazing. 'Want to know what I think?' he says.

'What?'

'What?'

'I think we're going to smash it in Italy. I really do. You two and me are going to blow them all into next year.'

I look at Tanya, who's retying her ponytail. She nods her head in agreement as if she knew this already. God, I wish I had some of their bottled confidence. I'd drink it by the gallon. I mean, I do think what we've created is impressive, but blowing people into next year? Mmm, not too sure. I'd say trio dancers in Spain, Germany and Ireland are probably thinking the same thing as us. We're not special, just hard workers.

We do some high fives and start gathering up our stuff.

'So, Anna,' Evan says to me. 'Your whole family are coming?'

I fiddle with the straps on my backpack and pretend not to hear him; don't want to be rude or anything, but, we're going to Italy, ITALY! I don't want to ruin the moment.

'Eh?' Evan pushes further.

'Shut up,' Tanya snaps … as all good pals should. 'Let's get our things first before we start having, like, discussions.'

'It'll be great, is all I meant,' Evan adds.

'It will be, won't it?' Tanya says to me with a ginormous smile.

'Amazing,' I say.'

'And what about you, Tanya?' Evan says. 'Both yours coming?' I can't make out if Evan is trying to stir the sewer or not. Me and Tanya glance at each other, then the floor.

'No, just my dad. My mum can't make it now. But Dad's dead excited, he's been to Italy loads of times, he knows all the best places.'

Evan's face drops a wee bit, he suddenly looks sad.

'Mine needs a passport to get out of the Borders so he'll be a no-show,' he says. Maybe he thought all our dads could hang around with each other.

He fixes his hair for about the sixtieth time and puffs out his cheeks. 'I don't know about you two, but I'm absolutely bursting.'

TMI, Evan.

When Evan heads out of the swing doors towards the toilet Tanya leans in and whispers: 'I haven't said anything to him by the way.'

'About?'

'Your dad and … you know—'

'Your mum?'

'Well, yes. I haven't said anything.'

'It's none of his business anyway,' I say.

'Too right it's not.'

'Anyway,' I say, keeping one eye on the door that Evan exited. 'It's no big deal.'

We tug the sleeves of our hoodies and look at parts of the hall we've never really noticed before. I stare at the long, thin lights on the ceiling. Tanya mostly examines the floor.

'Is your mum OK, Anna?'

No, Tanya, she's not OK with a capital NOT OK. She's as happy as a bag of frogs about to be shoved in a blender. When she's not crying or worrying about our Anto, she's working her socks off so she can give us the best. The best of the best. So maybe OK doesn't cover it. But it's nice of you to ask. It is.

'She's fine,' I say. 'The house is quieter.' If you exclude brother noises and late-night sniffling. 'But I'm sure that things will be better soon.'

They really should paint this ceiling and put up some better lights, modern ones.

'How is your mum?' I ask.

'The same, but different too.'

'Hey, I bet we won't even be thinking about all this stuff in a few months,' I say, trying to make her feel more positive.

311

'Hope so,' she says. 'Fingers crossed.'

'And toes.'

'As long as no one gets killed.' She nudges me on the shoulder.

'Well, it won't be me.' I nudge her back.

'Yeah, as long as we're all right, eh?'

'We will be,' I say.

We laugh. Then chuckle. Then stop.

'Anna.'

'What?'

'Can I still come to your house sometimes?' I stare at Tanya with my best don't-look-confused face. 'We don't need to dance or anything like that. We could just watch Netflix or you can tell me what the best books to read are.'

'Erm … yeah … if you like.' My mind is already swaying between Judy Blume, Nancy Drew and the look on Mum's face when she sees Tanya charging through the door as if she's just another routine pal. 'I can recommend tons of books.'

'It won't be too weird though, with your mum and that, will it?'

'Probably.'

'Right.'

Evan waltzes back through the swing doors. No, literally

waltzes. He's doing a three-four count and his arms are raised like he's swinging a partner around.

'This time in two days we'll be Italyed out of our nut,' he screams. 'You ready?'

I've been ready for ages.

Twenty-Six

Right, so, we're all sitting on this big fancy airplane. I'm next to Mum, who's squeezing the bones in my hand cos she's *completely petrified of flying*. The man next to me is watching *Game of Thrones* on his iPad. He's all elbows and sniffles. After take-off he ordered a panini sandwich, a packet of cheese-and-onion crisps and a glass of white wine. Man, he eats loud. Gran and Papa suggested that we stock up at the airport cos they were *rip-off merchants on the plane*.

Why do I have to sit in the middle? I mean, Anto gets to have a window seat and he's not even scared of flying. In fact, he's been excited all week. Dad has to sit in the middle of their row. They're across the aisle from us. Anto's nose is pressed against the wee window searching for other planes, tiny towns below and migrating birds. I did tell him that all he'd see is clouds and blue sky. I've done my research. Occasionally he'll turn and look around. I try to get his attention so I can do googly eyes at him, but he's got no interest in people.

Mum's eyes are closed. Head tilted backwards. Her neck is long and slender. Planes are torture for her; she needs a cuddle. Every time it makes a mid-air movement she squeezes harder on my hand and tightens her face. She definitely needs a cuddle. Who doesn't?

I lean forward to get Dad's attention. Maybe he'll like my googly eyes. Anto's now fiddling with the buttons above his head. The air steward has already been up to him twice. Dad apologised but didn't look embarrassed. It was a male air steward, which I thought was quite funny cos Papa kept calling them *trolley dollies* before we left.

When the plane is flying calmly Dad orders a wee bottle of red wine. Me and Anto get a fun-size picnic box. Mum goes for a salad. Dad leans forward and shoogles the little wine at Mum. She smiles, lifts her bottle of water and shoogles it back. I haven't seen her drink wine for ages.

'You excited, sweetheart?' Mum asks.

'I can't wait,' I say.

'It'll be great.'

'I think so too.'

When the plane jerks a bit she clutches her chest; *For*

God sake, she says loudly. We all hear it. I look across at Dad and Anto. Anto's inhaling cheese sticks, and Dad flicks his eyes to the roof as if to say his very own *For God sake*. This is the moment I finally get to do my googly eyes. He does his too. We tee-hee-hee.

I suggest to Mum that she watches something on her iPad. You know, to take her mind off the fear.

'That might be a good idea,' she says.

'I've got loads of them,' I say, which is true. It was me who told her to get a new bed, repaint the walls in her bedroom, and throw all the ashtrays out. All great ideas.

She plugs herself into *Modern Family*. That's her favourite at the moment. She's always watching that these days. I guess that's what we are now. Dad's got his iPad – the one he bought for his new house – and is playing a game with Anto.

Being wedged between *Modern Family* and *Game of Thrones* isn't much of a laugh. Maybe I should go to the toilet. Bit of a wander. Speak to the others. Probably better to get some sleep, or close my eyes for some imagination time.

Could all passengers please return to their seats.
'Anna!'
The Captain has switched on the seat belt signs.
'Anna!'

Please return your tray table to its full upright and locked position.

'ANNA!'

I open my eyes. Mum's fretting about my tray and seat belt.

'We're about to land,' she says.

I feel a twinge in my stomach as the plane descends; twinges flushed with excitement. It'll be far too hot to put my ANNA hoodie on, so I tie it around my waist. As land emerges, Anto gently starts tapping his new coat hanger off the window.

'The local time in Rome is three thirty-five,' the Captain says.

Wow!

Rome.

Italy.

Wow!

When the ping goes off, everyone clicks open their seat belts and, for some reason, stands up in a very uncomfortable position. I wave to Tanya five rows down, she blows me a kiss and we do huge *Oh-I-can't-wait* googly eyes to each other. Her dad nods a hello at me. We met at Glasgow airport when Tanya showed me her new NEW trainers. He wore a gold necklace and seemed nice. Evan got a fresh hairdo for the trip: dyed in the three colours of the Italian

317

flag. I think it might prejudice us in the trio, to be honest. But that's OK, as long as he's happy. As long as we're all happy.

Cos of Anto, we have to exit the plane last. He watches as everyone walks into the terminal building and out of sight. Then it's just the four of us left. Dad goes first, followed by Mum. Before he starts to walk he turns, says something to her and gives her a beaming smile. She shoves him forward. I know she's laughing cos her shoulders bob up and down.

'Come on, Anto,' I say, and wait for him to slide out of the row, shaking his coat hanger in front of him. If coat hangers could grin, this one would be grinning from ear to ear. 'Want me to go first?'

He pushes me ahead of him and starts to tap me on the back with his new coat hanger. I try swatting it away from behind me, but Anto catches my hand; our fingers loop around themselves and I practically have to drag him off the plane. On the tarmac, standing side by side, he doesn't let go of me. I hold him firm. His fingers, like mine, feel twiggy. As if they're from the same tree. I guess we are, really. See, that's the thing about twins; even if the branch gets chopped down, our roots will always be physically entangled. Actually that's the thing about families as well; you might be in separate places, doing separate things, having separate experiences, but you'll never be able to chop down that family tree. You can't hack away their love.

'Come on, Anto, we're not here to look at the bloomin' planes.'

We walk, holding hands, and catch up with Mum and Dad. I'm happy. He's happy. Sometimes words aren't needed. No bricks required.

Have you read

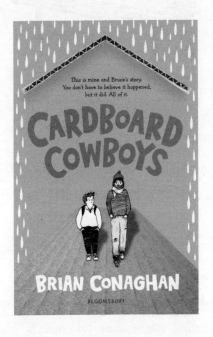

A funny, life-affirming, unforgettable comic drama about
Lenny and Bruce:
an unexpected friendship, an epic plan and
a road trip that will change their lives.

AVAILABLE NOW!

Turn the page for a sneak peek …

Bench

Imagine being trapped in a world with everything you hate. Picture how that makes you feel. Well, that's school for me.

So, today in English Liam McAvoy called me Fatso. Sometimes he's swallowed a dictionary and says Chunky. Other times Blubber. But Fatso is the main one. Teachers have never called me it, but I know the word pinballs around their brain cells. I caught Mr Sutton, the PE teacher, giggling his head off when I was playing dodgeball once. He tried to hide it but I snared him, standing there like a human letter A, arms folded, legs spread and cheese-faced.

Our English teacher, Miss Kane, is quality though. Before the *Fatso* abuse she told us what a haiku poem was by writing this on the board:

2

- They came from Japan.
- They <u>must</u> have 3 lines.
- Line one = 5 syllables.
- Line two = 7 syllables.
- Line three = 5 syllables.
- So, they <u>must</u> have <u>17 syllables in total</u>.

'So, with haikus you tend to do a lot of syllable counting on your fingers,' Miss Kane had said. Then did a wee syllable rap demonstration to show us what she meant, which was supposed to be funny. Nobody laughed. Except me, inside.

'Miss?' Liam McAvoy had thrown up his hand.

'Yes, Liam?'

'What kind of sad maddie writes poems?' He then chucked a pencil, which could've speared my eyeball. *This* made people laugh.

She read my poem at her desk and kept me behind to say, 'If you ever need to talk about anything you can always come to me, you know.' She shoulder-squeezed me while saying it. It's mad weird when a teacher touches you.

My poem was called 'The Future'.

Here it is:

Here is what I think:
People like me won't find love
I will not be found

(by Lenny Lambert)

Afterwards Miss Kane wrote *Amazing stuff!* in my jotter and big-ticked a beauty underneath. Funny how one little red pen flick can make you feel all snuggly inside. But that feeling was taken away in a flash. Outside the window I spied Liam McAvoy scratching a line across his throat while Grace McKenna inflated her cheeks, and gave me the bad-word finger. But then Trisha Woods passed and smiled at me. Not a teeth-showy one, but still a smile. It all happened so quick that I didn't have time to return mine, which really gutted me.

Next up, French. Eh, *non merci!* Don't fancy an entire lesson hearing shouts like:

Mademoiselle Murphy, how do you say 'whale boy' in French?

Mademoiselle Murphy, what do French people say for 'five-a-day'?

Mademoiselle Murphy, what's French for 'piglet'?

4

That's when your topsy becomes turvy as fast as. And when things are turvy I don't want to think about haiku poems or learn stupid French or be in school. So, lots of times I go to my bench instead.

The green paint is peeling off and it's made of metal; it's super uncomfortable, but peaceful. I can eat without a thousand eyes peering at me. Since it's still autumn the weather is kind enough for stretching the mind and watching fish swim along the dirty canal. I've never been fishing. Loads of times I sing songs in a very low voice. You name it, I sing it.

It's supposed to be some type of nature trail, but it's too soggy and overgrown. Even the tree trunks look like misery statues. In all the times sitting here I've never seen anyone trail walking or chilling in nature. I saw a jogger once, who stared me down. *Should you not be in school?* Him and his skinny pins haven't returned.

I've just started big school, which is a bit of a madhouse. If I lived in America I'd be known as a 'freshman'. Fresh man. Like, brand-new man, innocent man, happy man. Not so here. In Scotland we are simply called *first years*.

I wish I could just stay in my bedroom and sing into the mirror instead of going to school. There's no way I'm telling

5

anyone this though. Not after what happened with our Frankie. So, he might not be living with us at the moment, but that doesn't stop Mum and Dad adoring the life out of him; thinking the sun shines out his bumbaleery, always chatting about him when they think I'm not listening:

'Des, I hope our Frankie's going to be safe,' she says to Dad, almost nightly.

'He'll be fine, we know he's a good lad,' Dad returns.

'Think he misses us?'

'Course he does.'

'Breaks my heart, all this.'

'Don't, love. Don't.' And then Dad'll pat Mum's lower arm. Without that arm pat I think she'd be sobbing the walls wet.

Sometimes I wonder what they'd be like if it were me who was in Frankie's position:

'Think our Lenny is going to be OK, Des?'

'Aye, probably.'

'Right, let's see what's on the telly.'

On the bench next to me I place a chicken and mush-room pie, a can of Irn-Bru and a packet of Flamin' Hot Mega Monster Munch. Four quid from the wee shop next to school. They know me in there now. The guy always asks,

'How's it hangin'?' and I always answer, 'Hangin' good.' That's our banter, which I quite enjoy. He knows I dodge school but doesn't give a monkey's cos I'm crossing his palm with dosh.

I'm not thinking about school or the Liam McAvoys of this world. No, I'm thinking about how our Frankie and me are so different. He's got a handsome face, stomach muscles and jaggy chin stubble. In five years' time, when I'm seventeen, I'd really like to look like him. Wouldn't want to be him though. Not on your nelly.

About the Author

Brian Conaghan lives and works in the Scottish town of Coatbridge. He has a Master of Letters in Creative Writing from the University of Glasgow. For many years Brian worked as a teacher and taught in Scotland, Italy and Ireland. His novel *When Mr Dog Bites* was shortlisted for the 2015 CILIP Carnegie Medal, *The Bombs That Brought Us Together* won the 2016 Costa Children's Book Award, *The Weight of a Thousand Feathers* won the 2018 Irish Book Award for Teen/Young Adult Book of the Year, and *The M Word* was shortlisted for the 2019 An Post Irish Book Awards. *We Come Apart*, a verse novel co-authored with Carnegie Medal-winner Sarah Crossan, won the 2018 UKLA Book Award. *Cardboard Cowboys*, Brian's first middle-grade novel, was published in 2021 and is full of his trademark heart, humour and crackling dialogue. *Swimming on the Moon* is his second novel for middle-grade readers.

@ConaghanAuthor